D1005688

GRAVEDIGGERS
ENTOMBED

GRAVEDIGGERS
ENTOMBED

CHRISTOPHER KROVATIN

KATHERINE TEGEN BOOKS
An Imprint of HarperCollins Publishers

DEDICATED TO THE CITIZENS OF KUDUS

AND THEIR FALLEN ASSAILANTS,

ALL THOSE GUILTY AND INNOCENT . . .

TO THE DEAD.

Katherine Tegen Books is an imprint of HarperCollins Publishers.

Gravediggers: Entombed
Copyright © 2014 by HarperCollins Publishers
All rights reserved. Printed in the United States of America.
No part of this book may be used or reproduced in any manner whatsoever
without written permission except in the case of brief quotations embodied
in critical articles and reviews. For information address HarperCollins
Children's Books, a division of HarperCollins Publishers, 195 Broadway,
New York, NY 10007.
www.harpercollinschildrens.com

Library of Congress Cataloging-in-Publication Data
Krovatin, Christopher.
    Entombed / by Christopher Krovatin. — First edition.
        pages   cm. — (Gravediggers ; [3])
    Summary: "In this final installment of the series, Ian, Kendra, and PJ
face their most dangerous zombie-fighting mission of all, deep in the caves of
Indonesia" —Provided by publisher.
    ISBN 978-0-06-207746-2 (hardback)
    [1. Zombies—Fiction.   2. Friendship—Fiction.   3. Horror stories.]   I. Title.
PZ7.K936En   2014   2013047950
[Fic]—dc23   CIP
                                                                             AC

Typography by Carla Weise
14 15 16 17 18   CG/RRDH   10 9 8 7 6 5 4 3 2 1
❖
First Edition

ACKNOWLEDGMENTS

Heaps of thanks to Claudia Gabel, Alex Arnold, Katherine Tegen, and everyone at HarperCollins who made the Gravediggers series a reality; to all of the authors and publicists who joined me on tour; and to my family and friends for their undying support, especially my mother and father, Anna and Gerry, who believe in me. Hails to the many artists and musicians who have inspired me throughout the writing of this book, specifically the Misfits and Cannibal Corpse. Special thanks to Max Brooks, Mike Mignola, and, of course, H. P. Lovecraft, whose unorthodox interpretations of terror have always inspired me to push the boundaries of my own understanding.

And finally, I humbly bow to Ian, Kendra, and PJ, my brothers and sister in arms. It has been an honor to walk alongside you in your battle against the cold and the dark. Thank you.

From
The Warden's Handbook
by Lucille Fulci

Chapter 3: The Cursed

3.5—The Bite

The curse, ever insidious and persistent, attacks in two significant ways. One is its presence in the very air of a cursed landscape, which allows it to not only cloud the mind, but also to attach itself to any recently deceased human body within the boundaries of the afflicted area. Anyone unfortunate enough to pass away within the confines of a cursed area, even if their demise comes from natural causes, will have their body inhabited and taken up by the dark powers that run through this place. However, the other and perhaps more recognizable method through which the evil is spread is through being bitten by one of the cursed.

While the act of biting itself does not cause damnation, it is the most common method of damnation. In general, physical contact of any type with the undead is discouraged. In some cases, seemingly harmless scratches have caused death and reanimation, and some who have gotten the blood of the cursed in their eyes and mouth have perished from it. But because of the undead's insatiable hunger, they will more often than not attempt to bite their victims before scratching them or passing their ichor along to them. Thus, we must observe the bite as the most potent method of attack amongst these creatures.

Observed cases of bites have shown the following: that the undead's teeth must break skin to taint the blood and pass along the curse. (Perhaps due to some sort of functional imperative, the teeth are one of the last parts of the cursed to rot away, though toothless undead have been encountered.) Once the skin is broken, the bleeding stops swiftly, and the victim usually feels stronger, even more vitalized than before, for between thirty minutes and two hours. Soon after, however, the victim becomes feverish and light-headed. Then come dizziness, nausea, and an impossibility to catch one's breath. At this point, the afflicted person usually experiences numbness, with subsequent injuries painless and unnoticed. It has been posited that this is a response similar to that of the venom of certain snakes and insects—to incapacitate the victim so that they are easier to catch and devour. After this, the afflicted begins both visual and aural hallucinations. Many victims have reported a dull, low moaning or droning, like that of a heavy wind, as well as voices speaking violent and suicidal thoughts within their minds. Approximately twelve hours after this, the victim will simply close their eyes and stop breathing. At this point, the Warden has approximately thirty minutes to disassemble the bitten person's body. After that, it is officially reanimated and therefore untouchable by the hands of a Warden.

It should be noted that, unlike other entries in this volume, the above sequence of events is not set in stone. Depending on the location of the curse, the severity of the bite, and other mitigating factors, the speed at which infection and death occur can vary. In certain cases, such as the Chimney Rock Massacre (see *The Fugue*, p. 138), bitten individuals were reported as dying from their wounds and reanimating all within an hour. Similarly, many Wardens have reported spells and poultices staving off the curse for days before the afflicted succumbed to their wounds. However, there is a moot point throughout all of this that any Warden will agree with, and that this author cannot stress enough to any young Wardens believing themselves to be unique in their abilities:

The bite is a death sentence.

To forget this fact is to create false hope and put yourself, and others, in severe danger. When a person is bitten by one of the undead, they will die, and they will return. No spell, totem, sigil, or any other magical tool can stop this—they can only delay the inevitable. To this date, no one has ever survived a bite from one of the cursed, and no one has ever died without coming back as a mindless drone. Time spent hoping against hope is better used gathering one's wits, making peace with what has happened, and either destroying the specimen or putting distance between it and one's self.

CHAPTER ONE

Ian

"Help!" I scream. "It's tearing my face off!"

"Calm down, Ian," says PJ. "I know. I'm sorry. One more piece . . ."

PJ reaches up to my eyebrow, his face super intense like he's some scrawny mad scientist, all tongue between his lips and eyes wide, no blinks whatsoever. For a second, I hope that this last piece isn't a bad one, and then I feel his fingernails curl around the edge of the latex, and he slowly peels it back, and my skin tugs and pulls and stretches, and then *SKRRTCH*, it comes off, taking a nice amount of brow hair with it and stinging like crazy.

Sitting on the edge of the tub, Kendra's got her head

lowered so that all I can see is a big brown ball of hair, but I know that under the 'do, she's trying not to laugh. Don't know why, just *know*. Man, look at her—so weird to see her in a *dress*, let alone this yellow Easter-type number she dug up to help make PJ's movie.

"There," says PJ as I rub my eyebrow, "all done, you baby." He lays the brow appliance on the sink next to the others, and it's kind of cool, man, looking down and seeing my werewolf face staring back at me in pieces. Two heavy brow prosthetics, two brown latex pointed ears, a dog nose and lip muzzle, and a chin piece, all stinking of acidic chemicals and face paint. Part of me kind of misses being the werewolf in PJ's movie already, like maybe I could put the stuff back on and do another couple hours of howling and snarling, but then I remember only, what, thirty minutes ago, when there was fake fur in my nostril and everything itched and sweat had started pooling up in the rubber chin, and I'm totally stoked I no longer have to wear these things, ever again.

"My face hurts," I say, because that's pretty much what I've got going on right now.

Kendra raises her eyes to me, and yeah, look at her biting her lip, her cheeks blushing dark brown. She's been cracking up at my shouts and yelps. "Interesting," she says, "because it's killing *me*."

Silence, crickets, then it sinks in. See, Kendra's been trying to learn jokes lately. "Oh," I say. "That's not *really* how that goes." The smile and the bright sunny look on her face vanish, and suddenly I wish I could slap that last comment out of my own mouth. "See, it's 'Does your face hurt?' It's a question. And then they say no. It doesn't quite work if my face actually hurts."

She nods, all determined, in a way that I've slowly learned is sort of like saying, *Thanks, you've taught me something.* It's crazy to think about earlier this year, when we hated each other and all three of us were these complete messes, you know? Me, Kendra, and PJ, wandering through the woods, crying and sniffling and eating termites to keep from starving, but now, here we are: PJ being a crazy genius with a totally hardcore look on his face as he makes us up as monsters and directs blocking in my backyard, and Kendra, looking . . .

I mean, she's . . . in a *dress.*

PJ hands me a jar of makeup remover and a washcloth and nudges me slightly toward the door. "I'll yell for you when we're ready for your training," he says. "In the meantime, go use that."

"You sure?" I say. "Maybe I should see the process—"

"That would defeat the purpose," says Kendra. "Don't worry, it shouldn't take long. Right, PJ?"

"Probably not," says our tiny, dark-eyed friend in that quiet, intense voice he gets when he's working. He turns to his monster makeup kit, spread open

7

in two diagonal stacks of bins overflowing with glues and rubbers and face paints and prosthetics. He cracks his knuckles like some *extra*-scary evil genius. "We'll go simple this time around. No wounds, just coloring. Well . . . maybe a few wounds."

"Well . . . if you're sure," I say.

Kendra grins at me, and it's like the inside of my brain melts into a puddle. "See you shortly, Ian."

"I guess—" The minute I'm past the door, PJ slams it in my face. Part of me gets all intense and angry inside, wondering what's going on in there and what Kendra and PJ are saying about me, only I know what's going on, so why does it matter?

Lower your temperature, O'Dea told me two weeks ago. *Save it for the fight. Then, you need to be hot enough to cut through steel.* All right. Get all this gunk off my face, then an ice-cold soda. Should lower me right down to a nice cool.

My mom's in the kitchen sticking a lasagna in the oven when I get there. At first, she smiles when she sees me, but then she puts her hand to her mouth and tries not to laugh. Yeah, yeah, hilarious, I'm sure.

"Can you help get this crap off?" I ask, holding up the jar of remover.

She nods, takes the washcloth, and starts rubbing globs of creamy hospital-smelling remover into my cheeks and chin. Every time she pulls the cloth away, it's smudged a little darker brown.

"I almost forgot PJ was over here," she says as she dabs. "Samantha hasn't called the house five times today. How'd he like your werewolf?"

"Think it went okay," I tell her. "Got to run around growling."

"I heard," she says. "Kendra was screaming her face off for the last two hours. That girl has some powerful lungs on her."

"Girls do that a lot in horror movies, Ma."

The corner of her mouth goes up in this crooked way that makes her look like there's a joke I'm not getting. "Kendra sure looks cute in that dress."

Blecch. It's like she's reading my mind and trying to make me yak all at once. "I guess," I say in a way that hopefully tells her I have *no idea* what she's talking about. "She won't be in a little bit. PJ's working his movie magic on her right now."

"Oh yeah?" my mom asks. "Do you slash her with your claws or something? I thought you promised me this wouldn't be very violent. . . ."

"Nah, she's getting a . . . different thing done," I say, my mouth going dry and numb, like I'm just back from the dentist. It's like the island all over again. "PJ's . . . trying something out. A new makeup technique."

"Does this have anything to do with your big weekly phone call?" she asks.

"Nope."

Man, I'm *so* bad at lying these days. I've never been great at it, but lately, I've just been the worst, scrambling and failing left and right. Maybe it's because I've just been so busy hanging out with Kendra and PJ all the time, and we can talk about what happened whenever we want, like the more I'm used to the truth, the harder it is to lie. I feel like both those guys have mentioned the same thing—their parents getting suspicious.

But my mom can't know, which I still agree on, which all three of us agree on. None of them can know that the dead walk the earth, that on our last two trips away from home we ran into cursed places teeming with bloodthirsty zombies looking to eat us, and that if it weren't for this insane network of witches called Wardens, we'd all be corpse chow. Because even if they don't believe us and they think we're crazy, then we've got *that* to deal with, the counselor and maybe pills or special classes, and then we can't do our job, which is kicking the butts of these horrible things whenever they show up.

That's why O'Dea, our local Warden, calls us once a week—she's helping us train to be what we are, these sort of famous zombie killers called Gravediggers.

Gravediggers. I know. After the first time, I didn't believe it. We really just stumbled on those undead modern dancers by accident, and we sort of killed them by accident, too, tricking them to tear each other apart. But after last time? Swinging a machete into an oncoming horde of melty zombie tourists on some desert island owned by a freaking *teenage supervillain*? Yeah, I'll bite. Since then, I've been operating under the idea that all of this is real, and man, it feels good just admitting it.

That's why none of our parents can know—they'll get in the middle of things and mess up what we're doing. They may not be destined zombie hunters, but they're still our parents. If we're grounded and the dead walk somewhere? Not a good look.

"There," my mom says, "you're pretty much good. Definitely take a shower before you go to bed, though." She squints at me, like she's trying to figure out whether or not to punish me for something I *might* be doing, which I totally am. "You know I love you, kid. Be good, okay?"

"Always," I say, and haul back to my friends, dying to be out of my mom's line of vision and to know what's being said inside our bathroom.

I rap my knuckles against the door. "You guys done yet?"

"Almost!" shouts PJ.

"Come on!" I say, knocking again, and when that doesn't work, this wicked thought pops in my head, and I start slapping my hand against the door and moaning low and deep in my throat.

The door cracks suddenly, and PJ's head pokes out, his dark-rimmed eyes wide and a little concerned. "That's not funny," he says. "You're a sick individual."

"It was a little funny. Come on, let me in, I'm ready to see this."

At first, I think that little smile that sprouts on PJ's face is because of my joke, like he's trying not to laugh. Then he swings open the door and says, "Voila."

Instant brain freeze. Like my heart shoves its fist in my throat and everything from my knees down is made of ice.

Kendra stands there, face gray and slack, eyes dim and glazed, as though she's seeing me for the first time. Her cheeks are sunken, the skin all wrinkly like it wasn't laid down right, and her lips are a dark shade of blackish brown, but the one corner at the right edge of them is all torn away, revealing a couple of white teeth and some pink-brown gums. Both the gash on her face and the one on her arm are shiny and wet with chunky black goop. But it's her hair, man—normally this one single, perfect ball of frizz that's now sort of clumped together and dirty—that just gets me.

"I'm sorry," says PJ, his voice taking that soft, understanding tone he does so well. His hand lands on my shoulder, and bam, I'm back, I'm here, with my friends, not lost in a state of blood-chilling terror. "I was just trying to get back at you for the zombie knock. Didn't mean to give you the full freak-out."

"It's cool," I finally gasp. "Had to see it eventually."

Kendra's face breaks out of its far-off gaze and blinks into a delighted smile. "Is it that accurate? Were you genuinely afraid?" When I manage a nod, she giggles and turns to PJ. "Well done, PJ. Apparently, you did an excellent makeup job!"

"I do all right," he says with a slight smile. "Let's go."

We step into my bedroom, and after I've kicked all of the dirty clothes, basketball gear, and homework books into the corners, we have a nice space set up for practice.

"You ready, Ian?" asks PJ as I face off with now-zombified Kendra, who's swiftly typing something into her smartphone.

"I would be," I say, "if someone got off the stupid internet."

"Sorry, sorry," she mumbles, pocketing her phone. "Redditors. You know how it is." As she turns back to me, she lets that same sort of mindless dead look go over her face, and my heart goes fast again. This is my training session—for Kendra, we jumped out at her nonstop to get her acting quickly, and for PJ we screamed horrible scary stuff at him while showing him pictures of spiders and dead bodies (what a gross Google search). Now, it's my turn: confronting the dead.

After our last fight with the zombies, I had a

real problem at first when it came to facing off with them—just kept freezing up with something like the heebie-jeebies on steroids. O'Dea said we've got to be "familiar with the enemy," to be able to stare at them head-on and not mistake them for or treat them like people, even if they're someone we know. The way she said that last part made us think she'd been in that situation.

"All right, Ian, let's do this slow motion," says PJ, using his camera to switch from his werewolf footage to a new file. "Kendra's going to come at you, and you're going to try and fend her off and take her out, but do it slowly so you can see and remember your instinct. Got it?"

"Sure thing," I tell him, trying to keep from breathing too fast.

"Good," says PJ. "Kendra, ready to roll?"

"Affirmative."

"Great." PJ raises his camera and, after a little moment, the red light comes on. "Aaand . . . action!"

Just like that, Kendra comes lurching at me, moaning deep down in her throat, and I have to admit, her zombie impression is pretty spot-on. She drags one leg like it's been broken midway through the shin and manages to twist her fingers in *just* the same way that the walking corpses we've fought have done. For a moment, staring at my friend, or this creature that's supposed to *have been* my friend, it's like I'm stuck again, frozen inside of my own body—

Then, those weird bent fingers lightly touch my arm, and everything comes back to reality, and my hand comes out in a flying chop, swinging down at half speed and stopping just in the middle of Kendra's neck.

"Wait, stop," she says, dropping the zombie act in an instant and leaving me stunned, blinking and sputtering, like she just pulled a magic trick. "You can't just go for the throat. That won't stop them, remember?"

"I just figured it might break their neck," I try to say. "Especially if I have a machete. Doesn't cutting off their head work?"

"Technically, yes. But!" says Kendra, raising a gray-painted finger in my face. "It's all about the spine, Ian. Remember what O'Dea said? Unless you fully rupture the spinal column, they can still attack. Here's what I've been choreographing mentally. . . ."

She takes one of my hands and puts it under her chin, the butt of my palm resting just at her throat, and then she, whoa, hold on, she takes my other hand, wait, and pulls me right up close to her, wow, and wraps it around her back, by her waist.

What is she. I don't even.

"Push with *this* hand under the chin," she says, "to keep the mouth away from you. Then, reach around in back and sink your fingers"—she puts her hand on mine, makes a claw, and presses it into her backbone—"in around the spine. Then yank hard, splitting the spine open. That should at the very least drop them and slow them down so you can finish them off. Got it?"

"Aguh," I say, like a huge doofus.

Thankfully, my dad comes barging in, giving me a good excuse to pull away from Kendra and try to blink away the weird spinning feeling in my head. Bad news is, of course, that Dad's got a basketball in his hands and that crazy grin on his face, which means he's here to try and yank me away from my friends.

"You done yet?" he says, slapping the ball with a hard *ping*. "Come on, Ian, we have work to do. I saw Larry Leider at the gas station yesterday, and he says he's happy to start you if you're back up to the level you were at before you were banned from the team. Says he thinks the time off might have even helped."

"Dad, we've still got work to do," I tell him. "There are a couple of shots to get down, and then we have the phone call with our producer."

His crazy grin turns into a sour frown, and his mustache does this back-and-forth thing it does when he's angry. "You've got to be kidding me," he says. "Ian, I thought we agreed. You could do your friend's monster movie if you spent some time getting ready for basketball season. It's just around the corner."

"We won't be long, Mr. Buckley," says Kendra. "A half hour at most."

Dad opens his mouth to respond to her, but then his

frown falls even further and he cocks an eyebrow, so I know something's up.

"Why are you dressed up like that?" he asks.

"For our monster movie," I tell him.

"But wait," he says, turning his eyes, finally, on PJ, the kid who got his sporty son all tied up in the scary movie biz. "Your movie is a wolfman movie. You won't shut up about it. So why's she dressed like a, what's it called, a zombie?"

Hearing him say the word makes the blood freeze in my face and hands, and when I look at PJ he's just standing there, mouth open, like he never knew my dad was listening all the times he talked about his movie in the car, like the fact that Vince Buckley knows the difference between a zombie and a werewolf never crossed his mind, and at a certain point it makes sense, 'cause that's not the kind of guy my dad is. Even Kendra looks frozen in her corpse makeup. None of us know how to get out of this one.

That's when Kendra's phone buzzes and starts playing a hooting owl noise—O'Dea's ring. She pulls it out and glances at the two of us before looking at my dad. "Mr. Buckley, may we have a moment alone?"

Dad crosses his arms. "I'd like to hear what this 'producer' of yours has to say," he says. "This whole phone call thing seems a little weird to me—"

"Dad!" I say. "Just give us a sec, okay? I'll be out to

shoot hoops in, what, twenty minutes. Geez."

He harrumphs and finally says, "Ten." Then he stomps out the door, slamming it behind him.

"Sorry about that, guys," I tell the other two.

"Not a problem," says Kendra. She taps her screen and holds out the phone. "Hey, O'Dea, it's us. You're on speaker. How are things going—"

"Kids."

It's like an electric shock—definitely O'Dea's voice, but not like we've ever heard it before, all scratchy and full of heavy breathing, kind of angry but kind of scared, like she's panicking. O'Dea doesn't panic, she gets all kung-fu Zen and takes everything as it comes. She keeps her eye on the ball. Around me, PJ's brow wrinkles, and Kendra holds the phone a little away from her, like it smells bad.

"O'Dea?" asks Kendra. "It's Kendra. Is everything all right?"

"Listen to me," she says, surrounded by the noise of crashing branches and loud banging. "Whatever happens, you can't come after me."

Whoa. The words feel like needles in the back of my neck. PJ's hand goes to his mouth. It's like the room is growing smaller with every second of this phone call.

"What's going on?" I ask.

"No coming after me," she snaps. "You've got to follow your training. Prepare for whatever comes your way. You three are too important, too talented. I can't have you risking that for me."

"O'Dea, what's wrong?" says PJ.

"Just remember what I've told you," she cries, the banging growing louder. "Don't be scared. You're powerful and dangerous, no matter what happens to me. I'm just your teacher, but you three, you're the chosen ones—"

The banging turns into a crash, and O'Dea screams, straight-up lets loose at the top of her lungs. As my head goes all wobbly and I feel behind me for my bed, the phone lets loose a loud booming noise, and then the scream cuts out just as the phone drops from Kendra's hands and tumbles to the floor. For a few minutes, we're all silent, and my heart pounds and my mouth goes dry and I wonder what could've made the strongest person I know, who spends her days looking after a horde of zombies, scream like that.

Kendra's phone buzzes on the floor. My hand snaps out and grabs it before anyone else's can, and when I see the screen, I can't help but gasp out loud.

"Ian?" asks PJ softly.

The picture message shows O'Dea, her face beaten purple and bloody. She's lying on the ground, chin pulled up. A huge hand in a black leather glove is pressing the blade of a massive hunting knife into her throat.

Stay out of my way, reads the message, *or the warden dies.*

CHAPTER TWO

Kendra

O'Dea's visage, battered and threatened at the end of a cruel blade, is all I can see out the bus window. Every passing billboard or solitary gas station looks like our Warden brought low. It is what has kept me focused as we've arranged this bizarre ride and made our inexperienced and bumbling phone calls and emails: the thought that our friend and mentor is in mortal danger. Time is of the essence. We must act.

The bus driver, corpulent and unshaven, eyes us warily as Ian, PJ, and I all step out at the hotel's drop-off area, and I am unable to make eye contact with him in fear that such a personal gesture might rouse his suspicion. Thankfully, as we exit the bus, I hear the doors close and the vehicle rumble to life, and soon bus, driver, and worry all wheeze through a roundabout and drift out of sight.

"What time is our return bus?" says PJ softly, his expression one of both exhaustion and determination.

"Nine," I tell him, calling up our itinerary on my phone. "We arrive back home at ten-twenty."

"And you're sure she's meeting us here?" asks Ian.

"There's no way to be positive," I tell him. "The email she sent me was from two days ago, from an internet café in San Juan. For all I know, she was stopped and interrogated at customs. But this is without a doubt the right hotel."

We trudge our way across the front lot toward an airport hotel, its modern design sleek and pointed, like that of a luxury car. A doorman wishes us a good night as we push through the glass doors and enter the brightly lit lobby, full of soft leather furniture and *lilting* (five! When I get home, I have to strike that off the vocab list for this month) elevator music over the stereo.

At first, all I see is the occasional guest trailed by rolling luggage and the well-dressed clerks behind the check-in desk looking expectantly at us, and then a figure from the lounge area stands and waves. We all blink for a moment, startled by her outfit—the last time we saw Josefina was on an island off Puerto Rico, dressed in cutoffs and a sleeveless T-shirt. To see the sweet-faced girl dressed in pants, a winter jacket, and tight-laced boots is startling.

After she hugs us one after another (let it be noted that PJ's face, frozen in a look of hardened depression since the terrifying phone call from O'Dea, softens considerably, his eyes closing and his nose burying into the girl's shoulder), she waves for us to follow her down a hallway of the hotel, and we scurry along behind her.

"You're not warm in all of that?" asks Ian.

"If anything, I'm still freezing," says Josefina, shuddering.

"How are the zombie tourists?" asks PJ.

"Sleeping soundly at the bottom of the ocean," says Josefina. "After we resealed their resting place, we've not seen so much as one trying to crawl onto shore. Even before you arrived, one or two would try to reach the island. Now, nothing."

"I'm impressed you made it here so swiftly," I tell her.

"It was surprisingly easy," she says with a smile. "My yaya has recently been teaching me spells of deception, making people see what you want them to see. My boarding pass was a shop receipt, and my hotel room was charged to a sand dollar."

"Nice," says PJ, but part of me cannot help but feel at least somewhat unsettled by the methods we're being forced to employ. As much as Josefina's magical trickery isn't harming anyone—O'Dea thought of it as "Wardening your way" somewhere—it's still, technically, stealing, which is something I feel conflicted about. We three Gravediggers are perhaps no better, having to lie to our parents about going to see a movie together so we could abscond to this airport hotel. Just because we're karmically assigned zombie assassins doesn't mean lying and cheating should become our tools of the trade.

Sorry, Kendra, but you need to get over that. Part of the training O'Dea has given you over the phone is an emphasis on the present, on figuring out, at any given moment, the single best way to destroy your enemy without getting caught up in your own thought process. Right now, your enemy is whatever attacked O'Dea.

After rushing down this hotel hallway, Josefina stops at a conference room and ducks into the open door, placing us in a spacious, well-lit room with a large wooden table in the middle and an intercom and speakerphone system.

"This is the room where I was told to meet you," says Josefina. "From what rumors I've overheard, it seems that O'Dea's kidnapping is part of a larger problem."

"Do all Wardens' Council meetings take place in hotel conference rooms?" I ask, a little skeptical.

"It's a tradition," says Josefina. "When gathering in nature, Warden meetings were often ambushed by those who thought they were holding an 'unholy Sabbath.' Hotels provide layers of security to keep anyone from infiltrating our ranks. And there is often free coffee."

"How much do you know about what's going on?" asks PJ, sitting down at the table and leaning forward on his elbows like a successful businessman.

"Very little," says Josefina. "When I contacted the Council, they informed me that they would be sending someone out to area forty-seven to see what happened."

"Area forty-seven?" I ask.

"That's the number of O'Dea's area of cursed earth," says Josefina. "Each area has a number. Isla Hambrienta and the surrounding sea is area one-oh-two. Wardens never use them, except when talking to the Council."

"Do you think they'll help her?" asks Ian, kneading his hands. "I mean, they have to, right? That's their job."

"Not quite," says Josefina. "What you must understand is that the Council is very official. All they care about is containment, keeping the balance pure. For Council members to even appear here means our situation is serious—"

The door swings open, and in enter three women and a man. The first is skinny, a redhead with pale skin wearing a yellow coat that tapers in at her waist. The second is a round-faced woman with dark rings under her eyes and a mess of gray hair, wearing a flowing black gown. The third wears jeans and a Slayer T-shirt, with an army cap over her spiky brown hair and sharp hazel eyes. The man is a hotel employee in a bright red shirt, his smile as artificial as the ficus tree in the lobby.

"Huh! Looks like your guests beat you here," he says. "All right, ladies, you've got your phone equipment, your projector if you need it—anything else?"

"We were told there'd be coffee," says the second woman in an operatic voice.

"Oooh, we don't do complimentary coffee anymore," coos the hotel clerk. "Though for five ninety-eight, I can have a pot brought over—"

"This is fine," says the woman in the jeans. "You can leave now."

"All right." The hotel clerk looks at us and flashes a confused smile. "Are these your nieces and nephews, or students, or what, exactly?"

"Leave, please," says the redhead, and though her voice is soft and melodic, there is an undertone to it that is almost tangible, that crackles in the very air in front of us—magic being utilized. A flick of her hand, and the clerk's eyes go glazed before he silently exits, closing the door behind him.

"Sisters," Josefina says, bowing her head. "Good evening. May your gardens thrive with life. I am Josefina Pilatón, Warden's apprentice of area one-oh-two."

"Good evening, sister," says the redhead, her official tone like the chirping of a bird. "I am Anne Farrow,

Warden of area forty-one. This is Sarah Cardille, War-den of area thirty-eight and Warden General of the Midwestern United States, and Blaze Creed, Warden of area fifty."

"Sister," mumble the other two Wardens.

"I have brought friends of our cause," says Josefina, motioning to us. "This is Ian Buck—"

"We are aware of who your guests are, and what they believe themselves to be," says Sarah Cardille in her booming voice. "They would do well to remember that their presence here is a privilege, and they should not attempt to alter the proceedings of our business."

The words sting, but are not unexpected. Even Josefina and her grandmother Jeniveve were reticent to know us when we first met. Hard though it is, I swallow my pride and exhale slowly, keeping myself composed. Glancing over, I see PJ doing the same, his eyes closing in a brief moment of meditation. Ian, of course, is not so meditative.

"Excuse me?" says Ian. "Lady, our friend's hurt and you're telling me—"

"Ian!" snaps Josefina as the Wardens sit down, their eyes focused fiercely on my friend. Without compre-hending my actions, I reach out and grab Ian's hand in my own, and his look of rage seems to slowly *abate* (a little easy, but why not—one).

"If we may begin," says Sarah Cardille, clearing her

throat and never offering us a seat around the overly lacquered table. "Two days ago, Ms. Pilatón contacted us concerning the possible kidnapping of a Warden, one O'Dea Foree. Ms. Creed, did you visit area forty-seven?"

"Yup, I rolled through today," says Blaze Creed, leaning back in her chair. "Containment's pretty solid, all sigils regularly kept, seals and beacons well placed. Looks like she did a big recent resealing. This O'Dea knew what she was doing. She only has one cursed walking around anyway, hiker with a broken leg, so it's not like her being gone is going to cause a breach."

"But she *is* missing," I say. Every eye in the room darts to me. My question hangs in the air like a vapor.

" . . . yeah," says Blaze Creed finally. "Nowhere to be found. Her cabin looked like there'd just been an earthquake—furniture everywhere, windows broken. There was some blood, too, on the floor."

The words bring a sick feeling to my stomach, as though my bile had just turned cold and gelatinous. Not only is O'Dea missing, but she is bleeding. For all I know, she's beyond saving.

"Did it look like an attack by the cursed?" asks Sarah Cardille.

"Nope," says Blaze. "Too organized. Plus, there were boot prints, fancy ones—Italian designer. That poor cursed hiker wasn't wearing anything like that. If I had to guess, I'd say your idea about Savini might have some legs on it."

My mind explodes with instant recognition: that name. "Dario Savini?" I ask, sitting forward in my chair.

"We know that creep!" cries out Ian. "He tried to sic a mutant zombie on us on whatever area that is, Josefina's island!"

"He's a maniac and an imitation Gravedigger," says PJ in a spiteful tone. "Do you think he has O'Dea? Why? Where's he taking her?"

"Ms. Pilatón," sighs Sarah Cardille, "please remind your guests that their interruptions do nothing to help their friend, and only serve to irritate the Council. They may think they are something more than mere citizens, but I assure you they're not."

Keep it together, Kendra. Yes, this woman is obnoxious for no reason, and yes she and her cohorts seem unfeeling toward O'Dea's current kidnapped state, but that's no reason to have an episode and endanger your chances of ever helping find her.

Really. It's not.

Suddenly, I am standing, my hands planted firmly on the table. "My name is Kendra Wright," I say loudly. "With me are Ian Buckley and PJ Wilson. We are Gravediggers."

Why do I even try.

"There are no Gravediggers," snaps Anne Farrow.

"And who has decided that?" I ask the three witches, doing my best to keep my voice from quivering, though it feels as though I am jamming my finger in an electrical outlet. "You? Your Council? From what I have learned from my friend Warden O'Dea Foree, my role as a Gravedigger is my destiny, which no curse or enchantment can deny. I have felt the power of karma drive me as I fought the breach in area forty-seven by convincing the living dead to tear one another apart. I felt it at area one-oh-two when I struck down hungry zombies in the humid jungle. But now, I must fight for my friend's life. So Wardens, do me the favor of setting aside your reservations and allowing us to save one of your own."

Absolute silence. The three Wardens stare at me, mouths agape.

"So what you're telling me," says Sarah Cardille slowly, her dark eyes meeting mine, "is that you took part in two undocumented breaches of containment?"

My adrenaline rush turns sour and clammy. On my one side, Ian slaps a palm to his face; on the other, PJ exhales softly and whispers, "Ho boy."

"Well," I say through partly numb lips, "given the circumstances—"

"Enough," says Cardille, slamming a palm down on the table with a resounding smack. Her smile radiates smug self-satisfaction—she must have been aware of these breaches if she knew who we are.

Which means she played you, Kendra. She made you admit them publicly. Step up your game.

"Let me make something clear to you three children," continues Cardille. "Had this Council been informed of these breaches when they occurred, your friend Ms. Foree might not even be alive to be kidnapped. We have a time-honored policy of removing the heads of those who fail at their duties as Warden, depending on the extent of their infraction."

"She ain't lying," growls Blaze Creed. "We put it in a box, throw it in the river."

"Perhaps you are what you claim to be," muses Cardille. "You've certainly brought enough catastrophe, suffering, and consternation to the Wardens you've met, just like Dario Savini's father did some time ago. But we do not recognize Gravediggers. Not anymore. Your help is not needed, nor was it ever."

"But what about O'Dea?" says PJ, his eyes sparkling brightly. "Our friend is out there in the hands of a man who makes Bruce Campbell look like Shirley Temple. And she's probably hurt. What can we do to help?"

"Ms. Foree is trained in the ways of the Warden," says Anne Farrow. "Given what information we have, we can only assume Savini has kidnapped her to help him break containment at area five." The other two Wardens stare at their shoes at the last two words. "She will do whatever it takes to keep any secrets or talents she possesses from being used by our enemies."

"What does that mean?" says Ian, doing his best to ignore the horrible truth behind the woman's words that sends my skin crawling. "Sorry, are you saying she's going to *kill herself*? You're going to let O'Dea *commit suicide*?"

"It's our way," says Sarah Cardille matter-of-factly.

Her calm leaves me reeling, my head swimming with anger and betrayal. These are the people meant to be protecting our friend's life, and they're happy to watch her kill herself as long as none of their precious secrets get out. The lack of human emotion it must take to be this kind of person astounds me.

"You're monsters," says PJ, speaking my mind, his voice quiet but hard as steel. "Absolutely inhuman."

"Right on," snarls Ian. Joy passes over me in a huge wave as I hear my friends give voice to my exact feelings. It is good to be in this as a team. "Josefina, you can't be going along with this, right?"

Our young Warden friend stares straight ahead, her face frozen in shock and horror. "I don't . . . she is right, Ian. It is how Wardens have done things for a long time. If someone convinces a Warden to unlock the seals of cursed places all over the world, it could be disastrous. Death in the name of the balance, for the greater good."

"You're kidding me," says PJ.

"Do not presume to judge her, young man," says

31

Sarah Cardille, her round face clenched in a porcine sneer. "Had you not troubled the balance of things by killing those cursed, none of this would've happened."

"At least we did something," I say, leaning forward and looking into the old woman's eyes, my mind a vengeful blur. "Maybe you're right, maybe she would be all right had we not interfered. But without us, this countryside would be swarming with those things, and most of Puerto Rico might be overrun. I'd rather that than commit a pathetic sin of omission—"

Sarah Cardille rises, her dress billowing out around her, and suddenly her eyes burn with a cold light that seems to freeze me from head to toe. At my side, I feel Ian's hands shaking me and can barely hear Josefina crying out for the old Warden to stop, but there is nothing that can stop the electric tentacles of her power from digging into me, pushing down on me. Despite the overbearing pressure of her magic, some part of my mind recognizes what is happening, because O'Dea has done it to me before: the Evil Eye, the "oldest gag in the book," a Warden's most basic magic technique.

Wait, Kendra. Concentrate. If you can remember that, then you're not entirely under her control. Fight it. Concentrate your energy like PJ has been saying you need to. Feel her magic weighing on you, beating at your mind. Concentrate harder, Kendra. Force your own energy, your own neurons, to build a wall. Create a barrier to stop her power from spreading even further into you. Feel it? There.

Wait. Hold on. Something's not right. Something feels—

Sharp pain bursts in the front of my skull, and without meaning to I cry out. Sarah Cardille goes flying backward with a gasp, stumbling past her chair and collapsing to the floor. Every Warden in the room looks suddenly pained—Anne Farrow bites her lip, clutching her heart; Blaze Creed stomps her foot and swears in French; even Josefina pinches the bridge of her nose.

Dizziness overtakes me, and my feet stumble backward. Ian and PJ lower me into a chair just as Farrow and Creed help the Warden General to her shaky feet.

"What the hell was that?" asks Creed, nodding toward me. "Does . . . does she have the blood? You, girl, who's your mother?"

"Get out," snarls Sarah Cardille, blinking hard. "All of you. This meeting is over."

"Not a chance," yells Ian. "I don't know what Warden craziness just happened, but we want to help our friend. She's out there."

Sarah Cardille snorts and shakes off the helping hands of her cohorts. "Fine," she says. "You fancy yourselves Gravediggers? Very well. When we first investigated Savini's father, Joseph, after he murdered a Warden, he had repeatedly documented a desire to unleash the horde of area five. It's a city called Kudus. If our guesses are right, his son is heading there."

"And where's that?" I ask through my buzzing teeth and light head.

"That's all you're getting," hisses Cardille. "You have seven days to retrieve your Warden. If you succeed, we will recognize you as Gravediggers. If you fail, Ms. Foree and Ms. Pilatón here lose their positions as Wardens and will be punished for their breaches with death."

Before I can scream protest, the three witches storm out the door, leaving me to clutch my aching head and moan, my friends' terror palpable and heartbreaking.

CHAPTER THREE

PJ

Fear is, like everything I feel, a part of me.

This is something I first learned on an island off of Puerto Rico while a girl named Josefina refused to help me fend off a hungry zombie and my best friend, Ian, was having a panic attack. Caught in the spur of the moment, I managed to channel my fear into something stronger, kind of an . . . emotional assault? That sounds about right. This terror allowed me to see what a sad creature the monster coming at me was, and I put it out of its misery. At the time, I had no clue what that meant, only that something cool happened and I killed a zombie, which, for a horror movie fan, is up there on the bucket list. But the more I thought about it, the more I realized that that power to change my world is also something I've always known, every time I looked through the eye of a camera and saw the world as a film. It's the fear. It has always been a part of what I am.

My whole life, I've been afraid of almost everything that could possibly hurt me or the people I care about—bugs, dander, cell phone radiation, you name it. Part of that was my mom, I guess, who's always worried about my little sister, Kyra, and myself. Over the past couple of months, though, using the meditation technique Josefina taught me and the lessons O'Dea's been giving us over the phone, I've been able to channel all my fear into the thing I love most: writing and making movies. Before, the camera was my escape, but now it's my, I don't know, my vent, my soapbox. Kendra would probably call it something like "an outlet for unhealthy impulses," though that makes me sound like Michael Myers.

But what I'm feeling now, as I trudge through school toward the doors and my bike, the cold October air pricking my ears, isn't that kind of fear. The fear I normally get is kind of high-strung and sharp; it comes with a close-up shot and a violin shriek. This is despair, heavy and sick and sad. And try as I might, I can't shake it. Maybe I'm being emotional, or not meditating hard enough. But . . .

They're doing nothing. O'Dea might kill herself, and they won't do anything to help her. And O'Dea—how could she think about it? How could she take sides with a cosmic force that was this uncaring and cruel?

As I walk, an orange streamer catches my eye, and I begin to take in all the trappings of the month around me: cutouts of grinning pumpkins and fanged bats, dangling rubber witches riding on broomsticks, jointed paper skeletons dancing on classroom doors. And then, of course, there's the front office, which has a series of cutouts of walking corpses in rotting suits, made to look as though they're pressing their gray undead hands against the glass, trying to get at us. From inside, Ms. Brandt glances up at me with her bright, ruddy complexion. She smiles and proudly points at the cutouts, wanting to make sure I see them. I give her what smile I have left. For a moment, I picture me bursting in while she and Ms. Geofferies, the school secretary, sip coffee, and giving her a history lesson. *First of all, they'd come right through that glass. Second, they're never in suits, they wear hiking gear or beachwear, whatever they died in. And trust me, they don't just bare their teeth at you; they come growling with mouths open wide—*

Listen to me. Halloween, my holiday for cool makeup and scary movies on TV, and I can't even enjoy it because of all the real monsters in my life.

Ian waits by the bike rack, talking to Chuck Tompkins

and Sean Cunningham, who somehow have gotten even bigger in seventh grade without getting any more intelligent. As I approach, I can hear Chuck describing a football game, but can immediately see that Ian doesn't care; his eyes are wandering, his nods are slight and unenthusiastic. When he sees me, he waves a hand.

"We're shooting hoops this weekend," says Sean as I reach them. "Coach told us to bring you. Wants to get you primed for this season."

Ian shrugs, glances at me. "Maybe. I have a lot of work to catch up on."

Sean frowns, nonplussed, and glances over to me. That's never a good thing. "Hey, Wilson, where's your camera? You don't want to film this?"

"It's in my backpack," I say, unlocking my bike, "and there's nothing to film." Anger, like fear, is a part of me, too, and needs to be properly dealt with. As O'Dea put it, *One so easily leads to the other.* Besides, if he thinks this is going to faze me, he has no idea what's going on in my life.

"You used to film everything," he says, but I turn my back to him. "Fine, why don't *I* take it and get some footage *for* you—"

The minute his hand lands on my backpack strap, I close my eyes, let everything slow down, and focus my emotions on the necessary movements. One second, my hand is over my shoulder and my fingers are around his wrist. The next, I've spun to face him, twisting his arm in a painful direction.

Sean yelps and yanks his arm away. After a second, his face turns red and he snaps, "You're *dead*, kid." Before he can reach me, Ian is between us, his reedy muscle a match for Cunningham's girth.

"Leave him alone, dude," says Ian, glaring at his teammate. "You started it anyway."

"You've got to be kidding me, Buckley." When Ian doesn't say anything and Sean realizes he's not, he shakes his head and turns back toward school, Chuck following.

"I'll call you about shooting hoops," says Ian.

"Yeah, don't bother," chuckles Sean.

As we mount our bikes and begin pedaling away from school, Ian seethes visibly, and I feel like a jerk. "I'm sorry," I tell him. "I don't mean to cause trouble."

"Oh, dude, no worries," he laughs. "You were always right, that kid's a real jackass. Remember years ago, when I was so worried about impressing that bozo?"

"That was March, Ian," I say. "Remember? Homeroom Earth?"

Ian's eyes stare off into the past, and he whistles. "Guess it was. *Feels* like years ago, though." To that, I can only nod.

Kendra's mom's house is a massive new-looking number with a huge front lawn, a three-car garage, and a single uncarved pumpkin sitting by the columns around the front door. Kendra's bike stands carefully placed against one column, and we make sure to imitate her positioning. A few minutes after we ring the doorbell, her mother, Ms. Menendez, opens it wearing a suit that looks like it might cut you if touched the wrong way.

"Gentlemen," she says. "How has the new school year been treating you?"

"I can't believe our math teacher has never seen *Pi*," I tell her.

"*A Midsummer Night's Dream* sucks," says Ian.

"Splendid," says Ms. Menendez, opening the door wider. "Kendra and your friend Josefina are in her room. My daughter seems very excited about something, so please make sure she doesn't hack into an FBI server."

Ian says, "No promises," but I say nothing, my mind already wandering to Josefina. Maybe I can finally ask her about the dreams.

We walk through the massive marble foyer, up the carpeted stairs, and down the heavenly white hallway. It's like the set of *Moon* or something. The door to Kendra's bedroom is locked, and when I knock, Josefina answers, shooting us that perfect grin. "Boys! Finally, you're here."

"Is everything ready?" asks Ian, barreling across the room to where Kendra sits hunched over her desk. Josefina begins to turn back in, but I put a hand on her shoulder to stop her. Let Ian and Kendra talk a bit—especially with whatever's going on with Ian about her. (Yeah, well, he might as well have it written on his forehead.)

"There's something I've been meaning to ask you about—"

"We should get ready," says Josefina, darting away from me. My heart sinks. She's been like this since we got here—avoiding me, refusing to make eye contact. When we last saw her, just as we were leaving the island, she told me she'd been having dreams with me in them. She called them visions and said I was in danger. The fact that she won't talk to me makes me worry that I'm in bigger trouble than I think.

Up on Kendra's computer screen (which is larger than any I've ever seen) is the website for Melee Industries, mainly advertising their new game, *Dead Paradise*. The animated banner at the top of the page shows tourists in colorful Hawaiian shirts running from hordes of muddy, fearsome zombies.

"Still couldn't scrap the project," snorts Ian.

"This was not the project," says Kendra sternly. "Turning Puerto Rico into a zombie farm was the project. This is the best possible alternative."

"What have you found out about Kudus?" I ask her.

"Very little," she says. "Two websites mention that it was an ancient city off South Asia, and there are a few books saying it was renowned for its architecture and woven goods. There's not much else on it. One of them says it's fictional, similar to Atlantis."

"Let's hope our little psychopath buddy knows more," says Ian. "So what're we looking at? How do we get his attention?"

"Since I figure we'll get nowhere fast trying to email him, I downloaded this," she says, tapping the screen. "It's a modified aggregator that a friend on a computer science forum sent to me. It'll just plug these fields into the Melee Industries search function one after another. Call me optimistic, but I think we can pique his interest."

My eyes scan down the list of fields—*Isla Hambrienta, Isla Hambrienta zombies, Isla Hambrienta Kendra Wright, Wardens, Gravediggers, PJ Wilson, zombies, zombie spore, Dario Savini*, to name a few—and clap a hand on her shoulder. "This is genius. Thank you for doing this." Kendra doesn't look at me, but smiles into her keyboard and shrugs. Part of the job.

"And . . . here we go." She presses the Enter key. We watch the Melee Industries website flicker through countless screens, most saying they don't have any results and asking if we've spelled the words correctly. A silent minute in, I sigh, just a little heartbroken, and open my mouth to suggest we try something else—

Kendra's computer monitor goes blank. After a few moments, there's a crackle of static and a video window appears, showing us a familiar face with his greasy hair hanging in front of goofy *Matrix*-esque shades. By the looks of his scowl, he's upset.

"This is not cool, guys," says Danny Melee in a snotty tone.

"There he is!" I say. "Hey, Melee, how's the video game business?"

"My lawyers have advised me not to speak to you three," says Danny. I can almost feel his eyes darting between us behind those buglike glasses. "And as far as the things you were just searching for on my site, I have *no idea* what you're talking about." He trains his gaze on Kendra and sneers. "Really, Kendra? Like some Frankenstein-ed little aggregator is going to help you hack into *my* company?"

"Your attention was all that was required," says Kendra, "and apparently, I obtained it."

Danny looks like he's about to rear back with some insult, but then he freezes, and his face softens. "Oh, you didn't need some amateur's program," he says slimily. "Hey, Josie, how're things on the Isla? Sorry I had to bail early last time. Next week still work?"

One by one, our eyes turn and set upon Josefina, her sun-kissed brown cheeks even darker than usual, her arms folded over her chest. Her eyes, turned away, say it all.

". . . *Josie?*" I say. The word feels like a scab in my

mouth. Maybe *this* is why she won't look me in the eye.

"She didn't tell you about my follow-up visits?" chuckles Melee. "We've become *good* friends. She's taught me a lot about the island and Warden magic. Right, Josie?"

"I don't wish to discuss this," Josefina grumbles.

As I try to grasp what I'm hearing, Ian charges ahead. "I don't care about any of this," he says. "Melee, we need your help."

"Yeah, okay," responds the boy genius onscreen, laughing hard. "Sorry, kids. Take it up with a teacher; I have work to do."

"Too bad, nut job!" shouts Ian, jabbing a finger at the screen. "We're in serious trouble here, and the way I see it, you owe us for nearly getting us killed on that island."

"I don't owe you squat," says Danny. "It's really not my fault that you three can't stay out of trouble for more than a few months. What do you need, explosives? Bail?"

My eyes close, and I concentrate on my breathing, focusing all of the emotion in me—the irritation from his snarky voice and Ian's frustrated shouting, Josefina's embarrassment and the immense disappointment it leaves in me, the sadness and terror of losing O'Dea and the rage at the indifferent Wardens—into a point. As I exhale, I let the point guide me, become my energy, my voice.

"Danny," I say, staring into the screen. Danny's eyes go to mine, and something about the way his mouth settles into a straight line tells me he can hear more than my words. "Someone took O'Dea. We think it was Dario Savini, your former right-hand man. Please help us bring her back."

Danny exhales hard, sending an oily bang or two shaking, and then says, "Any idea why he'd kidnap her?"

"All we know is they're going somewhere called Kudus," says Kendra. "Is the name familiar to you?"

Danny hisses between his teeth. Slowly, he removes his shades, and the wet and wide eyes beneath chill me to the bone with the pure fear in them.

"That's . . . not great," he says. "It's a rumor, you guys. It's supposed to be a city of the dead that got swallowed by the underworld."

"Where is it?" I ask.

"Not sure, but let's think." Danny scrunches up his face. "Hm . . . Kudus, Kudus. Ain't English, that's obvious. What language is that, *kudus*?"

Kendra's fingers fly across the keyboard. "Indonesian!" she says. "It means *holy*."

"Can you get us there?" I ask.

Ian's and Kendra's eyes flicker up to me. "Dude," says Danny, "Indonesia? Do you know where Indonesia is on a map? No offense, but I bet you don't. Besides, if the little I remember is true, this is one of the more cursed places of, say, all time. You guys might have to bail on this one—"

No. I can't back down. I can't let this happen. "Can you get us to Kudus, Danny?"

After a moment where he obviously considers our sanity, Danny Melee sighs. "When do you need to go?"

"Immediately," says Kendra.

Danny nods. "Let me make some calls and I'll get back to you," he says. "No promises." He reaches a hand out, but then stops and glares hard into the screen. "And for the record, Kendra? You may have gotten my attention, but PJ reached me." Then, with a click, the monitor goes dark.

That night, we sleep over at Kendra's house, the girls in Kendra's room, Ian and me in the guest room. While I call home to say good night to Kyra, Kendra brings up a picture of Indonesia, wondering aloud how we could possibly get there.

For an hour after the lights go out, Ian rants from his air mattress about purpose and O'Dea and how he didn't think Danny Melee would go for it, but I'm barely present. In my mind, Dario Savini drags our Warden and friend kicking and screaming into a city made of skulls to the soulless moans of the dead. In my mind, he grins maniacally as he dangles her, hog-tied, over a slobbering mass of hollow-eyed corpses. This is the problem with being so into scary movies—you can vividly imagine the most awful things possible, in dramatic Technicolor with Dick Smith doing makeup.

Two hours pass after Ian's rambling dies down into soft snores, and I still can't get to sleep. Finally, I crawl out of bed and tiptoe through the darkened house into the kitchen. The fridge is full of fancy organic food and foreign-brand drinks, and I finally settle on some Georgian mineral water, which is actually not that bad—

"It will happen there."

My heart punches me in the rib cage and my every joint tightens at once, sending a spatter of sparkling water flying out of my glass and onto the counter. When I turn, Josefina, in a pair of Kendra's pajamas, stares at me. Her arms are wrapped around herself, and her eyes look damp and sad from beneath a veil of her hair.

A million things run through my mind—*You scared me, I couldn't sleep, what are you doing up, so this Josie business*—but what comes to my mouth first is what I really want to know.

"What will happen?" I ask.

"That isn't clear to me yet," she says. "The dreams are still just flashes, images and feelings. There's no order to them. But . . ."

"But what?" I say, doing my best to sound encouraging, the way I talk to my sister.

She gulps, blank eyed. "But there is always the cold,

dark place," she says. "Your friends surround you. They scream, long into the night. And then there is blood—red and thick and terrible."

My mouth goes dry and I lower the glass to the counter, trying to meditate on my feet, to push back the fear. "And then?"

"And then there's a flash," she says, "and you are gone. There is only one person there, someone new and frightening. I cannot see their face."

The concentration methods O'Dea and Josefina taught me are failing—terror tightens my throat, sends sparks down into my fingertips. "What do you think it means?"

"I think it means your destiny lies in that cave," she says. "But that you might have to deal with a great darkness to find it."

She walks over to me, pulls me into her arms, and presses her lips to my forehead. "I'm sorry, PJ," she says through a sob, and then turns and vanishes into the house's shadows, leaving me to measure my breathing, focus on my heart rate, and wonder how I'm ever going to get any sleep tonight.

CHAPTER FOUR

Ian

Danny Melee delivers. I mean, no joke, the guy *comes through*.

"My private jet is going to take you guys to Borneo tonight," he says over Kendra's smartphone. "That's where it seems all the rumors of Kudus are centered around. Someone'll be by to pick you up around six. On it, there'll be caving gear for the three of you, plus all the research materials I've managed to put together on Kudus. Once you're there, someone's going to meet you and take you on a cave tour. The cave system you'll be visiting as tourists is connected to the caves where we believe the city to be. The guy I'm hiring will wait

49

for you for twenty-four hours, but after that, he leaves and you're on your own in Indonesia, which, honestly, I wouldn't be too jazzed about if I were you. That work?"

The four of us trade oh-my-God looks across Kendra's room, and finally Kendra says, "Yes. This is incredible. Thank you, Danny."

"Whatever," says Melee. "Just make sure Dario doesn't do something stupid like release an army of zombies and end the world. I've decided I'm officially against apocalyptic scenarios. Bad for business."

The first thing that fires off my dome is *Aren't you a saint, Melee*, but I decide to shut up for right now; there's just too much going on, and besides, Danny's doing us a solid here. "We'll stop him," I say. "Thanks again, man. You're a good dude."

"Ian, I'm trafficking three underage killers halfway across the globe and dumping them in a cave full of flesh-eating dead people," snaps Melee. "I'm not a good dude; I'm just out of my mind apparently. Oh, one more thing, guys?"

"What's up?" I ask.

"Never contact me again." There's a click, and the phone goes dead.

At this point, one of the hardest parts of this whole Gravediggers thing is making up excuses to tell my folks. Standing in front of them the next afternoon in our kitchen, it's just killing me to keep a straight face, and honestly, given how quickly this has all happened, I won't be surprised if they just don't buy it. My mom's got that look that's somewhere between proud and worried, but my dad, he's the kicker, sitting there with his mustache drooping down, chewing his thoughts.

"But your movie's not done," he says. "I thought that's why we've had all these kids running around our house in face paint. To shoot this wolfman movie."

See, in this situation, my gut reaction is to ask him what he means with "*all these kids.*" This is Kendra and PJ, my best friends, who he should know by now, but that's not going to help us. I need to focus, do my part of O'Dea's Gravedigger training. In my head, I picture her face, wrinkled like crazy, glaring at me. *Calm down,* she says. *Look at you, getting all agitated and chasing the first thing you feel. Slow it down. Know what you're doing.*

"He only sent them a sample of the film and the script," I say, reciting Kendra's slapped-together excuse. "That's what's won us the award, not the movie."

"Must be some script if they're flying you to New York City," he asks.

"We have a sister school there that's hosting us," I lie. "Ms. Brandt's meeting us at the airport tonight." Man, even I'm impressed with how well I'm remembering this. I literally almost wrote it on my hand. "It would just be for a couple of days, and everything's already paid for, so it'd be kind of a big deal if I *didn't* go—"

"Wait," says my old man. He squints, then shakes his head. "Nope. Can't do it. You have a scrimmage Thursday, and Coach Leider told me he's going to try to set up a casual weekend game for you and the guys on Saturday morning. That's too much practice for you to miss."

"And school," notes my mom.

"Dad, come on," I say, trying my hardest not to sound whiny, which would totally just make him more hardcore, thinking I need to be toughened up. "This is a big deal for me, getting sent to New York for something I'm part of. I can miss a little basketball—"

"You've missed plenty of basketball with this movie nonsense already," he says. "You can't just be good at a sport, Ian. You need to work at it."

It'd be so easy, just to spill the beans all over the kitchen floor, that my friend's life depends on this, that there's a man who is trying to release a couple thousand living dead people into the world, that I *am* "just good at" something and it's whackin' zombies upside the head, but none of that's going to get me to Indonesia. What'd O'Dea say to me? *You're like a gun, Ian, always ready to go off; you just need to be pointed the right way to do your job.* "I'll do suicides on the plane, I promise."

"Ian, you agreed to be on a team," he says. "You can't

go back on it just because you won some weird prize."

Nah, none of it's working. That hot anger seeps through the cracks of my whole story, and I run my mouth: "These days, it's like *you* agreed to be on the team," I tell him. "I'm just the one who has to do all the running."

"What's that supposed to mean?" he snaps.

"Okay, guys," says my mom, "let's keep this reasonable."

"Ian, what's gotten into you?" says my dad, just totally ignoring her. "You're upset you're not allowed to play school sports, and then when they let you back on the team, you'd rather fly off with your weird friends!"

"They're not my *weird friends*," I yell, "they're just my *friends*! They're more important to me than anyone on the team!"

"Exactly my point!" says my dad with this little laugh, like he's laughing *at* me, like he thinks I'm some kind of *idiot*. "No one's going to want you as starting point guard or team captain if you don't show up for practice! Your coach, your team, they *depend* on you to be there! That's important!"

"Maybe some things are more important to me right now," I tell him, feeling my fists clench and my forehead get a sweat going. Gotta stay focused, point myself in the right direction, blah blah Gravedigger blah.

My dad shakes his head and waves a hand at me, like

he's brushing me away like some bug. "You're talking crazy. Obviously, you're in no state to be traveling anywhere."

"Vince," says my mom.

"Emily, he doesn't know what he's talking about. He's forgotten who he is."

And no, oh no, it's too easy, he set himself up for it, and listen to him, calling me crazy, *driving* me crazy is more like it. I can't stop myself: "Apparently, I forgot who you are, too," I spit out, "a real *jerk*."

He's on his feet faster than I could've ever planned, sending me back a couple of steps as he jabs a finger out toward the stairs. "Room," he yells. "Now. While you're there, email your friends and tell them you're grounded."

My mom calls my name out after me, but by the time she's done, I've slammed the door behind me and I'm in my room, just charging back and forth, feeling like there's exhaust coming out of my nose, like I could just punch my wall and watch the whole side of the house come flying off, that's how angry I am. The clock says five, my gym bag's loaded with clothes on my bed, and here I am, grounded, stuck in my room while the whole reason I'm around is going to be waiting outside in no time and I won't be able to go out and meet them. All because my dad thinks that me playing sports, being the kid he wants me to be, is the most important thing in the world.

O'Dea's advice about pointing my energy keeps coming into the back of my head, so I just start doing push-ups and crunches, trying to burn off some steam and do something, *anything*, with all of this anger I've got running through me like a hand made of fire grabbing me by the heart and shaking me back and forth, over and over.

Time flies when you're ticked off, and midway through my third round of looking in the mirror and telling my dad what he can do with his basketball team, I get a text from Kendra.

Outside in 5. Ready?

My fingers go to the keys of my phone—still some clamshell; Mom says I don't need "another screen"—and begin to type that I can't, I'm grounded, my pops won't let me because of his stupid rules, sorry to leave you guys stranded where I can see you right outside my door—

My fingers freeze as the idea hits me. And man, does it hit hard.

There's my window. There's a, what does Mom call it, a *trellis* outside of my window? Rules aren't, like, physical things, so nothing's actually keeping me here.

Out the window, the night air is super cold, but maybe that's just how nervous I am looking down. My duffel hits the bushes in our backyard with a little crashing noise that I'm *sure* will get me noticed, but thankfully it doesn't. Then, it's one inch at a time, hooking my hands and feet into the shallow diamond-shaped holes in the wood of the trellis. Every second I move down, I'm sure I'm going to put my foot through a piece of wood or the whole thing's going to lean away from the wall and I'm going to go right backwards, but somehow it holds, and I drop the last five feet into the bushes, grab my duffel, and *motor*, just *sprint*.

My luck must be good, because just as I'm coming around the front of my house, a stretch limo rolls up. The back door opens, and PJ's grinning face grows big as I launch toward it.

"I know we've got bigger worries, but there's a TV back h—" PJ yelps, and sits back as I launch myself into the limo, Kendra peering at me as I sprawl out on the floor.

"Drive!" I yell at the confused-looking chauffeur glancing at us in the rearview.

PJ shrugs and slams the door, and the limo goes shrieking off just as, through the window, I catch my dad throwing open our front door and my mom pressing a hand against her chest. Dad yells and screams my name as we speed off around a corner and out of sight.

Kendra squints, confused, but PJ gets it immediately, and smiles in that sad sort of way. "Ah geez, Ian," he says. "Guess they didn't buy the story, huh."

"You *snuck out*?" gasps Kendra.

For a little while, I can't say anything; I'm just stuck

catching my breath and waiting for my heart to slow down, but then all I can do is replay that last image in my head—not my dad at the door, but my mom, mouth open, looking stunned. Slowly, my hand fumbles my phone out of my pocket, and I send a text to her cell:

im sorry

Thirty seconds later, it vibrates.

Me too.

"You going to be okay?" asks PJ.

"Let's just get to Borneo," I tell him, feeling like my heart just ate something bad.

My fingertips run over the little rubber bumps on the ball, and I can really feel every single one of them as I charge down the court. All of the other players are dead as disco, green-skinned corpses with white eyes and black, chewing mouths, wearing ripped-up uniforms, who come at me with their hands straight out, the worst defense ever. My dad and O'Dea are in the stands, screaming at me to focus and work and give it my all, but then O'Dea's face turns all swollen and bloody and my dad becomes Dario Savini, laughing at me. I go in for a layup, and then *whoa*, the whole court jerks sideways and I sit up.

After a few seconds of blinking and shaking my head back and forth, my body tells me that the world is tilting, that everything is shaking. The dark metal tube of Danny Melee's private jet lies before me, shuddering with turbulence.

Slowly, the picture comes together—PJ across the row from me, asleep and wrapped in a blanket, the other seats lined up in front of us, each with enough legroom for an extra person to lie down in . . . and there, up at the front of the plane near the passage to the cockpit, a light. Once the shaking of the plane gets a little less intense, I unbuckle my seat belt and shuffle forward.

"Can't sleep?" says Kendra as I come up behind her. She's in a little circle of seats with a polished wooden table in the middle of it, and it's covered with old maps that are brown around the edges, big dusty-looking books, and computer printouts. Her laptop sits open by her side, glowing with even more information.

"Yeah," I say, taking a seat across from her. "Just a little shaken by everything that's happened, I guess."

"That's totally understandable," she says, still not looking up from her research. "We've been thrust into this situation swiftly, unlike the mountain, or the island."

"You think it's all going to be like this from now on?" I ask. "Just nonstop Gravedigger-ing, no warning whatsoever?"

She finally stops reading, and looks up, not really at me but kind of past me, at what's in her head. She blinks, and thinks. And it's funny, 'cause that used to really get to me, when she did that. I'd just want to shake her and shout, "JUST SPIT IT OUT ALREADY, QUEEN BRAIN," but these days it's maybe the most incredible thing about her, how she can stop and take everything into account and think. How she does it is beyond me, but it's so cool. *She's* so cool, in her own weird, nerdy, psycho way.

"I think we might be in the middle of something," she says. "Meeting O'Dea, dealing with Dario Savini, these seem like pieces leading toward an end. At this time, I'm just following them."

Again, so smart. Makes so much sense. "What do you think is going to happen?"

She shrugs and smiles. "That, I can't tell you. I'm just the brains."

"Ah, you're more than that," I say. "I mean, you're in our front line. You're the bomb." Yikes. Where'd that come from?

Her cheeks turn a little darker, but the smile doesn't move. "Thanks, Ian," she says. "You're also not all you appear to be."

Okay, time to hit the brakes. I'm in no way ready to deal with this right now. Gotta focus on something else. "So, what have you found out about this Kudus place?"

"Well, it was a city in ancient Borneo," she says. "According to the web transcripts I've found, it was a city in the twelfth century made up of artists, poets, and . . . the word here is sorcerers, but they probably mean philosophers. But that's just one document I found online. This one"—she points at a mossy-looking scroll with a white computer printout paper clipped to it—"was written a century later and already describes it as a kind of underworld, full of demons and ghosts. The question is, what happened in between the writing of these documents."

"My guess is, something bad," I say. "The kind of thing that can curse an entire city, make it a zombie town."

"Obviously," she says. "Since it was made up of creative thinkers, it would be unsurprising if they were just overwhelmed by a local tribe. The Dayak headhunters had a prominent presence in that area at the time. What I'd like to know is, how'd it go from being a normal city to one only found"—she peers at a translation— ". . . *through the dark holes in the earth, down in the depths of hell.*"

Good question—how do you sink a whole city? My eyes go over the old documents Kendra's absorbing into her giant brain. One is a huge map of what could be Kudus, spread out across a brown flimsy scroll. Another is a page of weird squiggly characters surrounding a second, small map, this time with Kudus marked out in black and covered with a skull—obviously the second map of Kudus, the evil-place-beneath-the-earth one.

"Is this a fence or what?" I ask. My finger outlines a border on the second map, the skull one. It's a thick black border with these old-looking suns around it, the kind with faces—or it's more like there are suns, and there are lines connecting them. Each sun has a symbol over it. "Why's this map got this border and the other one doesn't?"

Kendra stares at the map, going totally still—and then *bam*, she's flying into action. Her one hand goes rifling through all of her documents while the other starts typing furiously. An Indonesian/English dictionary comes flying out of nowhere. The sound of rustling papers and tapping keys reaches this crazy pitch and then stops all at once. Kendra, sits back, mouth open, dazed.

"Ian, you continue to amaze me," she says.

"Well, yeah," I say, having no idea what I just did.

"I . . . I think they're Wardens," she says, pointing at the suns. "This symbol means *pendeta*—the word for 'priestess.' " She rubs her chin thoughtfully. "I think the Wardens sunk the city. I think whatever happened here was bad enough that they used their magic to hide it away in the earth itself."

A shudder goes down my back at the thought of something so evil and terrifying to the Wardens that they had to jam it below the surface of the earth. But it's not just that, it's Kendra. All this talk of sorcerers and witch doctors gets me thinking about that meeting with the Wardens, when she blew that Goth Warden chick off her feet. That's not normal. Kendra's not normal. I mean, obviously she's a Gravedigger, normal's out the window, but she's even not normal at *that*. It's like the minute I got to know her, I found out she was nothing like what I thought; she was something stronger and crazier than I could be.

"Well, okay, so why bring O'Dea there?" I ask her. "You think it's like back on the island, that Dario Savini wants to release the zombies into the world and get back at the Wardens?"

"Maybe," she says. "My problem, though, is that he shouldn't need her. We destroyed all the protective seals and special sigils on the mountain, and he destroyed the ones on the island. It didn't take a Warden to do that."

Ugh. This sick feeling spreads deep in my guts just thinking it: "Maybe this is something new," I say. "Something we've never dealt with before."

Kendra laughs a little. "I don't know, Ian," she says. "We've seen the dead walk. I suppose anything is possible. But if it is a foe we've yet to experience, what might it be?"

My mind tries to come up with answers, but that only makes me feel sicker to my stomach, and suddenly I'm feeling worried about the whole thing—Kendra, O'Dea, my parents, this trip. "Well, good luck with the research," I blurt, and stumble back to my chair.

PJ shakes me awake and tells me we have about an hour before we land, and we all take turns changing clothes and taking showers (you heard me, man—Melee's got *a shower on his plane*). Once we're all ready to go, a flight attendant feeds us breakfast, and then we bump and shake our way through a mass of gray wet clouds onto a private airfield on the Indonesian half of Borneo. One by one, we shrug on our backpacks, huge black canvas numbers loaded down with caving gear—cords and carabineers and harnesses—and covered with buckles and straps. Mine goes on easy, but PJ nearly falls over—the thing's almost bigger than he is—and Kendra and I have to steady him as he gets geared up.

"Some Gravedigger, huh?" he laughs as he tightens his straps.

"As long as you kill zombies, I don't care if you wear your shoes on the wrong feet," I say, and get a laugh from him and Kendra.

It feels good, hearing them laugh. Something tells me it's going to be the last time I hear it for a while.

Whatever I expected, it wasn't anything like this. Part of me thought it was going to be all dusty and sunny, with long snakelike dragons and roofs with spiked shoulders, if that makes any sense. Like Japan in one of those samurai movies PJ made me watch.

Instead, the whole place is damp, and the gray sky stretches on over the airfield and over the bright green trees just past it. As we leave the jet and walk along the wet tarmac, planes and towers and fences on one side and swaying green trees on the other, all with this rumbling storm overhead, I begin to wonder how real any of this could be. Even with the sleep I got, I can feel the time difference already messing with my head, and the dark rings under Kendra's and PJ's eyes tell me the same.

An Indonesian man in a suit shakes our hands as we arrive, calling himself Mr. Kusama, an employee of Melee Industries Indonesia. Once we're all checked in and our passports have been reviewed (someone must have called ahead, because we get brushed by without so much as a second look), we're shown to a car waiting for us. For the record, it feels really dumb to take off your ultra-cool caving gear after getting all suited up and strapped in.

"All right, friends," says Mr. Kusama through a heavy accent as we leave the airfield. "Straight to the Bangyan Caves, correct?"

"That's correct," says Kendra. "We're heading there to take part in a new tour that's going on—"

"I have been instructed where to take you and how long to wait," says Mr. Kusama, "but also not to ask about or listen to any other information about your trip.

So, please: Bangyan Caves, correct?"

"Yup," says PJ.

"Splendid," he says.

As we drive, a city—Kendra says a name I can't in any way reproduce, "Ban-yar-museen"—passes in the distance and I watch its skyline roll by, surrounded by waving trees and scummy clouds. Everything about this place, even the city out my window, feels new and crazy, like none of it fits right and I don't belong here. Maybe it's the jet lag and the rain getting me down, but it's like everything's happening too fast, like we're running headfirst into a totally nut-bar situation where people's lives are on the line, and are supposed to accept it. And I think about my dad. I feel lousy about lying to him, and if I hadn't, I'd still be at home.

It's too much. All I ever wanted to do was play basketball and chase deer.

CHAPTER FIVE

Kendra

Obviously, our current situation is dire. With that said, I cannot help but think of how lucky we are to get opportunities like this.

Indonesia is as we speak transitioning from its dry season to its rainy season, which lasts throughout the winter, resulting in a sky dark with a massive gray Cumulus Arcus cloud. Out my window, the skyline of Banjarmasin shines over the thick green canopy of trees, looking both old world and ultramodern simultaneously. Part of me wants to tell our driver to get off at the next exit, take us through the busy streets, get us bowls of the local cuisine (I'm almost positive it's a tripe dish here—cooked intestines—but given what I've seen as a Gravedigger, I think I could handle it), and maybe escort us to the nearest Buddhist temple, where we could pray to the powers that be for good karma on this upcoming mission.

There's no time, Kendra. This isn't a research trip. You are not here to learn, or teach, or discover. A man has kidnapped your friend and may feed her to monsters. It might be your job to kill him.

As I think it, a shudder runs down my spine, and I watch Ian staring out his window, PJ with his eyes closed and his breaths measured. No one has mentioned this yet. If I had to guess, I'd posit that none of us are prepared to confront it. So far, being a Gravedigger has entailed murdering monsters, returning the dead to their appropriate state. All of O'Dea's long-distance teachings made sense in the context of battling zombies. But if Dario Savini is threatening to harm our friend or release a horde of the undead, our options may be limited. We may have to be assassins on this trip. A heartbeat will stop. I am unsure if we can handle that.

"What's the game plan once we get to the cave?" asks PJ.

"That's where Danny's research ends," I answer. "There are apparently caves over the city that may be able to lead to it, but no one seems to know how one goes from the former to the latter."

"Are you kidding me?" says Ian, looking amazed. "We're just going to these caves and *hoping* we'll find an entrance into Kudus?"

"We may have to do some searching," I say with a shrug. "We'll have to keep an eye out for signs of Savini or O'Dea having been there. If we don't see an entrance quickly, we may have to split off from the tour group and explore some less-traveled corners of this place."

"We'll find it," says PJ, eyes closed, voice almost sad. He sounds so sure, but in a grave and *fatalistic* way (appropriate for our trip, and a helpful distraction—one).

PJ, what is going on in your head? What am I missing?

"Let's hope," grumbles Ian. He raises a hand and starts writing "Kudus" in the steam on the window with his fingers, his brow furrowed.

This won't do, Kendra. You need your troops rallied. PJ may be in his quiet meditative head, but Ian can't afford to be petulant. For an adventure like this, our physical center is vital.

"You'll probably have to run the Eddie Haskell routine when we arrive, Ian." PJ's name for it, not my own. "Sorry to impose, but they fall for it every time."

He smirks a little. "Yeah, they do," he says, and finally looks at me. "No problem, I've got it covered." Something about the way he looks at me makes my cheeks go warm. It's as though someone wiped a layer of grime off Ian, and suddenly I am seeing a glow coming from inside him.

Listen to yourself, Kendra. This is Ian Buckley. Ian Buckley who once called you a pathetic loser in class. Ian Buckley, who got you all mixed up in this zombie business to begin with. You must be jet-lagged.

With the city long gone, the highway turns into a rural country road. An hour later, we see our first billboard, depicting a towering cave surrounded by brightly colored Indonesian characters. We turn off at an exit and head down an unpaved road, the car shuddering, a stretch of hills growing in the distance. Finally, we see another series of signs depicting stalactites and bats, followed by a metal fence that a man opens for us, ushering us toward a sizeable cave mouth with a small white shack next to it.

As we pile out of the car, Ian turns up his smile and ruffles his blond hair. Sometime in the last few months, PJ and I decided that Ian had to be the face of our Gravedigger unit. While he occasionally overspeaks and will often straddle the line between crass and unmentionable, Ian Buckley is a blond athletic young man with an upbeat attitude, and people seem to respond to that well. When information is needed, I'll dart in. PJ is, in his own words, "permanent background." Ian's our best face forward.

As we approach the shack, we see a small crowd of

tourists waiting nearby, wearing ponchos and sorting cameras. Tuning in my ears, I acknowledge three Germans, four Indonesians, and a Chinese couple speaking Mandarin. As we step up to the shack, a box office window greets us, where a teenage girl mans a battered cash register.

"Hiya!" says Ian, putting his biggest, dumbest smile forward.

"Apakah anda memiliki reservasi?" she asks.

His shoulders slump as quickly as his grin does, and he looks at me in sudden terror. I myself feel naked and embarrassed in my ignorance.

Didn't study your phrasebook enough this time, Kendra. Didn't think you'd need to. That's some sloppy work. Did you expect Ian or PJ to know Indonesian—

"We should have a reservation under 'Melee,' " says PJ, lightly pushing Ian aside. "Tickets for three."

"Oh, absolutely," says the girl. "They're right here." She slides three tickets through a slot in the bottom of the glass. "Everyone who works here speaks English, so feel free to ask questions."

"How did you know that?" I ask PJ as we make our way toward the cave mouth.

"Look at this place," says PJ. "It's a total tourist trap. Of course they speak English."

PJ is not wrong. The cave entrance, an egg-shaped stone mouth opening up in the side of a nearby hill, is surrounded by signs, trash cans, and even a battered vending machine. There appear to be no shrines or ancient carvings, only a series of damp-looking tourists and an uninterested tour guide in an orange jumpsuit and a helmet lamp. When we reach him, he's speedily talking to the Germans and hands us each a helmet lamp without looking at us.

When he finishes his announcement in German, he turns to us and rattles out: "Welcome to Bangyan Cave. Bangyan Cave is one of the largest caves in Indonesia and has a diversity of wildlife, there are also many rare geological formations, some even say the water from Bangyan is medicinal, Bangyan Cave was said to be formed over a thousand years ago, artifacts and fossils found in Bangyan Cave have been dated back for as long as twelve hundred years, more information can be found at our visitors' center, ready to go?" I can't help but blink, trying to digest the blast of information just fired at me, but our tour guide doesn't even wait for an answer, merely turns and begins leading us into the cave. One by one, we and the rest of our tour group snap on our lamps as the shadows close in.

A distinctly spooky ambience seems to settle over us as we enter the cave. The air is cool with darkness, and dusty and mildewed in my mouth and nostrils. Every sound seems *cacophonous* (one of the first self-quizzed vocab words), echoing along every surface. Our guide leads us through a narrow tunnel, the smooth gray stone walls descending around us until we walk in single file and our shoulders occasionally brush the walls. For some time, we amble forward in this way, glowing silhouettes in the light of the lamps. Soon, I feel an involuntary pang of claustrophobia, and I hope we're not just squeezing our way farther and farther into a stone coffin. My head goes a little light, and my hand reaches out to steady myself against the wall.

From behind me, a hand lands on my shoulder and squeezes. "I think it opens up ahead," says PJ.

"Right," I say, taking a deep breath. "Am I that obvious?"

"You're breathing really hard," he laughs. "And besides, I know about freaking yourself out. I'm good at it." I force a chuckle, if only for the splash of levity.

PJ is, once again, right. A few feet ahead, the tunnel leads into a dark mouth, which then opens up into a massive brown stone chamber, the air cool and earthy. Perfect blades of light pour in from one or two small cracks in the ceiling, and between that and my headlamp, I can make out the spindly, clawlike stalactites hanging down over us and a huge glittering black pool sitting in the center of the chamber, teethlike stones creating a path across it. Ian whistles, and the sound reverberates in a shrill echo.

Our tour guide makes another announcement in

German, Indonesian, and Mandarin before turning to us. "Here is one of the many underground pools of Bangyan Cave. These lakes are fed by wells beneath the earth's surface, they are famed for being—"

"How deep is the average underground pool?" I ask, trying to gather as much information as I can along the way.

The tour guide stops, his face sour and bunched. "The pools are very deep," he says. "They are famed for being rich in minerals and—"

"Are there any wildlife that live in them?" I ask.

"Look, *gadis*," says our guide, leaning in close, "I have a rhythm going here. With every question, I must start over. Keep asking them, and we will be here all day."

"Sorry," I say, though his brush-off has left me angry.

"Never mind us," says Ian. "Pretend like we're not even here."

We move on to another tunnel, one we have to navigate by getting down on our hands and knees and crawling through. The next cave chamber is decorated with hanging encrustations of epsomite and gypsum that resemble melting candle wax. My mouth opens to ask our tour guide further questions, but I shut it quickly. This man won't be much help to us, and besides, Ian's maneuver was the correct one. Our presence should garner as little attention as possible.

The entrance to Kudus hits me before we even infiltrate the next chamber of the cave. As we crawl nearer and nearer to the mouth of the tunnel, I feel a buzzing deep inside my body, running through my teeth like a live current. There's a sound, too, not unlike the rushing of water, which grows in my ears until it drowns out the shuffling of the German college student in front of me.

"Do you hear that?" I ask, my teeth chattering.

"Hear what?" Ian says, barely audible over the din.

As we enter the third chamber, there is no doubt in my mind that some sort of magical influence reigns over this place. My hands are vibrating. The room seems to throb with a loud sound like waves against rocks. While most of the smooth-walled chamber lies in the same state of still air and impenetrable blackness, one corner of the room burns with a hazy light that seems to rise from the ground in smokelike clouds.

"It's in here," I whisper.

"How can you tell?" asks Ian.

"I feel it" is all that I can whisper in return. He frowns and looks away.

The plan is simple; I just have to ignore the overwhelming blast of magic energy that courses through me. Our tour guide's mind-numbing descriptions seem to go on for an aeon, but this time around he actually skips English—perhaps my nosiness helped rather than harmed our ability to disappear into the cave—and swiftly turns to lead our crew through another small stone passageway. One by one, as the adults turn their backs to us, PJ, Ian, and I click off our headlamps, hold our breaths, and step back into the shadows.

As the last of our tourist companions vanishes into the shadows, darkness overwhelms us, so thick and inky you can almost taste it, lit only by the bright, shimmering aura rising from one small corner of the room.

"There," I tell them. "Where that column of light is."

"Column of light?" says Ian. "What are you talking about?"

"It's pitch-black in here, Kendra," says PJ. "What do *you* see?"

I flick my helmet lamp back on and approach the glow. There, in the floor, is a circular opening, its edges surrounded by intricate shapes and sigils that hum with an unnatural gray light. PJ and Ian turn their lamps on and illuminate a tunnel, descending directly into the earth.

"Ho boy," says PJ. "Talk about a metaphor for the past year."

My fingers press into the sigils, but feel nothing— these symbols are enchanted onto the stone, not carved. Yet as my hand rubs along the tunnel entrance perimeter, the pads of my fingers touch a series of impressions that don't take whatever these strange new visions are to identify. They speak with perfect clarity:

"Claw marks," I whisper, the shadows around me seeming to chill my voice into vapor. "These feel recent—" My lamp follows the scratches to their end . . . where what appears to be a human fingernail juts from the dusty ground. On closer inspection, I find my initial hypothesis correct. Revulsion quiets me as I visualize O'Dea, clawing for her life, being dragged down this hole.

"Oh my God," whispers PJ. "We need to get down there."

"Time to crack into our goodie bags, kids," says Ian, dropping his Melee Industries backpack. He unzips it and retrieves a pair of night-vision goggles, their verdant segmented eyepieces making him resemble a chameleon. PJ and I follow suit, and soon we all shut off our headlamps and switch on our goggles. For a moment, the darkness remains, and then with a flicker our jagged cave world appears to us in pixilated green.

"Nice," Ian says. "This is some Navy Seal stuff right here."

Bit by bit, we "suit up," as Ian repeatedly calls it—gloves, jackets, work belts containing flashlights, hammers, and other small caving needs. At the bottom of the bag, I find a rubber handle attached to an unknown object. One yank, and a machete comes free, awkwardly held in my hand.

"We better each have one of those," says Ian.

"I don't think I'll need mine," says PJ softly. "Okay, let's talk belaying. How do we do that?"

Between Ian and me, a plan is constructed: spike the rope at the cave mouth, link it through our belts, drop the remainder into the opening, and belay down. It all sounds perfectly logical if one doesn't take into account that none of us have ever climbed a mountain, or belayed down anything, or gone caving before.

I hold the spike, PJ loops the cord through it and ties a knot, and Ian drives it tightly into the rock, his hammer ringing *cacophonously* (again, old school) with each strike, echoing madly through the cavernous darkness that surrounds us.

"The tour will probably hear us," I say, brushing stone dust from my sleeve.

"Then we'd better get going," says PJ, looping the remaining rope through his belt. "O'Dea needs our help." I follow suit, and Ian takes the third loop. He then holds the remainder out over the hole, opens his hand, and lets it drop into the blackness.

There are exactly nine seconds before we hear it hit bottom.

Do the math, Kendra. If time until impact is nine seconds, then you have approximately two hundred meters until you reach the bottom.

Enjoy your climb.

"You're first," PJ says to Ian.

"*That's* original," he responds. He pulls out a pair of gloves from his pack and slips them on. He then grabs the rope, leans back into the hole, and scoots bit by bit down until he vanishes. A few seconds later, the cord stops pulling through our belts, and we hear him call out, "Okay. Next, Kendra."

Doing my best to be fearless, I recline gradually, pressing the soles of my boots against the stone walls at all times and allowing my weight to tighten the cord in my hands, suspending me. Below, I hear the zip and chuckle of Ian being an adventurer, and I attempt to imitate him by increasing my downward speed. Inch by inch, I sink in the enclosed silence of the hole, its smooth edges slowly engulfing me until I'm surrounded on all sides by walls of stone, all illuminated in spectral green.

And yet, in this clammy darkness, my goggles are nearly blinded by light.

Sigils. They descend along the walls of the stone tunnel in glittering lines, each intricate and careful in its artistry. My hand involuntarily rises to touch one, only to find a cool, smooth surface beneath it; either these sigils are painted onto the wall, or they're enchanted into it.

Though they resemble no alphabet I've ever encountered, both their swooping designs and faint glow speak to their meaning. I do not simply know it, like a piece of trivia, I feel it, like a belief, deep within my core.

Go back, they say. *This is a terrible place. They are here.*

For how long we drop, I can't tell exactly; PJ lowers down above me, and for what feels like hours we sink deeper, the sigils on the walls continuous and consistent. Suddenly, I hear Ian beneath me gasp.

"Guys," he whispers, "we're here."

"Is it the city?" I ask him.

"Nah," he says. "But I'm guessing we're on the right track."

As the walls finally open up into a cave ceiling, the view appears, and I, like Ian, find myself breathless. Before us stretches a vast cavern, with dozens, perhaps hundreds of stalactites descending from the ceiling, interspersed with the skinny tendril-like formations known as "soda straws" and jagged, monolithic pieces of epsomite crystal. Enormous columns of rock stretch between the floor and ceiling of the cave, creating sloping oval openings in the sprawling interior cave. And all along it, sigils, glowing white against the green background, thousands of them stretching in a spiderlike web that spans the entire floor and walls and through a darkness so huge and cold that it feels like we've arrived on the ocean's floor.

With no rock to brace against, I descend quicker than

planned, but thankfully Ian is there to help catch me, and PJ shortly thereafter. The sensation of solid ground is reassuring beneath my feet, but my focus remains on the stunning cave all around us. As PJ and I make noises of wonderment at the incredible geological formations, Ian drops his backpack, sorts through its contents, and hands us each a plastic-wrapped item.

"Food," he explains as I stare dazedly at his offering. "Those are Danny Melee Noob Chewers. Protein bars, basically. Eat; we'll need the energy."

Only Ian could eat at a time like this. My mouth barely registers the flavored protein cud I gnaw upon. (If my tongue is accurate, Danny has chosen a hazelnut-graham cracker flavor here that will no doubt have a sour aftertaste.) Slowly, just to be sure, I lift my goggle from my eyes and stare out at the cave. And I am correct—even without the goggles, in the lightless subterranean void, the sigils continue their soft glow, giving the invisible space depth and shape even in the dark.

"Kendra?" asks a black space where PJ was. "Are you okay?"

Great idea, Kendra. Take your night-vision goggles off while your friends watch. That doesn't look suspicious, does it?

"I'm fine," I respond, flipping the lenses over my eyes once again. In the green electronic glow, PJ nods with a knowing smile. Ian, meanwhile, chews his pressed protein supplement with a look on his face that suggests it has spoiled.

"What did you see?" he asks.

"Nothing," I tell him. "It's . . . a scientific experiment. Total darkness. Can the eye adjust itself to the dark in a totally lightless space? Sensory deprivation has been said to cause interesting effects on the human brain."

Ian chews a bit longer and then says, "So . . . are you seeing things?"

"Ian, stop," says PJ.

Ian's eyes narrow behind his goggles, whether I can see them or not. "Warden things? Sigils and stuff?"

An influx of heat coats my face. My involuntary power immediately becomes my shame. "It's fine, Ian. All I saw was the dark."

"You should tell us, you know," he says. "If you notice anything."

"Ian, what are you even talking about?" asks PJ, measuring his breath.

"I want to know, is all!" says Ian. "If Kendra is developing some kind of extra senses or magic powers, I think it's important we talk about it."

That's a thought—why aren't *you talking about it, Kendra? Why aren't you shoving your face in Ian's, laughing, shouting, "Maybe I do, jerk, so watch it or I'll make a Hand of Glory out of you"? Suddenly, it feels like his words, his* knowing, *is some sort of spotlight focused on you. It feels anxious, and creepy, and sad. What is that?*

"Guys, focus," says PJ. "We're in a cold, lightless space with no one around. Things are bound to get a little claustrophobic." There's a distinct waver in his voice on the last word. PJ, it seems, is fighting his own fears as much as ours. "Whether or not Kendra's seeing things, we need to find O'Dea, and it's looking like this place leads to Kudus. We just need to figure out how to get there. Kendra?"

My fear swells up in my heart again, taking shape and lashing out. "I didn't *see* anything."

"I mean, do you have an idea for a plan?" says PJ, sounding disappointed.

Ah, yes, Kendra. You're the smart one, remember? Focus on your brain.

"Well, obviously, we have to feel the air for current," I say, doing my best to sound analytical. "If there is a passageway out of here, it probably has wind blowing out of it."

My statement is true, but I know it's unnecessary. My eyes have already settled on a spot, a circular shadow in the distance where the sigils amass, forming a ring.

Play along, Kendra. Lick your finger and hold it up. That's it. The air is coming from over there, right? Why, you didn't need magical powers at all *to figure that out—*

"Stop," says PJ, aiming an ear upward. "Do you hear that?"

At first, I want to accuse him of being preposterous, but then my ears find the strange sound in the air—a scratching noise that seems to get louder with each second. My mind runs through a list of wildlife found in Indonesian caves, but none of them make a noise as loud and unsettling as that.

My mouth opens to speak. Before I can, it appears.

The hole in the wall is too small for any human being to fit through, yet somehow the repugnant thing unfolds out of it like a spider—long thin fingers first, torso and head following. Slowly and silently, it creeps from its crevice and crawls along the edge of the cave wall insect-like, bones popping. From our vantage, its spine, thick, ridged, and discolored, bulges from its back at us. With every painstaking stretch of a hand or foot, the scratching noise rings through the cave.

Ian and PJ follow my gaze and both go dead quiet. We observe as the thing inches along the wall, stopping every so often to tilt its head to the air and sniff loudly.

Good Lord, Kendra. You looked at pictures of axolotl and cave cockroaches and hairless bats . . . but you never planned to see anything like this. What in the world is . . .

Wait. Is that a zombie?

The bead of sweat that forms at the rubber seam where my goggles meet my face is barely noticeable until it descends down my cheek rapidly. I am only truly conscious of it as it dangles momentarily from the very edge of my chin, allowing me a brief moment to paw at it before it drops from my face and hits the cave floor with an audible *pat*.

And, as expected, my heart explodes with fear as the creature freezes, twists its head in a complete reversal with a loud crunch, and looks directly into my eyes with orbless sockets.

CHAPTER SIX

PJ

Something has happened, down in the cave.

In our run-ins with the living dead, something I always find upsetting about them is that, when all is said and done, they're people. It's what separates them from the other movie monsters. Zombies don't become zombies under the full moon. They don't turn into dust when you drive a stake through their hearts. Bela Lugosi and Lon Chaney and Christopher Lee never played zombies, because walking corpses are not fancy or nuanced. They're just human beings, only the script got downgraded and the stunt wires are showing. Our first zombie horde was a group of college dance majors, and the second was a cruise ship full of tourists. Both were dead, and ugly, and ravenous, but they were people.

How did George Romero put it in *Dawn of the Dead*? "They're us, that's all."

Which means this is, or was a long time ago, a person. It was us.

Which means things have taken a terrible turn in this place.

The cave zombie on the wall is a skeleton wrapped in gray chipped skin, its fingers long and knobby, its dusty eye sockets black and empty. Its backbone is like a Stegosaurus's spine, lined with bumpy, discolored ridges. The nose, the ears, all the extremities are gone, leaving this skinny skull-faced lizardlike thing that is, somehow, *climbing the wall*.

When it pulls its Ashley Bell impression and meets our eyes with its back turned to us, my stomach tries to turn itself inside out, but I manage to stave off my fear. Then, the rest of its body lowers gracefully off the wall and twists itself to meet its head, and I manage to croak out, "Oh *GOD*."

"Okay," says Ian, teeth chattering. "Oh man. Okay. It's coming for us, isn't it?"

"No," says Kendra. "It can't. The sigils won't let—" She gasps and looks at us, eyes wide, mouth open. The words make me cringe, revealing what I've known since Kendra blasted that Warden across the room. Our friend is more than meets the eye.

"So there *are* sigils," grumbles Ian.

"Well, look on the bright side," I stutter. "At least we know it can't get to us."

The cave zombie responds by carefully moving its foot forward and placing it on the dusty ground. Then, with a dancer's grace, its scarecrow body steps forward, balancing on—oh, what is this—on the very tip of its big toe. As it moves, its body bends and twists horribly, the arm and ribs shifting fluidly while the face stays set on us; the air is full of popping bones and creaking dead skin.

"Kendra," I say, "what's happening?"

"It appears to be moving *between* sigils," she says, voice sinking with hopelessness. "It must have been down here long enough that it has learned how to navigate around them."

"Everyone get ready," says Ian, dropping his bag and scrambling to find his machete. "We don't know how tough this thing might be. They might—"

The zombie takes a quick lunging step toward us and snaps out a long, bony arm, which sends us all stepping back with a cry. For a second, its grasp looks like it has just barely missed us, and then I see the finger hooked in Kendra's backpack strap.

Kendra yelps as the bony long-dead corpse yanks her toward it, doing its best to stay carefully standing between the magical symbols none of us can see. Her hand flies to her helmet, which is about to fall off, and by accident her headlamp clicks back on, filling my goggles with blinding light. As I yank them off, a cry leaves my throat, but it's drowned out by the raspy hiss of the cave zombie, which recoils from the light, acrobatically lurching away from us and back toward the wall.

Suddenly, it dawns on me—its lack of eyes, its twisted body. This thing has lived in darkness for years. It must find its way around using vibration, smell, or sound. And it must not like direct light.

So let's overexpose this sucker.

When I switch my headlamp on, I'm staring directly into the shadow where its head should be. My aim is good, and my beam strikes the thing in the face, sending the creature recoiling with another high, nails-on-chalkboard hiss.

"Aha!" shouts Kendra, her voice deafening as it bounces around the quiet, smooth stone of the cave. She points her lamp directly at the zombie. Ian follows, and the three of us slowly advance, watching its nearly translucent skin throb beneath the glare. By the time it's back at the crevice that it sprouted from, all three of us have our lights aimed directly at its back, framing it like a prison escapee.

Hands clawing at the crack in the wall, the undead creature seizes up, going into a round of quick, twitching convulsions before it tumbles to the cave floor.

In the pool of light at our feet, the strange insectlike corpse curls up. Its legs and arms twist in close to its chest with snaps, crackles, pops. Its mouth splits into a silent, lipless scream, and it tucks its head down, as if protecting the eyes it no longer has. Finally, entirely balled up like one of those Mexican mummies, the cave zombie is barely bigger than, say, a suitcase. We could probably fit it in one of our backpacks.

The cave, once filled with the shuffling of feet, popping of bones, and shouting of terrified Gravediggers, returns to its pitch-black silence, heavy with tension. The blade of Ian's machete appears in the light and softly taps the zombie. When nothing happens, we all exhale at once.

"I guess light kills them," says Ian. "Maybe they're just not used to it." He pauses and gulps audibly. "Shoot, guys, what . . . what do we think happened to this thing?"

"Their physiology must have changed due to its extended subterranean existence," says Kendra. "It's common—animals lose their eyes over generations from living in total darkness for too long. And—my word, look." She points to the zombie's hands and feet, gnarled near its stomach. When I see them, panic and confusion shoot through me—its fingers and toes have some kind of claws at the end, white and pointed . . .

Oh. Oh, no.

Bones. The zombie has worn away the skin at the tips of its fingers and toes, leaving sharpened ends of bone to poke through and form needlelike claws.

"They must utilize those for climbing along the walls the way this one did," mumbles Kendra. "And look. Notice the prominent spinal column. Remember, Danny determined that the zombies keep their 'brains' in their backbones."

"This one must have gotten very smart," I mumble, kneeling down next to the withered thing and poking the creature's spine. The ridges on its back are white, spongy looking, and as I poke them I realize that they're not made of bone as well. "I think these growths are fungus. Like those flat mushrooms that grow out of trees."

"Shelf fungus," confirms Kendra. "It's actually growing shelf fungus out of its spine. This is incredible."

"Watch it, dude," says Ian. "Maybe I should get in with the machete—"

"I think it's dead," I mumble. "For good." Hatred and disgust for the cave zombie radiate off my friends in waves, but something about its willowy body and blank, skull-like face makes it seem sad, pathetic, to me. As I get closer, my eyes find blue veins webbing through its skin and take in the deep indent beneath its rib cage. Is this what happens when zombies have nothing to eat—they just wither away? Imagine starving, every day, for hundreds and hundreds of years. It's enough to make you climb the walls.

Which this thing learned how to do.

My eyes drift up to the crack in the cave wall where the zombie emerged. It's a small crevice, but might be enough for us to crawl through. Switching from my headlamp back to my goggles, I peer into it, trying to see where it opens up, but its twists and turns eventually just drift out of sight. There's nothing visible inside, just smooth rocks and the occasional piece of moss—

Not moss. My hands reach out and grab the thin, grassy follicles in front of me, and looking at them up close sends my nerve endings screaming.

"PJ, what is that?" asks Kendra.

". . . hair," I choke out. "It . . . could be O'Dea's."

"Whoa, wait a second," says Ian. "Let's not freak out quite yet. It could be anyone's hair. Could be a zombie's hair."

"Does this thing look like it has hair?" I snap at him. My mind is trying to force my heart into Calm Down mode, but it's not working; my deep measured breaths are slowly becoming hyperventilation. In my mind's eye, O'Dea smiles at me, her face hard but warm and welcoming, only when she opens her mouth to give me sage Gravedigger training advice, she screams and blood pours out. "Dario, or one of these things, took her through that hole. We need to get in there."

"PJ, I'm surprisingly inclined to agree with Ian," says Kendra. "That passageway is a tight squeeze. It would likely be impossible for anyone other than a desiccated zombie to fit in there."

"If it fit in there," I say, jabbing a finger at the balled-up corpse on the ground, "then we can most likely fit in there—"

Something impossibly hard closes around my wrist, squeezing a screech out of me.

The zombie's hand holds tight onto my arm even as I pull away. Before our horrified eyes, its body slowly unfolds, popping and crunching along the way. My meditation methods fly out the window, and my scream deafens us as it bounces around the pitch-black shadow. I tug hard against its grip, but for how skinny it is, the cave zombie is incredibly strong.

Ian raises his machete, but Kendra holds up her hands. "You could hurt PJ!" she shrieks.

For a second, I consider urging Ian to go right ahead, as any minute now I'm waiting for the corpse's bony face to dart forward and take a chunk out of my neck. But the bite never comes—the zombie steps a bony leg into its tunnel in the wall and yanks sharply, pulling me after it. Before I know it, my arm is into the crack, and then my feet are lifted off the ground as I'm yanked hand first into the stone wall.

As my feet disappear, I feel a hand clamp around my ankle and the extra weight of my friends being dragged after me.

The tunnel is too narrow to have ever been used by people, and even in my night-vision goggles everything is a blur of jagged rock outcroppings. As the zombie drags us along, my head, hips, shoulders, knees, elbows collide with sharp pieces of stone. Bolts of pain blast through my bones. My wrist and ankle both go numb with the two weights yanking at them, and one or two pops in my back and ribs warn me that I might end up with a dislocated *everything* if I'm not careful.

After what feels like an eternity of jostling and slamming, a rush of cool air hits my face, and my head emerges from the tunnel and into another cave, the points of stalactites jabbing down at me from the ceiling. This cavern is even larger than the last, sprawling out endlessly around us like a set piece from *Temple of Doom*. A glance down makes my breath seize up in my chest—we're a good fifteen feet up, being pulled out of a crack in a sheer rock wall, and the cave zombie is yanking me out of the crevice with all its might. This fall is going to end with broken legs unless we have something to cushion us—

Wait. My eyes shut. O'Dea's advice comes back into my head, and my mind goes into my breathing, each inhale and exhale like a bow moving across a violin, creating a focused note out of my fear and panic. As the world slows down, the answer comes to me in a slow-crashing wave.

The minute I'm able to pull my foot out of the rock crevice, I plant it against the rock wall and shove, hard. My other ankle slips free of Kendra's hand, and I fly backward. My body collides with the skeletal cave zombie, and we go tumbling off of the wall, its arms closing around me in a steely embrace, my hand coming up under its chin to keep its chattering yellowed teeth from sinking into my flesh.

The cave zombie is mostly skin and bone, so the landing isn't *comfortable* per se. For a second, all I see is Kendra's hand growing smaller in my view, and then there's a hard slam in the back and a crunch like a million flashbulbs going off at once. Everything goes white, and my breath flies out of my lungs, but a quick mental check reveals that nothing is broken and my mouth doesn't taste like blood. Small victories.

When I roll over, the zombie's broken body shudders where we landed, sharp hunks of bone rending open the tough skin and showing deep gouges full of foamy black liquid. The mushrooms from its spine fizz as they melt into pools of gray muck. Its misshapen form suggests I managed to crush its spine in the fall, and it lets out a last hiss as its carcass finally goes still.

"PJ!" calls Kendra, her voice echoing through the

cavern. "Are you okay?"

"Yeah," I mumble back, my eyes frozen on the cave zombie's body. That's weird. Why's the blood bubbling and hissing like that? That's not normal. I hear myself whisper, "I'm sorry."

"In which case," she calls out, her voice edged with panic, "maybe you can help us down from here?"

"Right, right!" My shoulder screams in pain as I climb to my feet, but I can't think about that now. In the distance, I can see Kendra's top half sticking out of the crack in the wall of the cave, arms flailing. As I run under her, the lightness on my shoulders hits me—my Melee Industries backpack must have gotten yanked off along the way.

"How do you want to do this?" I ask, staring up at what looks like part of a magic act.

Kendra opens her mouth, then freezes. ". . . unsure," she finally says. "I take it you lost your backpack."

"Yup."

"Mine as well." She frowns. "No rope. This will prove difficult."

"I could move the zombie remains over here, for you to fall on."

She grimaces. "While not preferable, that is a viable option. Well, perhaps if we take off our clothing, and tie it together, we could use it to rappel—"

This is quickly becoming the wrong kind of horror

movie. "I'm very against getting naked in the zombie cave, Kendra."

"As though I'm all for it?" she cries. "PJ, we're very low on options here. Sacrifices must be—" Suddenly, her eyes go wide, and she gasps. "What—no, no, NO, IAN, DON'T—"

There's something like a popping sound, and Kendra goes shooting out of the hole, flying through the air. Once again, I close my eyes, breathe deeply, and let the scene slow down. Her speed and distance become obvious to me, and I manage to run directly under her just in time for her to come down and make a sprawling heap of arms and goggles out of the two of us.

"Thanks," she groans, rolling off me. "That fall might've killed me."

"No problem," I say, feeling something in my back shriek with pain.

Of course, Ian doesn't need to be caught—one minute he's in the hole, the next he lands on the hard rock floor with a *boom*, crouched perfectly to break his fall and sending up a small cloud of dust, his machete held out in terrifying Jason Voorhees fashion at his side. I can't help but blink at him in awe—jumping fifteen feet like it was nothing. When I notice he still has his backpack, and one of ours in his hands, my breath jets from my lungs in a grateful sigh.

"You could've seriously injured me," snaps Kendra.

"While you guys were talking, I was stuck in a crack like some kind of cockroach," he says, rising and brushing rock dust from him. "I was suffocating in there."

She says no more, just snatches the backpack from him and begins rifling through its contents. Ian hauls me to my feet and brushes me off.

"You okay?" he asks. "What's this black stuff on you? That zombie blood?"

"Yeah," I say. "I bodychecked him and crushed him on landing."

Ian grins. "I would've never thought of that, man."

"Perfect." Kendra pulls a thin rod from her backpack and twists it, making it flare bright white in my night-vision goggles. "We'll leave glow sticks at important points along the way. That way, if we need to backtrack, we'll know where we are." She looks into the bag. "Hrm. We have to hand it to Danny; he made sure we had everything we might possibly need."

"Okay, this is zombie kill one," says Ian. "Where is it?"

"Right over there—" I turn, finger pointed, to show Ian, but the words turn to a ball of ice in my throat and refuse to move further.

Crouched on its haunches at the edge of the shadows, leaning over its brother's broken corpse, is a second cave zombie—thin, leathery, eyeless. It looks almost identical to the first, save for maybe an extra wisp of hair. Its nose, or the hole that once was its nose, hangs over the crushed remains of its buddy, taking deep sniffs of its carcass.

On my one side, Ian latches onto me, hands digging hard into my shoulder. Kendra keeps examining the supplies in her backpack. "Our map is still secure. There's even a satellite phone in this one. Hopefully, once we discover the city of Kudus, we can find somewhere to try and call—"

"Kendra," I stage-whisper, "stop talking."

"What? Why—" Behind me, I hear her twist to face us, and then all noise stops and she goes deathly still.

Of course, there's no hope of going unheard. We know very little about these zombies, as they're nothing like the ones from the countless monster movies I've watched. But given the last zombie's response to very little noise, it's heard us.

Slowly—always slowly—the head rises, the gaping eye sockets aiming at us, its gross nose hole fluttering as it smells the air of the cave. For almost thirty seconds, we remain perfectly still, watching it take us in without any sign of hunger or hostility. The dusty air tastes dry on my tongue; the total lack of light puts a deep, resonant chill through my bones.

"It's not moving," whispers Ian. "Why's it not moving?"

"Maybe . . . they've evolved into vegetarians," says

Kendra, "and it doesn't want to eat us."

"Maybe it can smell the Gravedigger on us," I whisper, the idea sending a surge of raw power through my body. "It knows what we are, and that we pose a threat. It's . . . scared." I love it. Things have made a reversal. We no longer fear the dead for trying to kill us. The dead fear *us* for succeeding in killing *them*—

Suddenly, a rhythmic tapping, *tak-tak-tak*, echoes through the chamber, making us all jump and gasp. My eyes whip around, looking for the source of the noise, when I notice the zombie's hands and feet twitching. Sure enough, as I focus in, I watch as the zombie taps his pointed finger and toe bones against the floor in a careful, quick way, sending sharp noise echoing throughout this abyss.

"I think it's attempting to communicate," says Kendra.

"Is that Morse code?" asks Ian.

"I don't think it's trying to talk to us, Ian," says Kendra.

As if on cue.

First, one huddled shape crawls into view behind this new cave zombie, then a second, then four more, then eight more, ten, forty. In the distance behind it, the cave grows thick with slow, skeletal shapes that seem to emerge from the shadows like the night just spat them out. Not just on the floor, either—suddenly, over the walls, even along the ceiling, the cave fills with a scuttling swarm of thin, bony beings, creeping into view. As they make their way along, their own fingers and toes tap out a similar rhythm to the one being played before us.

"Kendra," I call above the deafening tapping of bones, "tell me you see some sigils in this room that I can't see."

She gulps and squeaks, "I'm afraid not."

CHAPTER SEVEN

Ian

Oh man. Oh man. Okay. Oh man. Here they come.

There are a lot of them. No, scratch that, too many of them, a bazillion, creeping slowly at us all crouched with their arms curled up at their chests like T-rexes, or moving across the ceiling and walls like a bunch of undead Spider-Mans, and it's like my goggles go from seeing a green cave to some kind of barrel of ants, moving all over each other, each one more covered with flat mushroom scales than the last. The sounds are creepier than the other zombies we've fought, the ones that moaned and snarled and gurgled, 'cause with these guys all you get are these low-pitched scratchy hisses and the sound of their old skin rubbing together with this noise like bedsheets being gathered and the tap-tap-tapping thing they seem to like so much. I'm guessing that's a cave zombie's dinner bell. I don't know. I'm officially back to square one when it comes to dealing with zombies, because *what the heck are these things* and *how are there so many* are pretty much all I'm dealing with here.

They fill the room, forcing us to scoot away from the front line of them like three scared poodles. Here PJ was, talking about them being afraid of us, and now we're falling back faster than you can say "hopeless."

That's when cold lumpy stone hits my back, and as hard as I push with my feet I can't move another inch. My head whips up, and I realize we're at the rock face we just popped out of, that the way we came in here is at least ten feet over our heads, so there's no hope of getting to it now. We're stuck here, in a giant stone coffin with no way out and a couple thousand flesh-eating skeletons coming at us. So, *that's* awesome.

"We need to fight them back," I finally stutter. My hand remembers the machete in it, and I give it a toss in the air and tighten my grip on it. "It's the only way."

"You're right," says PJ, setting his feet, holding up his arms like he's Bruce Lee or something. "Headlamps on in three, two—"

There's this *WHUNK* and a blur, and PJ goes down screaming and scrambling, and before I can tell what's going on, something heavy lands on my back, the *WHUNK* sounding through my body in this sharp blast of white, and then I feel claws on my shoulders, bony arms on my head, and I realize that they're cave zombies that have just jumped down on top of us. They must have been crawling on the ceiling and let go directly overhead, death-from-above style. Suddenly, I go from butt-kicking Gravedigger to headless chicken, jabbing my machete into the thing on my back over and over again while trying not to stick myself.

And then they just swallow us up. Kendra's screams and PJ's repeated "I'M SORRY, I'M SORRY" go muffled as a few thousand zombies leap on us in a great big pile of corpses.

Imagine being thrown through a jungle gym, hard, for, like, fifty seconds. That's what's going on here, only every so often this tunnel of hard limbs has a rotten bone-tipped hand or a hissing skeleton's face. After a second, I'm not even screaming; I'm just making that karate-chop-on-the-back motorboat noise, *uh-uh-uh-uh-uh*, as my green night vision reveals a mishmash of seven million hard, undead knees, elbows, knuckles, fungus-covered spines. Are they even trying to bite me?

One of the hands snags onto my ankle and doesn't let go. I'm ready to get pulled in half like a gory piñata, but then the hand feels kind of cold and fuzzy, like the Icy Hot that Dad has me put on my ankle when I'm hurting after a long game. Suddenly, the whole tangle of zombie hands lets go of me, and I go flopping on the floor with a little puff of dust, my body feeling something different, not normal, definitely nothing like the chalky blackness of the cave. This feels powerful and bright and . . . alive.

Kendra's got my ankle in one hand and PJ's in the other, and man, whatever's going on, she's just burning up. Literally, there is *steam coming off her* in my green night vision. Sweat's dribbling down her face and even soaking the edges of her goggles. Her teeth are gritted hard with her lips all peeled back. She looks like how I felt when I sprained my ankle two years ago.

"What are you even doing?" I ask her.

"NNNNGGGGI DON'T KNOOOOOW," she shrieks.

"She's keeping them back," says PJ. "Look."

He's nailed it—the whole squirming wall of claw-fingered bone-thin dead people around us is keeping this nice little three- or four-foot distance. I mean, they don't look happy about it, and their hands come out like they want to snag us and pull us to whatever dark hole they eat in, but they can't, and instead it's like they're warming themselves at the fire of Kendra. When I look up, my stomach goes flat—the wall of clambering zombies continues at least ten feet up. We've got a few thousand hungry dead people here, minimum.

"What do we do now?" I ask.

"HEDLNSH," growls Kendra.

"What?" I ask.

"HEADLAMPS!" she shrieks.

Oh, *yeeeeah*!

PJ and I flick on our helmet lamps, and man, do the zombies not like that. The whole mass of interconnected crawling bodies shifts and shrieks wherever we shine our lamps on them. When we climb to our feet, Kendra lets go of our ankles and sways for a second, and PJ's there just to time to catch her, but it makes him turn away, and immediately a hissing zombie is leaning in, his sharp, skinny fingers going right for the helmet. If only I'd held onto—

Wait. Hold on. Right hand—hey! I *did* hold onto my machete!

At least today's improving.

A leap and a swipe later, the zombie backs away snarling, its fingers tumbling to the floor. PJ and I crowd around Kendra, keeping our lamps moving in a wide circle, me striking out with my machete, PJ doing his weird meditation-based closed-eyed zombie judo and tossing them away, but every time we turn away from one part of the horde of undead things around us, another begins to fold in toward us, hands out, mouths open.

"There are too many of them!" shouts PJ, swerving

out of the way of a swift gray hand, and I'm pretty amazed by how well he's doing staying away from them. He dodges them like he knows where they're coming from, like he can hear them ahead of time, and it's cool to watch, his skinny little body twisting and lashing out over and over.

"Kendra!" I shout. "Can you give us round two on the juju?"

My answer is Kendra straight-up lurching forward and throwing up on the cave floor. It ain't pretty, and the sharp pukey smell gets me coughing, so I focus on swiping out with my machete and blasting the hissing mass of shadows with light. Whatever, it was bound to happen. One thing I've learned, man, you fight zombies, someone's gonna ralph.

We try to keep the perimeter around us tight, but I can't help but know we're losing mad ground with every second, and I'm feeling more and more of these creepy skinny cannibals connect with me, no matter how much I slash at them. There's a sharp-ended hand clawing at my hair, there's a pair of jaws coming hissing out at me from the pile. It's like they don't have any joints, just bones in a bag, and we can't win against something like that, no matter how ready and trained we are this time around, and I do exactly what O'Dea told me not to and start stiffening up inside, because let's face it, O'Dea's dead, she's gone, there're just too many of them for her to make it through this, no matter how tough and sage and wise and kind she is, she's dead, we're *dead*—

And then, it stops.

Seriously. Every shuffle of skin or pop of a bone in a socket, every gasp and shriek and hiss, they just end. The zombies freeze, all stuck in their big tangled heap. All you can hear is the sound of my, PJ's, and Kendra's panting.

Then, it's like this rumble, deep and loud, like the earth's stomach is growling, just shakes its way down the tunnel, growing louder and louder until it fills the room, making the floor tremble beneath us. This rumbling moan sounds like some kind of angry animal, something old with a lot of scales and eyes. Suddenly, the night vision doesn't mean a thing, the dark and cold of this place hits me, making my skin go all goosebumped.

The zombies start crawling backward—and I mean that—they don't turn around and leave; they back off—those black hollow eye sockets still zoned in on me, PJ, and Kendra the whole time. It's like they're being rewound in slow motion. They probably don't even need to see to know where they're going, which is the kind of idea that makes you want to cry.

And soon, the last few of them back up into the dark and vanish. There's a final *clik- clik-clik* as a final skinny one with a head of tattered gray hair crawls back along a wall. He lets out a loud, angry hiss as he disappears.

"Where do you think they're going?" I say.

"It must be something about that sound," Kendra says, standing and wiping her mouth. "Something is calling them away."

"Do you think it's a Warden?" asks PJ.

"Wardens repel zombies," says Kendra. "Besides, this place has been out of reach for hundreds of years. Nothing could have survived down here."

"Maybe it didn't," I say. "Maybe it's some kind of . . . super-zombie." Kendra gives me this look like I'm being an idiot, and it stings inside. "Hey, look at those things. If the zombies can turn into some kind of skeleton-spiders, anything can happen."

Her eyebrows raise and she nods. "That's actually a fair point. Well said, Ian." And the sting is gone, and I can feel my blood running through my face, like I'm full of lava or something, 'cause she said I—

I don't know why I'm thinking about this. Think of anything else. My shirt is ripped. Black foaming goo all over my machete. This room smells like barf. Where did the zombies go?

"Where do you think they went?" I say, jabbing out my machete toward the deep black shadow where the dead people disappeared. "We should follow them to find out."

"Careful, Ian," says PJ holding out a hand. "You don't know what could be down there."

"You sound like your mom," I say, storming fearlessly into the tunnel before me.

Of course, I've taken maybe ten steps before the floor just disappears from under me, and I go falling, like, midair falling, arms and legs wheeling. It's lame, too, because I looked so cool jumping out of that crack in the wall earlier (they can't lie; I was awesome), so to suddenly be screaming and tumbling blind in a shower of dirt and rocks is just not a cool look.

Fortunately, I land on my backpack, so it just feels like a giant punching me in the back and not a person actually taking a stone club to me. My breath flies out of my chest, and everything's a cloud of dust and PJ screaming.

"IAN!" he cries, his voice echoing all over the place and basically stabbing me in the eardrums. "Are you okay? Say something!"

"Stop . . . yelling," I manage to cough as I climb to my feet. Once I'm upright, I take in all the dark shapes around me in creepy green night vision and see a curving wall, a set of blocks, leading . . . wait.

"It's a staircase," I call, waving my hand at the two pairs of red power lights and thick lenses shining overhead. "Throw down a rope and let's follow it. It can probably lead us to wherever these zombies are hiding."

It takes some figuring out, but Kendra and PJ manage to drive a spike into the floor near us and drop one of our remaining ropes. PJ goes down first, but he's sort of clumsy doing it and I have to help him. For a second, I think of my dad—*If it weren't for you, that kid would be dead by now*, he likes to say—and I feel bad, wondering if he's right, wondering how PJ can throw a zombie around like he's a Shaolin monk but he still can't climb a rope right. Then, Kendra zips down, but of course she goes all creepy and weird the minute she looks around.

"Oh, wow," she whispers, wandering up to a wall and running her hands across it. "Look at these hieroglyphics. Incredible."

"I don't see anything," says PJ.

"What are you—oh," she says. "You should get close to them with your lamp on. Then you can see them."

Switching my goggles for my headlamp, I see what she's talking about—the walls are covered with these old-looking scribbled drawings of people running from other people with big sticks and skulls on their belts, all surrounded by a ton of weird, swirling sigils. But what leaves a sour taste in my mouth is that we need the light to see them, and Kendra didn't.

"Are they glowing or something for you?" I ask her. She doesn't come back with anything, so I try again: "Kendra, do you see some kind of magical—"

"I can feel them," she says calmly. "That's all."

"What do you mean, *feel them*?" I ask. "Are they hot? Do they give off some kind of smell or something?

Work with us here."

"I just . . . feel them here," says Kendra, wrapping her arms around herself. "It doesn't matter. We should follow the staircase. If it goes to Kudus, it goes to O'Dea."

"Wait, hold on," I say. "Kendra, if you've got some kind of crazy Warden powers now, we should use them. Like, back there, I know you lost your Danny Melee power bar afterward, but that was a clutch save. We need more of that—"

"They don't work that way," she snaps. "I don't want to talk about this."

"What? Why not?" I say. "We're Gravediggers. Any tool we have against the zombies counts—"

"I'm not a tool!" she yells, her face scrunching up beneath her goggles. "I'm a Gravedigger, Ian, like you. Our Warden is somewhere down here, and we need to find her. That's all that matters." She storms off down the stairs, shaking her head and grumbling to herself.

"What's her problem?" I whisper to PJ. "*Not a tool? We're all tools. Zombie-hunting tools.*"

"That's a little creepy, man," says PJ, and when I look at him he's kind of shaking his head, like he can't believe what I'm saying.

"Isn't that what O'Dea wants us to be? Trained zombie killers?"

"But we're people first," he says. "Kendra's your friend, not a weapon. Whatever's going on with her, she's having a hard time with it. You need to just let her deal with things at her own pace."

"Easy for you to say," I tell him. "You're all Zen about Gravedigger-ing these days. If you were smart, you'd be scared. You'd want to use every strategy available to you."

"Trust me, Ian," he says, trotting off after Kendra, "I'm very scared."

Great, so now I'm the jerk, and for once I'm the guy being left behind instead of forging ahead, which is a feeling I'm not that big a fan of, let me just say. As I power walk to catch up with the two lights ahead of me bobbing in the darkness, I just keep wondering why I'm the only one having the normal reaction to this. Dad would get it. Coach would get it. Why pull punches? Why do I stay the good old-fashioned zombie fighter while Kendra gets to witch out and PJ's some born-again mercy killer or something? What's the big deal with wanting to do what we came here to do?

CHAPTER EIGHT

Kendra

The cave is like outer space—the darkness is oppressive, all-encompassing, and carries with it a deep and lonely cold. Or so I think. As we descend farther into the cave, I cannot help but wonder what is making me feel so isolated and outcast. Is it our current situation, or Ian's awful comments that have my cheeks burning and my fists clenching?

It's not as though I disliked things the way they were before.

If I had my way, these unsettling developments—O'Dea kidnapped and dragged to a sunless crevice where she might kill herself rather than divulge the tools of her trade, a new breed of inhuman zombie that behaves like a skilled predator, my emerging talents for an energy conveyance that some might call *magic*—would not be happening. O'Dea would be giving us phone tutorials, the zombies would be slow and unintelligent, and I would be nothing more than a karmically destined zombie killer. And, of course, Ian wouldn't be acting so awkwardly around me, alternating between reverent and aggressive.

Three more years. All I needed was three years of learning, training, understanding what we are. We'd be teenagers, ready to deal with an abundance of displacement and change in our daily lives, not only in our karmic standing. Instead, we're shoved into this our first year, belaying down a centuries-old abyss to a sunken city filled with mutated corpses.

And don't forget the powers, Kendra. You saved your friends' lives earlier with that Warden trick, but you left no room for speculation. You've got a power beyond that of mortal human beings (be honest; somehow you always knew), and you used it to get those zombies away from you.

Remembering the feeling of those strong, dead hands clawing at my flesh sends a chill down my spine. But it's not simply their new forms, their new abilities . . . it's what these cave zombies *didn't* do. Everything observes a set of rules within this world of karma and curses, and one seems to be that zombies devour human flesh. Danny Melee once speculated it was to allow the fungus that reanimates them to spread, but whatever the reason, it's consistently been the case that the zombies eat the living.

So why didn't these zombies bite us? They had plenty of time to do so, yet they never did. It makes no sense. None of this does. What *happened* down here?

The sigils on the wall, both those carved by hand and those glowing softly in my vision that must have been enchanted through witchcraft (if O'Dea is still alive, ask her if that term is considered offensive or insensitive), scream at me in some kind of hidden electrical dialect that feels slightly painful. But to some extent, Ian is right—I've got to try and make sense of their message. If we're going to save O'Dea, we need to do so any way we can. Whether or not we're "tools," as he so idiotically put it.

My heart beating fast, my mind racing, I close my eyes and put my hand to the wall, drinking in its strange empathic—

DOOM PAIN DEATH BLOOD CHAOS

My hand flies back, my mind stunned by the blast of discord that swept over it. Ian and PJ stop in their tracks as my gasp bounces between the darkened walls, filling the dusty silence. "I'm fine," I stutter, trying to blink the dots of light out of my vision. And yet, as they start walking again—PJ quicker than Ian—I feel the loss of that new and somewhat harsh power, which was both shocking and thrilling.

Easy, Kendra. Don't rush into this. Tiny steps. Try again.

Mentally, I focus on O'Dea's lessons, her calm growled words on escaping my own brain and letting go. As my hand approaches the wall, I take several deep breaths, doing my best to put all extraneous thoughts from my mind. As my hand collides with the sigils, the energy flows freely through me, filling me. But rather than clashing with my active cerebellum, it finds an empty space to burn out its dark, ancient message.

Before the warriors came, the wall explains in a blooming of raw data, Kudus was known as a heaven on earth.

Great thinkers, artists, and wise men from all over the island, and from many lands a great ways away, came to Kudus to learn under its many brilliant citizens. Pilgrimages to Kudus were seen as a necessary rite for any monk or mystic, and peace, harmony, and freedom were the governing principles within its walls.

For ages, the warriors, the great headhunter tribes of the island, had a fine relationship with the city's strange residents, trading furs and meat for medicine and spiritual guidance. Though brutal and cruel, the king of the warriors saw the good that the people of the city brought to the land and made a law that the city was to go undisturbed. But the king died during battle with a neighboring tribe, and his son, a vicious killer and inhuman monster, took over. Immediately, he demanded better trades, began to question the importance of the city, and more than once threatened the city elders during a bargain. Unlike his father, he would come in full war paint when entering the city, complete with enemy heads around his neck or on his spear. Finally, the people of Kudus cut the headhunters off, forbidding them from entering the city and forbidding its citizens to do business with the warrior tribe.

One week after the decree was made, the warriors attacked. The guards of the city walls were no match for them; the weapons they bore were sold to them by the very warriors they fought, and they were not well trained in handling them, given their environment. Within minutes, the walls had been breached, and the headhunters entered the city. Though the warriors were greatly outnumbered by the citizens of Kudus, the thoughtful and generous citizens were easy pickings for the skilled soldiers. What followed was horror—slaughter in the streets, blood sacrifices, temples burned, countless heads lopped off and carried as trophies through the city. For miles in every direction, the screams of the dying could be heard filling the night.

My feet slow, my breath catches in my chest, and tears burn the backs of my eyes. No voice speaks to me of this horrible killing—it is transmitted directly into my heart. The fear of the citizens, the bloodlust of the headhunters, the sickening smell of carnage, the agony of a city dying in one unspeakable night.

"Kendra?" whispers PJ. His hand lands softly on my shoulder. "You all right?"

"What's the holdup?" asks Ian, trundling up behind us.

"Kendra just needs a second," says PJ, thankfully saying what I wish I wasn't too emotionally compromised to express. "But she's fine. Right?"

"Right," I manage to utter.

"You feeling sick still?" says Ian. His hand takes mine and puts a water bottle into it. "Here, if you want it. Not too much, though; we only have a little."

The simple action makes me feel somewhat better about Ian. He helps when he can. The water is good, washes the taste of my post-magic regurgitation out of my mouth, centers me. "Perfect," I whisper. "Thanks. We can continue."

The boys quietly walk off ahead of me. My hand attempts to touch the wall again, but it hovers an inch above the dusty surface. The cold, overwhelming darkness of the cave feels safer than the ravaged horror of Kudus.

But I have to know. It could help us find the city . . . and O'Dea.

Closing my eyes, I move a few inches down the line of hieroglyphics, hoping to miss any further slaughter, and press my hand to the wall. The energies fill me once more, pouring their story behind my eyes. . . .

The sacking of Kudus was spoken of through all the land, causing much sorrow and agony. And while some cried out against the tribe that would so willingly butcher a peaceful city of freethinkers, other tribal leaders respected the viciousness of the headhunters. They had been suspicious that the people of Kudus practiced black magic and consorted with demons. Many local tribes made their way to the city, ready to ransack what loot the warriors had left behind.

The tribesmen who made it back spoke of the dead.

Those people of Kudus who had not lost their heads had risen and were devouring any living person, pilgrim or bandit, who made their way to the city. Soon, some of the dead began escaping and wandering the countryside, seeking warm flesh and hot blood. The warrior tribe who had destroyed the city vowed to do it a second time and marched proudly into battle with spears held high and war cries on their voices.

That night, the people of Kudus had their revenge. The headhunters were overwhelmed by their lifeless adversaries and fell. Of the hundreds of headhunters who entered the city, only two made it out, and they were gibbering madmen for the rest of their days, haunted by visions of the living dead.

Defeated physically, the tribesmen brought together every sorcerer and priest they could find and had them use their magic to cleanse the city. The dead came, and in a last effort to free the land of the scourge, the gathered mages used their power to cause a massive earthquake that split the mountain in a great jagged vent that swallowed up the entire city. Many lost their lives using their magic to create the quake, but when they finished, the city and its thousands of undead monsters sat a mile below the surface of the earth. In an act of bravery, a team of powerful Wardens made their way down through the caves and into Kudus to lay the final containment spells onto the city, to ensure that it could never escape. The last of the mages, a woman named Yanta, completed one last task over twenty years of sunless living and dodging the cursed. Her last act as Warden of these caves was to carve . . .

". . . this staircase."

"What was that?" asks PJ, looking back at me.

"What?" I ask.

"What about this staircase?"

My stomach sinks. I'd been so good about taking in the story of the city without mumbling it out loud, and here I am revealing my bizarre magical powers at the last minute. "Nothing," I say. "Just had a thought, about the city. I'm thinking we might be getting close."

PJ nods, but doesn't say anything. No one, not even myself, is interested as to how I might know it is close.

The answer's the same, Kendra. Because you feel it. Because a new sense of which you were previously unaware, somehow simply knows.

We finally turn around a new corner on the staircase, and a pile of stones blocks any further progress. Ian gives it the Buckley Test—a sharp kick—and a bit of loose rock comes crumbling off of it.

"We might be able to break through this," says Ian, poking at the stones with his machete. "It'll take a bit, but I bet we can do it."

"Wait," I say, approaching the wall. The sigils glowing from it speak to me of a barrier, built and enchanted to keep the undead at bay. But there's something else, too, laid into the magic surrounding the wall. A warning, an explanation, and a series of instructions. As I close my eyes and empty my brain, a picture begins filling my mind. . . .

"This wall is meant to keep the undead from leaving," I tell them, "but it's not the only way in. One of the stairs lifts up and creates an entrance into the sewers beneath Kudus. We can get through that way."

"You got all of that from a *wall*?" asks Ian, his voice high and incredulous. "How's *that* work?"

"There's something here that's sort of a . . . magical message," I say, trying to choose my words carefully.

"And you can, what, speak ancient Indonesian?" asks Ian.

Once again, his words make me feel useless and freakish all at once. "It doesn't matter. The sewers into the city are under a stair. I'm positive of it."

We backtrack the stairs one by one, checking their edges in the hopes of finding a hinge or seam. By the fourth one, I'm officially beginning to feel foolish—here we are, three minors in the dark wearing over five thousand dollars' worth of expensive caving gear, tugging at stairs—until Ian gives the fifth one a pull, and there's the unmistakable sound of stone against stone. He and PJ pry the heavy slab of rock out of the ground and push it aside. From beneath it comes a heavy, rank must that fills the room and stings our nostrils, and we retreat coughing. With a second glance, I see a rusted metal ladder descending into the green pixilated depth of the hole.

"I told you," I gag and hack. "Once the bad air clears . . . we can get down there and into the city."

"This is probably the most booby-trapped place on earth," coughs Ian.

"Forget booby traps," gasps PJ. "These are probably crawling with zombies. The sewers are where all zombies end up in the movies."

"Would the Wardens have left us this message if they were unsafe?" I ask, my throat still swollen with stench.

"Kendra, think about this," says PJ. "Maybe these things are crazy wall-climbing freaks these days, but at one time, they were regular stupid zombies. If these people had sewers, they had entrances to them. You don't think that over hundreds of years, zombies might have squirmed down by the dozen? Or just fallen down manholes? Zombies are bad with gravity."

Ian nods. PJ is our zombie expert due to spending much of his life watching movies with the plural noun *Dead* in their titles. To be fair, he's normally trustworthy on these issues. But I can feel, in my very gut, the magic at work here. We can't be afraid of some disgusting sewer if there's a chance of finding this lost city and locating our Warden while she's still alive.

"I can feel it," I tell them. "It's magic. I don't know why, or how, but I can hear the walls. Something really bad occurred here, and that gate just informed me of this sewer entrance. It's our only hope. Think about O'Dea."

"O'Dea would want us to be careful and think," says PJ, taking what I think is a dramatically long breath.

"Can you really feel, like . . . magic in this stairwell?" asks Ian.

"It's like the walls are screaming in my head," I explain.

"Ugh," he grumbles. "I'm not sure you hearing voices beats PJ's movie monster knowledge."

"Ian, you need to trust me here," I tell him. "This is something you cannot understand, but I promise, I have this power. Breaking down that wall is a very bad mistake."

Ian nods, but doesn't look at me. PJ sighs and throws up his hands.

"All right," says Ian, finally turning and stepping out a hesitant foot onto the ladder. "But if it's all a bunch of booby traps, or zombies, or booby traps *involving* zombies—"

"It won't be," I say. After he finally disappears down, I follow him, and PJ, shaking his head, finishes up.

The ladder ends about five feet off the ground, so we have to jump. Ian spots me, then turns away and wipes his hands on his pants, as though I'm covered in some kind of sheen of grime.

After PJ touches down with a splash, we stare into the tunnel. Hanging clots of filth and rot drape across the passageway like fat in a clogged artery. In my night vision, it's all the same bright green filter, and yet somehow I can feel the lack of light, that lost change in energy that one *should* feel when descending into a sewer pipe. A claustrophobic shudder throttles me as I truly think about it—moving from one darkness to the next. No wonder the zombies mutated into those insectile aberrations.

The tunnels are long, hung with huge growths of mucuslike sediment from dripping water and covered with an ankle-deep slosh of scum at the bottom that gives off the unholy smell that still assaults us. Still, I cannot help but admire the architecture. For a city over eight hundred years old, this sanitary sewer is up there with any Renaissance city in Europe.

You'd imagine, Kendra. Luckily, this is your first trip down a sewer pipe. Maybe someday, you'll travel the world and spend your days wading through the sewers of cities like London, Paris, even Prague. Ah, the life of a Gravedigger. Or Warden. Whatever you are.

Up ahead, the muck becomes thicker, rising to our knees. At this point, its phlegmy texture makes it harder and harder to pull through. In my night vision, I can see the lumpy mess coating the floor, quivering and gelatinous with filth. A collection of branches or pipe parts strikes my leg, and I yank my foot up and bring it down with a wet, meaty crunch.

Something slaps the back of my calf.

"Hey," I say, turning back to the boys. "Who did that?"

They blink. "Who did what?" asks Ian.

As if on cue, there's a sound, deep and bubbling, as

though an amphibian were gargling.

"YAH!" shouts Ian, yanking up a foot scum-covered. He looks toward us, frantic. "There's something down there. Oh man. There . . . there might be a zombie in all of this filth—"

"Stop," says PJ. His voice is calm, barely a whisper, but it has a sickened tone to it that gets our attention. "Nobody move. I think I know what's going on here." He sighs. "I just . . . really hope it's not that."

"PJ?" I ask.

"In three, we pull up our goggles, we turn on our lamps, and we run," he says. "Got it?"

Ian and I share a glance. Whatever PJ's thinking, his demeanor suggests complete confidence in this plan. We nod, slowly, and reach for our goggles.

"Three," says PJ. "Two. One. Now."

In a single, swift motion, I yank my night-vision goggles down around my neck and flick on the lamp on my helmet.

As the light crosses over the pale quivering muck beneath us, it contracts, pulling backward. Huge, bulbous shapes move through it and push up toward the surface as the gargling noise becomes a shuddering throaty howl.

And that's when I begin understanding. Before my eyes, the mounds of twisted arms tear wet, bloated skin from each other. Rib cages push up as though they were sea turtles beneath pale and veiny-marbled muck. As I survey our own footprints, each one opens a scabby hole into a solid layer of putrefaction zigzagged with bones. The first of the skulls rises free from the mass, turns its near-liquid eyeballs on me, and shrieks through thick bubbles of flesh.

CHAPTER NINE

PJ

Unfortunately, I'm right.

The whole thing is zombies.

If I were making the movie of our trip down to this place, this would seem so blatant. Obviously, without sunlight and fresh air for over a century, the zombies evolved, conditioned themselves to no longer be the simple staggering monstrosities that we've dealt with all right. From what I know about these zombies—and believe me, I know zombies—there were two types down here in this lightless maze: those that clawed at the walls trying to get out, and those that stumbled into the sewers and wandered around in the wet and the filth for ages. The ones at the walls eventually sharpened their fingers, got skinny enough to climb, and began to communicate through vibrations.

And from what we've seen, water speeds up zombie deterioration. It melts them down, if it's too hot. But it was nice and cool down here, so they didn't melt all the way.

They just kind of . . . fused together.

The whole blob of merged human corpses rises up like a garden of death, like a swelling lasagna of dead people sloshing up around us in festering waves. The basic laws of zombie nature have gone horribly wrong here, the conjoined dead deformed beyond reason—there are zombies with three arms, two torsos, four people's worth of intestines spilling out of them. They all come pouring from the horrible pool of reanimated flesh around our feet.

"This is *the grossest thing I've ever seen*!" yells Ian, pulling back from the writhing mass. With every second we stomp through the flesh-muck, more arms, legs, faces, teeth, come shuddering out of the mound with soggy, burbling growls. My mind races, taking in the lake of dead bodies, the whirling of my friends' arms, the noise of our screams and their moans echoing through the tunnel—

—no. Eyes, shut. Mind, quiet. Put everything in slow-motion, bullet time. Think about O'Dea's advice.

Know your enemy, and turn your fear into something that will outlive this repulsive scene.

"Jump!" I scream just as a bushel of rotting claws comes snatching at me. "If they're still moving, it means their spines are undamaged somewhere down in there! Crush them if you can find them!" My feet launch me up into the air, and when I come down I hear the wet rip of meat and a muffled crunch. Immediately, two of the zombie faces twisting my way shriek and sink back down into the depths of their own mangled forms.

Ian and Kendra follow suit, leaping through the air and landing hard on the bloated multi-corpse. Automatically, the whole pale gray mass begins shaking hard, sending vibrations through the sewer tunnel. Every single jump fills me with a twisted mix of pity, pride, and nausea. This poor zombie-amoeba (zomoeba?) has laid down here rotting into an impassable flesh-slick for ages and ages, so I'm glad I'm putting the poor creature at least somewhat out of its misery. But every noise and stench that rises from a hole I stomp in its giant body sends stomach acid back up to burn my throat and tears to the backs of my eyes.

As we hopscotch across the sprawling creature, my headlamp catches something rusted and green, coated with slime, but perfectly usable.

"There's a ladder!" I cry, pointing. "Come on, let's get out of here."

"I guess you were spot-on about the zombies," pants

Kendra as we leap toward the ladder, protruding half zombies gurgling in agony and clawing at us with melting hands.

"Look on the bright side," says Ian, "no booby traps."

We take the ladder rungs two at a time. I barely feel the rotten iron grate that I heave up with my shoulders, but suddenly we're flopped out in the fresh air (fresher than the sewer, anyway—we're still maybe a mile underground), panting and desperately wiping the black gore from our boots on the dust-piled ground. Beneath us, the sounds of melancholy gurgling and the slapping of loose meat come in a horrible stomachache chorus.

"Okay," I gasp, trying to keep my head clear and my breathing steady. "Glad we made it out of that. Now, let's get moving. We have to find Kudus."

"Um, PJ," says Kendra, pulling on her goggles and taking in our surroundings, "I think we're here."

At first, when I switch back to my night vision, all I see are a few scattered huts and pueblos, and I can't help but think, *I expected more.* Then, I rise, and turn around, and I can feel my eyes bulge painfully from my head and my heart beat faster.

"Some city," laughs Ian. "Isn't our cul-de-sac bigger than—"

"Turn around, Ian," I whisper.

From behind me, I hear him follow my advice, and then a long low whistle leaves his mouth that echoes deep within the cave as he surveys what is easily the greatest set piece of all time.

The buildings start as small huts and crumbling houses, but soon there are multi-floor clay structures, huge longhouses with horned ends, one or two larger dome-topped buildings that could be anything from mansions to churches . . . but they are nothing compared to the temple. There in the distance it stands, a series of teardrop-shaped structures surrounding one main tower, the many-ledged point of its apex like a flame made out of stone, covered with leering statues of gods and demons and showing through its very size the sheer massiveness of the cave we stand in. The city of Kudus grows thicker as it nears these forgotten gates of hell, but though the buildings around it cluster together tightly, none match its height or its beauty.

And yet, seeing them this way, in green night vision surrounded by darkness and perfect quiet, makes my heart go numb in sadness and fear. Slowly, my eyes begin to take in more and more of the cave, the curtains of dust and filth that cover every hut and stone building, the piles of cracked and strewn bones jutting from the layer of cobwebs and rot that covers every inch of ground, the gaping black windows of the temple as it looms up in front of us like some kind of giant skull, staring down at the three puny humans who never should have seen it.

This isn't a city. It's a grave, one giant mausoleum. A hole for the murdered to wander aimlessly, never at peace, always hungry. Until three clueless morsels wandered into their domain.

I'm going to die down here.

My joints go weak; my head whirls. My eyes won't close; my breaths won't come. I am so tiny, the cave so huge, so endlessly dark, but so empty. There is only the temple, and all this death. My body lurches forward, and I fall to my knees. Kendra and Ian call my name and rush over to me.

"You okay?" says Ian. "You feeling sick? Need some water? We're running low."

"He might just be claustrophobic," says Kendra. "Remember, PJ, keep calm. Use the fear; make it function as something different."

Hearing her try to repeat O'Dea's advice to me gives me a light shake, enough to let me clench my eyes shut and focus. That's why we're here—O'Dea. Our teacher is somewhere down here in the hands of a supervillain. If she's still alive, we can save her.

And if she isn't—if she's taken her own life to protect her people—then we've got some revenge to take.

I've got to get up.

Get. Up.

As I rise to my feet and shakily dust the crud off of my knees, I manage to gulp away my dry mouth and say,

"Where do we begin searching?"

Kendra opens her mouth, inhales, and then makes a squeaky noise. "It's . . . anyone's guess," she says. "Maybe we should go house to house? They could be anywhere."

"Hey, let's not forget the zombie factor here," says Ian. "Aren't you worried we'll bother them?"

"I doubt the zombies are just sitting in their homes, Ian," says Kendra.

"Then where are they?" I ask.

The words freeze in the air as they leave my mouth, but I must strike a nerve—Kendra and Ian immediately whip around, scanning the streets. Here we are, on the outskirts of a city that should be swarming with horrible skeleton-people, and there's nothing, not even the tap of a finger bone. The sheer number of them means that there *must* be one or two around, and yet there's only deeper silence than ever.

"We need to get moving, at the very least," says Ian. "The longer we stand here, the bigger pieces of bait we are."

He's got a point. We scurry our way over to a nearby hut, throwing our backs against the wall. Huge drifts of age-old dust go puffing out around us, sending a sneeze rocketing through me.

Kendra stands and glances through the hut window. "Some bones, cracked," she says, "but no O'Dea."

Cracked bones. Something comes back to me from our time on the island—the zombies eat everything, even the bones. Danny Melee said so. So why all the bones? Did they go bad? Did the zombies have a change of heart?

"Let's keep at it," I say, darting around the side of the hut.

The zombie I nearly run into doesn't seem half as surprised to discover me as I am to find it. While I take a leap back and wheel my arms while yelping like I've stubbed my toe, it just turns its eyeless head with a sickening pop and then begins making its careful way toward us with its clawed hands stretched forward. It sniffs the air in great hissing gulps through its nose hole, shelf fungus bulging out of the side of its skull and shuddering lightly with every deliberate step forward.

There's a click, and blinding light fills my vision. Flipping my goggles up, I see Kendra standing over the zombie, helmet light illuminated. The creature hunkers low, hissing. I follow her lead and turn mine on, and we back the shrieking corpse down into the floor, until it balls up into a shriveled lump the way the last one did.

This time, though, there's no chance of it reconstituting and dragging us through some kind of chasm—the minute it finished popping and crunching down into its balled-up state, Ian darts in and begins stomping on it as hard as he can, bits of leathery skin flying and bones

135

cracking sickeningly, until the cave zombie is a mass of foaming black muck and shard-ended bone.

"There," whispers Ian, wiping the zombie gunk off his shoe. "Let's see him come back now."

As I switch back from lamp to goggles, I try to regain my composure. Deep breaths, blink hard, change the fear into drive . . . and always apologize. "I'm sorry," I whisper.

"Stop saying you're sorry, man," says Ian. "That's not a person. It would've eaten you alive—ugh, just *smell* it." He waves his hand in front of his face. "That's not a human smell."

No kidding—the foaming black blood coming from the zombie reeks, like old vegetables and spray cleaner rolled into one. It's the kind of smell only a dead thing that's been around for hundreds of years could have.

Wait a second.

Oh. Yes. This—yes. This is good. This is dynamite.

"We need to put it on ourselves," I say, pointing at the zombie. "The blood, the dust from the floor— spread it on your clothes."

"Excuse me?" says Kendra. "PJ, that's ridiculous. Zombie blood is probably poisonous—maybe even acidic."

"Did you notice that these zombies have been sniffing the air?" I tell her. "Zombies are dead, Kendra. They don't breathe. These things have evolved to use smell to detect prey. If we spread blood and cave dirt on ourselves, we'll smell like zombies and be undetectable."

Kendra looks from the zombie corpse to me, then back again. Finally, she huffs and says, "A layer of dirt first, then the blood. And none on our skin."

Don't get me wrong, I'm not overjoyed by this—but it needs to get done. Zombie horror is all about survival, and that requires sacrificing comfort. We all take our time with the dirt and dust from the floor, spreading it leisurely onto our arms and legs, none of us wanting to deal with the next part. Finally, though, it comes time, and I realize that since I suggested it, I have to be the one who does it first. Trying not to think about it, I grab the zombie's broken-off foot and begin rubbing the stump up and down my arms, smearing black gore on my Melee Industries jacket.

The first test, I pass—Kendra's thankfully wrong, and the blood doesn't eat through my jacket with a loud acidic hiss like Alien blood. But I can't hold my breath forever, and when I finally do inhale, the scent of it stabs at my throat. As I gag, I turn my face away, doing my best not to fill my expensive goggles with tears.

"PJ?" asks Ian. "You all right?"

"Fine," I cough, finally letting my nose and throat get used to the burning, toxic smell of age-old zombie. "Your turn."

Slowly, my fellow Gravediggers grab hunks of

stomped zombie—Ian an arm, Kendra a cross section of ribs—and begin adorning themselves. Both dry heave at the first close-up whiff, but they, too, seem to get their acts together.

"This better work," grumbles Ian. "This is worse than Mitchell West's gym shorts."

"Enough fond memories," says Kendra. "Let's continue."

Slowly, we creep our way from one building to the next, peeking into windows and whispering O'Dea's name. So far, we've got nothing—lots of cobwebs, furry piles of dust, outcroppings of festering mold, but no signs of people. No footprints. No O'Dea.

As we creep onto another street, two cave zombies come scuttling into view, hunched low to the ground. I throw up my hand, and my friends freeze behind me. With all my might, I try to keep my breathing slow and faint, my body absolutely still. Mentally, I urge my heart to beat quieter.

The zombies stop mid-stride, and one of them raises its skull face to the cold, dark air and sniffs. For a moment, they are perfectly still, and their gray colors and gnarled bodies make them look like they grew out of the rot piling around their feet. Their stillness is even more disturbing than any moaning or hissing. My legs shake; my teeth chatter.

Maybe I was wrong. Maybe it was all in vain. Maybe

now, we'll just die smelly.

After two more sniffs, the cave zombie lowers its head and turns to its companion. It puts its fingers to the floor and taps out another strange, clicking rhythm, like it did before. The other one responds in turn . . . and then another, and another. From somewhere deep in the sunken city, a whole stream of bone-claw clicks ring out through the air, traveling away from us like an echo. Like bats, the zombies use sound waves to send messages through the bottomless dark.

Maybe these ones are guards, sent to keep an eye out for us. *All quiet on Dayak Headhunter Boulevard. Keep looking—they're around here somewhere.*

Neither we nor the zombies see the sewer grate until it's too late. There's a loud crash, and a slotted section of the floor goes flying away. One of the two zombies, the one who almost detected us, hisses and rears back a claw as though to strike, but before it can, a bouquet of putrid congealed arms snatches it up and drags it down into the sewers, its partner scuttling off with a startled hack in its throat. The cave zombie's claws make a shrieking sound against the ground as it disappears down into the hole, and then its hisses give way to a chorus of crunches, slurps, and bubbling moans.

My face prickles with sweat and my throat swells shut. It's not just the horror of what has happened that wells up the terror inside of me, it's the . . . the *wrongness.*

"They . . . they're not supposed to do that," whispers Ian, pointing as though he's caught some older kids spray-painting a wall. "Zombies only eat people and animals, right? They don't eat other dead things." It's as though he's read my mind.

"Maybe, being down here long enough . . . they've resorted to cannibalism," says Kendra, trying to convince herself. "Or maybe the fused zombies in the sewers have some sort of . . . giant, single stomach."

But she knows she's wrong. We all do. So far, everything about them has been wrong. This evolution, or mutation, that the zombies have undergone down here in the caves breaks every rule I've ever learned about the undead, both on the big screen and through real-life Gravedigger-ing. Not just the rules of the zombies that O'Dea taught us to fight, but the rules of the movies, the comics, everything. Zombies are idiots—how are they communicating? And how is it the skinny zombies *aren't* trying to eat us—Lord knows they had the chance—but the strange mass of liquefied dead are eating *other* corpses? Even Kendra. If she has some kind of newfangled Warden powers, how is it she can still hurt zombies, something Wardens are sworn never to do?

What can we possibly do against an enemy we don't understand? What happens when our training and knowledge just aren't enough?

Josefina's words pound in my ears over and over.

It will happen there.

Your destiny lies in that cave.

Stop. Backpedal from the edge of the panic. Breathe. Think about O'Dea—no. Don't even think about O'Dea.

Think about you, the Gravedigger. Fear is a part of you. It's who you are, at your core. And if you fear this place, and these things, so much, then it is your job, your purpose, to make sure that they never leave this place.

Find your friend, and leave here forever.

"There's a lot of city to cover," I whisper. "Let's keep at it."

My friends nod, and we push deeper into the impenetrable blackout all around us.

CHAPTER TEN

Ian

This probably sounds weird, but I'm sort of down with how much this is freaking me out.

I mean, okay, *yes*, this is maybe the scariest, creepiest, most insane thing we've ever done, and we have a pretty solid history of undertaking absolutely loco zombie-filled adventures in our time, but this, this takes the cake. Sure, we are covered in a camouflage layer of cave dirt and zombie blood, looking through night-vision goggles at a massive underground city some crazy distance beneath the surface of the earth, while weird, reanimated blobs of dead bodies drag wall-climbing, mushroom-covered mutants into sewers to be eaten. And look, the idea that O'Dea got kidnapped and brought down here makes me chew the inside of my cheek and clench my hands into fists; fear for my friend is what's driving me here.

But sometimes, it's cool to be scared. There are times where you just have to go ahead and be frightened, but you have to do the right thing anyway. That's what we're currently working with. And I'm pretty down with that.

No matter how chill they're trying to be, I know PJ and Kendra must be feeling something similar. PJ's off in his own world, acting intense and cryptic, but I know that comes from him doing his fear-channeling craziness; and Kendra's figuring out she's a witch/X-Man, which is kind of awesome in some ways—reading the wall, zapping back the zombies with her weird cold-touch force field—but I can tell it's also freaking her out a ton, and she's not happy if she feels like she's not in control. I wish we could all just ride the rise we're getting out of this and push forward, braving this nutso scenario, and instead there's just me being brave and them being weird.

To be fair, this place is in a whole different division from our past zombie-hunting experiences. With every hut window we peek in and piece of tattered tarp we pull back to look for O'Dea, I'm seeing stuff I didn't think was possible. I'm talking cobwebs that fill whole houses, skeletons frozen with their mouths in silent screams, dust piled higher than snow during a blizzard. It's like being on another planet or something . . . which is scary, but cool.

We duck into one hut to find the same thing as always—bones, dust, decaying fabric—when something catches my eye. There's a huge shiny black pile in the middle of the floor that looks untouched, like it shouldn't be there. No dust, no spiderwebs—just these weird, glistening black lumps.

"Guys, look at this," I say, nudging it with my foot.

"Ian, leave that alone," says Kendra.

"Do you even know what it is?" I ask. "Is there some sort of glowing symbol on it?"

"It's not magical—"

She gets cut off by a loud hissing noise that comes out of the pile, sending me stumbling away from it with a hard slug of fear to the chest. Suddenly, the black pile splits to life and becomes about eighty tiny disks that go roaming around the hut, swarming over our feet and up our legs. PJ cries out, slapping them off his pants, while Kendra sort of tiptoes around them, kicking at the occasional black, slithering oval that goes rushing past her.

"I was saying," she continues in her hushed teacher's voice once the floor empties of creepy crawlers, "that they're cockroaches. Caves like these are crawling with them."

"Huh!" I say. "That makes sense, right? It's like we're under the world's refrigerator right now."

Part of me expects to get an eye-roll and some kind of insult to my intelligence like *Brilliant description, Ian Buckley*, but instead, she actually cracks a smile despite herself. "That's a comical mental image," she says. "You're funny, Ian Buckley."

"Thanks," I say, and wait for it. She opens her mouth and freezes, lost in thought. I go ahead and finish it for her: "Funny looking."

"*That* was what I wanted—ugh," she says, shaking her head and grinning. "I promise, I'll grasp this 'joke' concept soon enough."

"Don't hurt yourself," I say. "We've got all night."

"Thanks for your patience," she says sarcastically, but still smiling, and then we're just smiling at each other, and it's like the cave isn't so deep and dark and cold after all, like Kendra and I have a little fire going between us that makes this whole repulsive adventure worthwhile—

"Guys." We both turn at the sound of PJ's voice. He stands there, blank faced, staring at us. "O'Dea's down here somewhere. Enough jokes."

"You're absolutely right," says Kendra, trying to sound serious. My own embarrassment and guilt at getting sidetracked by . . . whatever I was feeling there is mixed with some anger at PJ. Leave it to PJ Wilson to remind you just how deep and dark and cold it is down here.

"Sorry, man," I say. "I just want to keep the mood light. I can't wait until we can get out of here, is all."

Something about the way PJ nods and doesn't say anything makes me uncomfortable. When I slap him lightly on the shoulder, I expect something, anything, out of the guy, but instead he just keeps staring straight ahead. Finally, he mumbles softly.

"What was that?" I ask.

"I don't think I'm getting out of here," he replies.

The words hit me with a cold wind on the inside, way worse than any of the quiet dark chills I've dealt with today in this giant bat cave. Kendra stares back at him with her mouth open, stunned. PJ's voice just sounds so hopeless and serious, like this is a fact that he's 100 percent sure of.

"Cut that out, dude," I say. "We've just got to find O'Dea. Once we have her back with us, we'll high-tail it out of here and leave Dario to the zombies. We've got this."

"Our progress so far has been incredible," chimes in Kendra. "You yourself have been exhibiting your skills as a Gravedigger—"

"I'm fighting off these things as best I know how," he says, shaking his head. "But Ian's got all the strength, and you have these new Warden's powers . . . and I'm just here, feeling all of this pain and hopelessness that's been trapped down here for centuries. It's like this place has it out for me. I can almost smell it." He sighs. "She was right."

"Who was right?" I ask.

"Josefina," says PJ calmly. "She had a dream, a vision. She said . . . that something happens here. Something bad happens to me."

For a silent moment, Kendra and I drink this fact in. "What happens?" I ask. "Does she know? Did she say where, or how it happens?"

PJ frowns hard and mutters, "No. It's a blur. But there's blood."

"PJ, that could mean anything," I say. "It could be about our time on the island. It could even be just a dream."

"Since we started fighting zombies, when has anything like this *ever* been what it seems?" snaps PJ. "I just want to find O'Dea before it happens. That way, you two can get out with her."

"We will not allow anything bad to happen to you," says Kendra. "All three of us are making it out alive."

PJ's face screws up, and I'm waiting for the outburst, but instead he just exhales and says, "Yeah, sure. You're right. Come on, let's keep looking."

PJ saunters away, and Kendra and I follow him, sharing glances of worry. It's obvious we didn't even get to PJ, that he's upset but doesn't want to worry us. It's a

shame, and I wish he'd told us about this sooner, but . . .
we needed him down here. Kendra and I couldn't do
this alone, and we all knew it was dangerous, but scary
Warden dream or not, we couldn't save O'Dea unless
he came. We're a trio, a team. That's something that
maybe O'Dea didn't teach me, but Coach Leider did
while I was playing basketball—you have to be ready
for anything, and you can't get all upset or out of line
just because things didn't go your way. No raging at the
ref, even if the call's a total crock. That's a personal foul.

Thinking about basketball gives me this shot of sadness and anger as I tiptoe through little mountains of
dust and corpse dandruff. My folks are probably freaking out right now. They've probably looked up the film
festival (which does exist—Kendra on the research
tip), but there's a pretty high chance they've contacted
our school and realized that they don't know anything
about it. Which means they're worried sick. My dad's
gotta be losing it, calling the hotel we gave them twenty
times a day . . . and my mom is probably crying. God, is
there anything worse than your mom crying?

No, you know what? Just like PJ, I had to be here.
O'Dea needs saving. She's somewhere in this gross hole,
and there's a total nut job holding her hostage. We need
to be here, even if it is a massive bummer.

Wading through piles of dust and decay, we get
deeper and deeper into downtown Kudus. The huts and

dirty igloos turn into these longhouses that look like Viking ships and white mansions with Hershey's Kiss tops. Our wandering leads us into the middle of a marketplace, with rotten canvas stalls lining either side of a big square. There are even some mummified goods lining the cobwebby shelves, mummified bowls and jars dripping with dust. We make our way around the stalls, glancing in one after another, but each one gives us the same view of cockroaches, dust, and the occasional headless skeleton.

"All the same," says PJ when we finish our seventeenth market stall in a row. "Maybe we're going about this the wrong way. We've still got a lot of ground to cover before we reach the temple."

Kendra stares straight ahead for a second and then nods slowly. It's so cool to watch something dawn on her, like you can see parts of her brain moving around like a, what's it called, a Rubik's Cube. "You're correct," she says. "Our current method is counterproductive. Besides, one doubts that Dario Savini would make his way down to Kudus only to hide out in a long-abandoned fruit stall. Surely, he must have more of an agenda than that."

"There's been no sign he's even down here," I tell her. "This all looks like no one's really touched it since the city tripped and fell down this awful hole."

Kendra nods, and then opens her mouth and draws

in a breath that's just hard enough to be a gasp. "Ian, that's it," she says, grabbing my shoulder. "You're a genius."

Coming from Kendra, about me, that's huge. Plus, she's touching me. And, well—wait. "Wait, how am I a genius?"

"I was just going to ask the same thing," says PJ.

"We're looking at it wrong," she whispers. "We've been looking for a specific thing, signs of O'Dea's or Dario's presence. But as you just said, much of this place has gone undisturbed for centuries. What we need to look for is *anything* different. Even the slightest alteration in the area is a sign that we're not alone." She plays with her massive fuzz ball of hair, lost in thought. "If only we had a map of this place."

The image of a map in my head—of looking down over the city—turns into a fully formed idea, one that feels equal parts crazy and totally brilliant. "What if I got up there?" I ask them, pointing to an old longhouse. "I could climb up there and get a good view of the city, see if I notice anything."

At the idea, PJ seems to buck up a bit, like finding O'Dea beats the fact that we're in hands-down the most horrible place on earth (and to defend PJ's mood, this *is* basically God's blind spot down here). We approach the longhouse, and the closer we get the taller it looms. When we reach it, I'm amazed at how big it is, but I can't help but notice that its triangular roof has low-hanging sides that level out.

PJ and Kendra cup their hands once we're under the roof's edge. After a few deep breaths and a quick stretch, I take two quick steps and plant my foot in their hands, and they toss me up with all their might (which isn't much—if only I had my teammates here). For a second, I'm in midair, hands reaching out, and I'm sure the only view I'm gonna get is of the inside of my broken leg—

My hands clap down on the edge of the roof, and with one strong pull I yank myself up onto the slanted surface. After a few moments of breathing and getting used to my steep new terrain, I climb to my hands and knees and start creeping toward the peak of the rooftop.

Bingo: once I'm straddling the pointed top of the roof, I can see all of Kudus, and it would be a beautiful view if it didn't look like a city after the apocalypse. The buildings continue growing larger as they near the temple, and now I'm really face-to-face with the massive pointed buildings, all covered with sculptures and ridges like big stone artichokes. The streets are stretched out in every direction, totally empty except for the shape of the occasional cave zombie stalking slowly through the blackness and looking like blurry stick figures in my night vision. All around us hang huge ceiling spikes and pieces of white jagged crystal; for a second, it's like I'm at the very center of the cave.

"Remember, just look for *different*," says Kendra.

There's not much "different" going on here. The city looks pretty dead, even from this height, and most of it is completely swallowed by dust from the past five centuries—

Hold on. What about that one?

"Ian!" hisses PJ. "Behind you!"

I turn just in time to see the cave zombie scuttling toward me, its fingernails tapping faintly on the slate beneath us, its backbone covered with one big flat slab of fungus, like it's got a spinal Mohawk. In a flash, I've ducked to one side of the roof and dropped to my belly, creeping backward down the slanted slope until my feet reach the edge and dangle over.

The zombie leans forward, its nostrils only a few inches from where my hands—one of my few body parts not disguised with zombie blood—just were, and sniffs loudly. Instantly, its bone fingers and toes begin tapping out a rhythm on the slate roof that gets responded to throughout the dead city . . . from nearby.

As I dangle from the roof's edge and drop to the dust-caked ground, I see PJ and Kendra looking over their shoulders and lowering into fight stance. They've got the same feeling I have, a kind of weird extra Gravedigger sense: they're coming. We gotta go.

"There's a building," I say, pulling my machete from my backpack and loving the weight in my hand. "A few blocks from here. It's got a bunch of boards on the windows and door that look kind of fresh. All the build-ings around it are deep in dirt."

"Great," says PJ, sounding ready for battle. "Let's get moving."

We run fast, staying low to avoid the cave zombies that come crawling toward the longhouse with their nose holes to the sky. All we hear are our soft footsteps in the piled dust, the hissing and moaning of the zom-bies, and, way off, like a typewriter in a church, claws tapping against slate. Every couple of yards, I hold up a hand to signal a stop and we watch as a group of spidery cave zombies go scuttling past us, no doubt headed to where we were last spotted. Given how creepy they are, I'm surprised they can't hear my heart thud-thud-thud-ding in my rib cage, but I have to assume that all that gear must have fallen apart in their skulls about two or three hundred years ago.

"How do you think they got this way?" I whisper as a cluster of three disappears around a corner.

"A lack of food," says Kendra calmly. "Without any flesh left to devour, their bodies probably began to mutate."

"But they didn't eat us before," PJ says. "They could've."

"Maybe they're too weak to digest us while we're alive," says Kendra. "They were taking us somewhere to . . . ripen us."

I'm about to tell Kendra that she's officially the

grossest person I know when my eyes finally notice a series of indents in the dust up ahead of us—big, boot-sized imprints, not like either our Melee Industries boots or the weird skeleton prints of the zombies.

"Guys, look," I say, nodding forward. Their eyes follow mine, and we all scurry toward the prints.

"They're old," says PJ, and he's right, they're sort of half filled, like footprints during a heavy snowstorm, as though they were made a while ago, but they're definitely boot-prints, large and industrial.

"If they're this old, they can't be Dario's," says Kendra.

"Then whose?" asks PJ.

"Let's find out," I say, following their path. My friends slowly take up the lead, and we head farther into the darkness, until in the distance I see the building I noticed from the longhouse roof, a clay house with its windows and gateway boarded up, the boot-prints leading beneath the barrier.

There's someone inside that hut. And we need to know who.

CHAPTER ELEVEN

Kendra

The huts of Kudus are strangely shaped, given their geographical location. Indonesian architecture usually leaned on the very angular and pointed Austronesia styles. The longhouses and the massive temple in the background have what I expected from that ancient style—jagged points, gabled roofs adorned with jutting hornlike protrusions, and hard angles. But these huts are domed and rounded, their edges smooth in an almost impossible way, one that would require an incredible amount of proficiency with clay, straw, and other natural materials. Now, buried by time, decay, and dark magic, they appear as great green lumps of unhygienic *detritus* in our night vision (that's two on *detritus*, somewhat of a cheap shot this time around), like warts of the earth.

Even among these strange structures, the one we're nearing is especially unsettling, drawing us in with *fatalistic* purpose (two on "fatalistic," as well).

The windows of the hut appear to have been barricaded somehow. Its few portals are entirely clogged with lumber and bones. It looks almost like a reversed beehive rising out of the ground, its ominous nature only emphasized by the corpses of its shelter brethren that loom around us in this dome of pure, clammy night through which we sneak.

And there's a set of footprints leading to it. Not fresh, but unmistakably not zombie footprints. Someone boarded him or herself up in this hut. The question is, is he or she still there?

The closer we get to the structure's silhouette, the higher my heart rate climbs. A cold sweat beads on my brow, and I'm forced to remind myself not to swipe a mutant blood-coated arm across my damp forehead. God forbid I somehow end up with this terrible slime in my hair—its consistency suggests it will take weeks to remove. Assuming, of course, it doesn't cause my entire scalp to go bare due to its toxicity.

"Okay," says Ian. "On three, I kick the door in, and we see what's inside."

This is the worst idea I have ever heard. "Ian, are you insane?" I whisper. "Every living thing in this cave will hear the noise caused by such an action! We will essentially become zombie bait."

"I side with that," says PJ calmly. "Don't do it, man."

"Dario could be in there," mumbles Ian, his stare never leaving the hut. "O'Dea could be. We have to look. There are footprints."

"Ian, this is a bad idea in any horror movie," says PJ, trying to sound soothing but firm. "This is the mummy's tomb, basically. If it was closed up, it must have been for a very good reason."

Ian nods. "Okay. On three. Ready?"

Ian's gone on autopilot, so I step between him and the door and put my hands out. "No," I tell him. "Not a chance. There's a smarter way to enter this hut, and I intend to find it."

As his shoulders sag and he exhales, I turn to face the barred door and consider our actual options.

Every crack and crevice, Kendra—scout it out; use it to your advantage. Pry the blockage off with the hammer? It doesn't look quite like that would work, does it? Or what about slowly pushing at whatever's filling the doorway. First, test your barrier's strength. Lightly press the item that's blocking your path and see if it resists—

"Three." Ian's leg rockets up from his side and obliterates the boards filling one window of the hut. A deafening crack rings out through the entire cavern city, echoing for what sound like leagues into the dark.

"Ian!" I stage-whisper. "You *idiot*! You're supposed to *count* to three!"

His response is a dead-on stare and a matter-of-fact smirk. "I'm sorry," he says, "was I not counting out loud?"

How I feel is at odds with common sense. The logical impulse would be to reach out and wrap my fingers around his corded and athletic neck. But some part of me feels amused by, and enamored of, his stupid attitude and straightforward thinking. I can't help but look away from him and do my best not to smile. Such a lummox, and yet so smart and . . . and *sharp* in his own right.

Don't forget that you had little to no idea of how you were going to get in there, Kendra. The lummox did you a favor.

One by one, we heft ourselves through the window, cartwheeling to the cobweb-laden floor, Ian bringing up the rear with a quick and easy hop. The inside of the hut is about what one might expect—a wide circular room, one or two rotting tables, some old vessels made of clay and metal. The bed jammed up against the door is somewhat disconcerting but entirely justified given what has been lurking outside this hut. But it is the smell that is most discomforting, that stings our noses and immediately triggers my gag reflex, a smell not unlike that of the sewers we just escaped. Out there is an ancient death scent, a musky and mildewy stench of long-form decay and bulging spinal mushrooms. (*No, Kendra, getting a sample to take home with you would defeat the whole purpose of this trip; don't even consider it.*) In here, there is the septic stench of rotten meat and neglect—fresh death, death in bloom. Like roadkill.

"Pfuh," hacks PJ, waving a hand in front of his face. "Whatever's in here, it reeks. Kendra, we were right—this was the worst idea we've had so far."

"Why's it smell so bad in here?" coughs Ian. "The cave zombies don't smell that bad."

My eyes scan the room, my brain doing its best to overcome the odor of the place and focus on our task at hand. At our feet lie the boards, their edges heavy with blackened lumps of mud, bone, leathery flesh.

"Whoever was in here was using pieces of zombies as some kind of mortar," I say, nudging the split wood with my foot. "See? He or she must have killed one or two and then used their blood and body just as we used them—to deflect attention. It's ingenious, really."

"Uh, Kendra," says PJ, his voice going deep and hoarse, "I think it may have just been him."

My eyes fly up, and I follow PJ's pointing, and nervously shaking, finger.

Beneath a table, in the corner where the left-hand

and far walls meet, is a dead body.

It is not sprawled out or splattered like the corpses I looked at when I, preparing myself to be a Gravedigger after our jaunt on the mountain, googled "dead people" (a truly nauseating afternoon on the internet). Rather, this corpse is hunched over in a sitting position, its knees bent up by its chest, its back to us. Something about the climate down in the cave must have kept it preserved in that position—a flash mummification, if you will.

Though perhaps I am just unused to seeing a corpse that is not attacking me.

As Ian and I slowly approach it and round its front side, we see its face between the table legs—male, older; eyes, nose, and lips long since rotted away; expression relaxed, calm in death; empty eye sockets focused on a large pointed object clutched in his hands.

"It appears to be some kind of bone," I whisper. "A tusk, maybe."

"Looks like it's all carved up," says Ian.

Indeed. As I crouch near the huddled cadaver and bring my goggles closer to the object, I can see the intricate web of sigils and swirling runes that cover every inch of the three-foot hunk of ivory, no doubt taken from an *Elephas maximus sumatranus* or *Elephas maximus borneensis*, the Sumatran and Borneo elephant respectively.

And the closer I peer at the sigils, the more I begin

to see a throb of light, heavy and slow, emanating from them. Soon, I can feel it on my skin, can hear the rumble of magical energy pouring out of it. This isn't the loud, communicative scream of the sigils I read along the tunnel walls earlier today. These ones are strong but unmovable, powerful but quiet. They are not intended to frighten or warn, but rather to hold, to contain. Given its unspoken language, this tusk will feel like it weighs seven hundred pounds when I hold it in my hands, though it is in reality much lighter, I'm sure.

"What is it?" asks Ian.

"It's the seal," I say, knowing I'm right as the words leave my mouth. "Every containment site has one—the dream catcher on the mountain, the *zemi* on the island. This is the magical seal of Kudus."

"That makes sense, actually," says PJ as he and Ian crouch next to me. "It's huge, and it looks as though there are a ton of really tiny sigils on it. This must have taken hours to carve."

"Days," says Ian. "Weeks. Geez, look at it."

"Hold on," I say, reaching out to—

Wait.

Kendra. Stop. Use your brain. All day, you've been manifesting the powers of a Warden in ways beyond your control. Now, you want to touch easily the most powerful magical item in this cave? Enjoy your seizure.

"Ian, can you grab the tusk?" I ask.

"Why?" says Ian. "You grab it."

I open my mouth to speak, but no words come out. Blood involuntarily rushes into my cheeks.

"Or not, whatever," says Ian. He grabs the tusk, and, with a dry crackling noise, manages to pull it free of the corpse's hands, a thick membrane of cobwebs stretching and tearing loose as he yanks. Up close, the tusk is even more magnificently carved; along its concave side is a spine of blue and green jewels, uncut and shining even in the faint light coming from our goggles.

"And look," says PJ, reaching deeper into the corpse's balled-up body. His hand returns with a wad of ratty papers, folded haphazardly. Before I can scream at him to please, please be careful, he unfolds them and begins reading.

"What do they say?" I ask.

"Oh wow," says PJ. "Listen to this . . . 'My name is Joseph Savini.' "

Cold strikes me in the chest and radiates along my veins. Ian mumbles, "Ho boy."

" 'I am a hunter of the cursed, the living dead that stalk the evil regions of the earth,' " continues PJ in the hushed tone of a boy used to reading ghost stories by the glow of a flashlight. " 'For years, I kept the world safe from the hungry damned. But my family was slain by these monsters because of the stupidity of the Wardens, sworn to contain and protect these beasts

162

from slaughter as though they were sacred cattle. In my rage, I came here to Kudus to free the masses of undead that haunt this sunken city. Instead, I found horrors beyond my knowledge. The cursed down here have transformed into strange new monsters thanks to the gifts of their foul lord. They are . . . lej-ay . . . leg-ee . . .' " He looks up to me, his brow furrowed over his goggles.

"Legion?" I ask.

"Right, right," he says, and then goes on: " 'They caught me as I had just discovered this, the uniting totem that controls the Wardens' magic over this place. Through my training, I fended them off and hid myself in this hovel. I cannot say how long I have been trapped within here, only that the cursed are no longer clawing at the windows. I am . . . sluggish. I feel the curse of Kudus all around me, pulling me in. When I try to destroy the totem and release the dead, it won't let me. I need their magic to break it. To stop . . .' " PJ grimaces. "Welp, the writing is getting really hard to read . . . and there's blood." He scans a bit and hisses. "Oh no."

"Dude?" asks Ian. "Everything okay?"

" 'There is no hope. I am a fool. God forgive me. They are everywhere. Victoria, forgive me. Dario, Danielle, forgive me. Death to them all. Curse the Wardens. Kill them all.' " PJ looks up, his face tightened into an expression of disgust and sorrow. His mouth is downturned at its corners, as though he might cry; even toward a man who might have ended the world, my sweet friend has sympathy. "And then it's just scribbling and lots of blood on the pages. I think it's blood, but I don't know."

"How long do you think he was down here?" asks Ian.

"Is there a date on the pages?" I ask.

PJ shakes his head. "Nothing like that. But he's not nearly as rotten as anything else down here. If I had to guess, I'd say he hasn't been here long. What, twenty years?"

"Probably more like thirty," I say, observing the desiccated corpse once again and remembering Dario's revenge story on the island. "No matter how dry or damp it might have been down here, the level of decay this has undergone suggests that it—"

"He," notes PJ.

"—*he* has been dead for quite some time."

"Not long enough to stop smelling, though," says Ian. "Those cave zombies smell like gym shorts, but not dead people."

"True," I say, "but this corpse has also been locked up inside of this tiny hut for quite a while. The cave zombies have a whole underground structure in which to air their rotting entrails. This creature has sat here in a ball, decaying, for quite some time. It's no wonder the rot has been contained, given this small hut."

"You had me at 'rotting entrails,' Kendra," says PJ. He tosses the pages down and sighs. "But no O'Dea. Not even a sign of her."

"This is still extremely useful," I tell him. "Think about it—this means that Dario is almost certainly on his way, and that he probably knows a way in—and out—if his father knew enough to get down here and escape the cave zombies."

"But we knew that!" says PJ, throwing his hands up. "We found claw marks up at the entrance! This doesn't help us at all! We're in the same place we were at when we got here, and O'Dea's still out there!"

He's right, Kendra. Panicking, overemotional, but right. What good did breaking into this hut do for you three? What clues have you picked up, other than a letter by a trained and established Gravedigger explaining that there's no hope of escape from this appalling place?

"We found the seal," I tell him, pointing to the long white shape in Ian's hands. "With that, we can hopefully fend off other undead attacks and make sure that Dario doesn't succeed in releasing the zombies down here. Right?"

PJ shrugs and mumbles agreement. When I look to Ian, he is a statue, face frozen in a blank stare and one ear cocked to the air overhead.

"Ian?" I ask.

"Someone's here," he whispers. "Someone alive."

"What?" I gasp. PJ and I share a glance of stark terror, then turn our eyes back to our bloodhound-like friend. "Are you sure?"

"Yup," says Ian, nodding surely. "Footsteps. And breathing. Somewhere out there."

We scrabble to the window, PJ and I peeking over the edge, doing our best to reveal as little of our faces as possible (though unless our intruder is as equipped as us, there's little chance he can see much at all).

At first, all that is visible are the buildings of Kudus in their cluttered rows, the piles of dust and rot on the ground. Then, my ears tune in to the sound as well—footsteps, deliberate and slow, muffled by the dust but still audible.

Into view moves a large, broad-shouldered shape, its head covered with a hood. His eyes are invisible, but his breath—Ian was correct, this new figure lives—rings out sharply into the air and pegs him as a man.

"Do we think it's Dario?" I whisper.

"Tough to say," responds PJ. "He's certainly big enough."

The shape freezes, its body crouched and taut. For a seemingly eternal period of time, it stands perfectly still. Then, gradually, its hooded face moves in the direction of our window.

A sharp crackling noise makes us jump, and turns our intruder's head toward us. I am about to admonish Ian for giving away our position when a hand, cold and impossibly strong, clamps down on my shoulder.

CHAPTER TWELVE

PJ

At least Joseph Savini's walking corpse is the kind we're used to. Without the chance to mutate or evolve or whatever horror has happened to the zombies out there, his body has stayed relatively normal and has returned that way. His hands go grasping out blindly in front of him, his teeth gnashing and his eyes rolling white and soft in his skull, his bushy white mustache giving him a walrus-like quality. The moan that comes out of his mouth is morose and sends me into a fit of something like ants crawling down my flesh, but they're the ants I know. He doesn't tap out messages with his feet or sniff the air; he just lumbers at us like he wants to eat us, like Romero made them do.

There's something kind of comforting about it. Like eating McDonald's on vacation—it's familiar.

All three of us cry out in what must be a deafening roar in the black, gaping, silent shadow of the cave encasing Kudus like a giant crypt. Kendra manages to shoot out a foot and knock the creature off balance, but he hangs onto her one shoulder and won't go down, instead dangling from her like an anchor and dragging her to the floor.

Finally, my mind cuts out of slow-mo, and I manage to climb to my feet and hook my arms around his waist. When I try to take a deep breath and concentrate, my nose and lungs are filled with the stench of a freshly hugged dead body (like cheese, really, like fancy cheese that has been forgotten in a warm place), but I fight through it and focus my overwhelming fear and disgust. My foot plants behind the zombie, and I throw all my strength into my shoulder and toss his body backward. Sure enough, his heel catches on my ankle, and the sack of rotting meat goes crashing to the ground.

At first, we're all ready to go back into fight mode, Ian searching frantically for his machete and me cracking my knuckles . . . but then we actually watch the zombie. We watch as he crawls to his knees and paws blindly at the air, eyes aimed dumbly at the hut ceiling. Twice he falls while he tries to get up. This poor, pathetic thing doesn't have the smelling power of its mutated counterparts—he hasn't been wandering the tunnels for year. He can't see a thing.

"It's almost sad to watch," I say.

"We need to kill it," says Ian. "Before—"

The zombie whirls with a wild clawed haymaker that barely misses my face.

But slaps off my goggles.

Darkness. Pure and impenetrable darkness, greater than that of any room I've ever been in, than any space I can imagine. As my eyes blink, taking in the pure nothing, I think about how foolish I've been, getting used to the goggles and believing that *that* was reality, with the world outlined in spooky Jodie Foster-at-the-end-of-*Silence* green. Wrong. We are basically in a black hole, only this one is full of noises—Kendra screaming my name, Ian bellowing curse words and dumping his backpack on the floor, a loud inhuman creature clamoring for my flesh with eyes as blind as mine. The mind-blowing noise throttles the endless night around me.

All of my training, all of O'Dea's instruction to capture my fear and make something of it, is gone. There is no thought in my head but pure, instinctive terror. At once, my pulse spikes, my brow glistens with sweat, my whole body shakes, my every breath carries a piece of scream on the end. The unfiltered fear of this vast space full of invisible monsters wraps me up and conquers me entirely.

Footsteps grow in sound and become a loud crash that shakes the walls around me. Kendra's shrieking cuts off with a gasp while Ian begins a chorus of, "OH MAN, OH MAN, OH MAN—"

A blinding beam of white light cuts through the surrounding void like some kind of powerful laser, making me cover my eyes and hiss through my teeth. Ian and Kendra duck down, pulling off their goggles and shielding their own faces. The light illuminates the green-gray gob of Joseph Savini, his skin cracking in wet black gouges and his teeth a snaggled yellow fence beneath his smoky mustache. The man holding the flashlight is huge, and I faintly see a handlebar mustache and two heartbroken eyes beneath his hood.

"Oh, Papa," whispers a hoarse baritone voice. "Papa, I'm sorry. I had hoped you hadn't . . . no. No, of course you did. Of course you're here."

The zombie snarls viciously and staggers toward the light, unlistening.

The flashlight clicks off, and then the air rings with the sound of a knife leaving a leather holster—*shing*—before a wet ripping and crunching fills the air, cutting off the zombie's moans. Ian cries out, Kendra makes a noise in her throat, and I'm suddenly choking on a stench unlike anything I've ever smelled.

A few seconds later, something nudges me in the hands, making me start. As I reach out, I feel my night-vision goggles.

"Put them on," says Dario Savini in his rumbling voice. "You're no good to me floundering around in the dark like a blind man."

My hands shaking, I yank the goggles to my head, clamping them on. My eyes are filled with a green silhouetted world—the hut, my friends staring dumbstruck, the zombie's remains piled in the corner, and Savini, his barrel chest, and tree-trunk arms, and hard gaze looming over me, bloody knife still in his ham-sized hand.

"There," he says. "Better?"

My mouth moves, but no sound comes out. My brain is still vibrating from the fear of the dark.

"Good," he says, taking a step back. "Now, stand up. We need to talk. All four of us."

My eyes shut, and I inhale sharply, trying to steady myself. But the stench of rotting flesh and subterranean hell just reminds me why we're here, and my focus is overwhelmed by emotion. I go ballistic.

My shoulder slams into Dario's stomach, making him cough out a "*WHUFF.*" In seconds, I've got my hands slapping around his thick neck, my mouth open and shrieking in his face, "WHERE IS SHE? WHERE IS SHE, YOU MISERABLE—"

One of his arms swings up and tosses me across the room like I'm nothing. This time around, my goggles stay on, but I land a lot harder—a flash of white in my eyes as I hit the wall, a dull pain in my back as I tumble to the floor. Ian yells out and takes two steps at Savini, but a hard glare from the large man makes him stop short, face twisted up in rage. Only Kendra, with her superior intellect, knows not to approach him.

"This helps no one," growls Savini. "I have no desire to kill any of you three, but the next person who tries to attack me gets cut down."

"*GOD*, you're a tool," snarls Ian.

"Permission to pick up my friend," spits Kendra.

"Granted," says Savini with a nod. Kendra walks across the hut and grabs me by the armpits, lifting me to my feet.

"Are you unhurt?" she asks.

"Yeah," I finally say, "just . . . upset."

"I guess it was foolish of me to expect anything else," says Savini. "It's in your nature, after all. Still, I'd hoped this would be a reasonable conversation." His slumped posture speaks exhaustion. His breath is heavy. It's not surprising, given that he's just had to re-kill his zombie father. Slowly, he bends to the floor, eyes sharp and intent.

"You *kidnap our friend*," snaps Ian, "and expect us to have a nice little talk with you? Eat dirt, Savini."

"Your old Warden friend is safe," he says. "I've hidden her in a side cavern that seems well protected by her people's magic . . . and I've managed to keep her from biting off her own tongue." He chuckles. "For so-called peacekeepers, their methods are particularly brutal."

Dario's words echo my own thoughts, but I won't give him an inch. "They're just worried about their secrets falling into the hands of people like you."

Savini stands, and I see what he's been reaching for: his father's papers. All three of us share a glance and a silence. Do we take them from him? They're not ours. He was forced to just put down his zombie dad. He has a right to know. And besides, he could probably crush us like flies.

"And what about my secrets?" he mumbles after a long silence, as he reaches the blood-soaked last page. The man's eyes come up to mine, determined and vengeful. "What about yours?"

"I don't understand," I whisper.

Dario lowers his head and heads for the door. "Follow me," he growls. "Let's leave this awful shelter. It's time we talked."

"We're not going anywhere with you," says Kendra, but as if on cue, the tapping of bone on stone rings out through the cave outside, followed by a round of clicking responses that make my blood freeze. Dario doesn't even respond, he simply turns his back to us and walks out of the hut. For some reason—be it our lack of options, the impending zombie investigation that's about to go on here, or the off chance he'll lead us to O'Dea—I follow him. Ian and Kendra both look somewhat shocked, but eventually come take up the rear.

The cave city of Kudus is as massive and unsettling as before, but something about walking with Dario makes the cold air feel less oppressively clammy, the darkness less all-consuming. As we follow him, it dawns on me that this is the first time since we entered the cave that I've walked like a normal human being—we've been crouched, sneaking through the silent darkness, trying to avoid the cave zombies that seem to come out of the shadows on a whim. With Dario at our head, though, we're strolling down the streets of Kudus with our heads held high. We were acting like horror movie survivors, desperate to not be caught, while he's all action hero.

"How are you not wearing goggles?" I ask, as much as I don't want to speak to him.

"The hood," he says, pointing to the leather hood hanging out of the neck of his jacket. "Your Warden friend enchanted it. It allows me to see through the dark."

"Did she do so at knifepoint?" asks Kendra.

"You think me a butcher," scoffs Savini. "I'm merely a man with a mission."

"And what is that, exactly?" asks Ian in a snarky tone. "So far, all I got was the part where you beat and kidnap our friend so you can pretty much end the world."

Dario's silent for a few seconds, and then says, "During the old days, the days when Kudus thrived and even some time after that, the Wardens were little more than hags and medicine women who knew some ways to fight off the evil. Containment rarely worked, and when it did, the Wardens used their powers of containment to threaten locals and use the undead for their bidding. If you've ever heard legends about witches summoning monsters and demons, that's why. The Wardens were not organized until centuries after Kudus fell, and even then, breaches in their little containment spells were common. The world lived in fear of these monsters because, despite their best efforts, the Wardens' attempts to contain them were futile. Evil would slip through the cracks, and innocent people would die."

"How do you know this?" I ask him.

"My father and his fellow Gravediggers—his cousin and their friend Octavio—worked with a Warden for many years in Italy," says Savini, solemnly, his voice tinged with sadness. "She trusted him with many secrets, and told him of the times long before he was born. She considered it part of his duty, to know his history."

"Is this the Warden he killed?" I say, the words bubbling up before I can stop them.

"Yes, that was her," says Savini. His tone of voice is surprising—if I didn't know better, I'd say that was genuine remorse. "Her name was Chiarra. She had been the Warden of the lands neighboring my father's home for ages. Unlike many Wardens, she always saw the purpose of Gravediggers. She understood that, sometimes, unbelievable people must be sent to confront an unspeakable problem." Savini shakes his head and stops in his tracks. "Her lapse in judgment—she forgot to properly mark and seal a cave in the mountains swarming with cursed—and the containment breach that it caused, cost my father his family, his fellow Gravediggers, and his sanity. It was a great tragedy on the whole, and he never forgave himself for ending her life. But you must remember that if he didn't kill her, another Warden would have soon afterward. By then, the coven was already amassing."

He says the word *coven* as though it tastes bad. The idea had never occurred to me, but hearing it out loud, I can't help but think of those women in that hotel, those three witches stacked against us and telling us we don't exist.

Two cave zombies round a corner and sniff loudly at us before hunching forward, claws spread wide, and stalking in our direction with a hiss. It's like a cut shot—one minute, Savini has stopped in this dust-covered street, lost in the sorrow of his father's death. The next, he's got the zombie's throat in his hand and yanks its shoulder forward. With a repulsive ripping noise, he tears the creature's head off and pulls its spine out of its back, the vertebrae swaying slightly in our field of vision, coated with foaming black blood and noticeably swollen.

The second zombie stalks toward us, and wordlessly, Ian thrusts the tusk in its face. The creature immediately hops backward on its ballet dancer feet, hissing and shielding its face from the conduit of good karma. Almost immediately, though, it begins tapping out a steady rhythm on the floor with its bony fingertips. Savini whips around and snatches one of its arms in his huge paw, tossing the frail creature over its head and swinging it into the floor with a blast of choking dust and a wet crunch. Even as he steps away from the mangled body, it still twitches, not quite entirely dead.

"You see?" he huffs, storming down an alley so fast that we're forced to trot to keep up with him. "Your Warden magic cannot actually stop them. They can still summon their brethren."

"Dude, the Wardens are *nuts*," says Ian. "They kept all these zombies locked up for a bazillion years. That's *real*."

Savini laughs, just a little. "You're lying to yourself," says Savini. "Do you believe any of the run-ins with the damned you've had would've turned out well, had you not been there to stop them?"

"Technically, we *caused* those outbreaks," says Kendra.

"Except for the one where a teenager with lots of money caused it," says Savini, his voice reaching an angry growl. His eyes turn to mine, and there's a fierce shine to them, visible even through my night vision. "And even the one you did put into motion, your stunt on the mountain—have the Wardens come after you for it? PJ, I can tell you know. Why do the Wardens threaten to kill their own, but they haven't touched you? Why are you beyond their reproach?"

"Where is O'Dea?" I say, doing my best to ignore his words.

"Why, PJ?"

"Because they're afraid of us." It's out of my mouth before I can even think of it. Savini smiles and nods.

"Indeed," he says. "They've never known what to do with us, because we have the power. Wardens need to be trained. Their blood has the potential for magic, but they need to be . . . *whittled* out of a person. Gravediggers are like *diamonds*." The way he says the last word lets me see the bright, glittering jewel in his mind's eye. "We have an inherent power behind us, an ability. The Wardens fear what they can't control, and so they fear us. Back when this city flourished, we were hundredfold." He sweeps an arm out into the inky shadows before him, displaying to us the deceased city full of the mutated dead. "Gravedigger clans roamed every land, defeating the evil as they came upon it. Wardens helped them, yes, but they were the law, the men and women who people turned to. It was understood that it was better to wipe the evil from this place than to try and keep it quiet and contained, hoping no one stumbled upon the cursed earth."

"So why are you trying to set it free?" Kendra asks.

"Yeah, man," says Ian. "Seems to me like the Wardens are doing their job and you're making things worse."

We exit an alleyway into a small street leading directly to the temple at the city's center. Before us, the three-pointed construction looms in the darkness, its statue-lined walls looking jagged and cluttered as they rise up toward the rock ceiling overhead. Again, Dario is silent, considering Ian's words, and for a moment, I hope we've reached him, that we've turned our villain into an antihero . . . but the furrow that crosses his brow, the way his jaw sets, lets me know that's only wishful thinking.

"What the Wardens need is a wake-up call," says Savini. Just like that, the impassioned Gravedigger is gone; this is the hard, cruel tone of a psycho. "Can't you feel it? Something is going to happen. Soon, these things are going to get loose, containment be damned. So why wait? Let's return the world to how it was meant to be, so that we can stop this infection from growing down here until it cannot be contained. It's our time, children. We need them to see that our way is the right way—"

"Your way," says Kendra.

"What?" says Savini, snapping out of his rant.

"This is not *our* way," says Kendra. "Don't speak for the three of us. We have no intention of letting you release a horde of zombies onto the world. No real Gravedigger would do that."

Her words center me. For a second, I'm ashamed that I felt for Savini, that I listened intently to his words as though they made sense. Then, I'm just angry again.

"Absolutely," I say, feeling my face grow so red it might glow in the dark. "Is there anything else you want to tell us? Other than 'Wardens lie' or crazy bitter Gravedigger propaganda."

Savini takes a deep, slow breath and screws up his mouth the way my dad does when I've said too much. "I know your Warden friend has put a lot of ideas in your head," says Savini, "but listen to me, the truth will set you free. With the right training, you can be shaped—"

"We don't need any of your training," says Ian, looking angry. "We've got, what was it, inherent power? All of these soldier-type shenanigans you're into sound like a ton of baloney. Us real Gravediggers, we're like *diamonds,* or whatever." He smiles. "See, that's you. That's how you sound."

Savini looks at Ian with those sharp, glinting eyes, and then with a blink they are soft and sad, like those of a dog. He steps up to Ian and claps a big hand on my friend's shoulder, making him flinch. "That you are," he says softly, nodding. "You're very powerful, Ian. Perhaps I'm too hasty to deny what you three are saying.

Maybe there's another way."

Ian slowly nods, and Kendra and I share a glance. Maybe it did work. Maybe he's seen the light. But this sudden change of heart just feels a little too, I don't know . . .

Convenient.

Dario's free hand wraps around the tusk in Ian's grip, and before any of us know what's going on, his palm moves from Ian's shoulder to his face, shoving him to the ground and tearing the tusk away from him.

"Give that back!" snaps Ian, scrambling to get back on his feet.

"Make me," rumbles Dario, admiring the intricately carved magical seal.

"It doesn't even matter," says Kendra. "That seal is more magically encrypted than a server at Google. You'll never be able to break its spell."

"Unless," says Dario, a cruel smile growing across his face, "I have a Warden."

CHAPTER
THIRTEEN

Ian

Oh man, we screwed up.

Maybe I'm not as smart as Kendra, but I've got a brain, and something rattling around in it clicks into the right slot, and the whole thing gets moving at once.

We could've done anything *but* go along with Dario Savini, like go running through the city or try to stab him with the tusk or stay put and use the rest of his dead dad to glue the hut closed while he stomped off doing his own thing. But instead, we wander after him listening to his super-sure speech and watching him break down zombies like it's nothing, and we even think we can reason with him, and then he just takes our stuff and kicks our butts to the curb once we're deep enough into the cave city to not have any idea where the heck we are.

Coach Leider calls that "rope-a-dope." It's what Muhammad Ali used to do, get your opponent all settled in thinking they've got you, and then when they let down their defenses you come out swinging. Dario just saved PJ from his zombie dad and got all cozy with us so we wouldn't be ready for when he snagged our magical seal and released a ton of zombies onto the earth. That kind of thing ain't cool. My friends, yeah, they can treat me like an idiot, but this nut-bar? Not a chance.

Staring at him, all smug with the tusk in hand and this giant evil-looking temple rising up behind him, it's like I already know what to do. Feels a little low, yeah—this kind of thing gets you kicked out of a game, heck, thrown off the team—but considering the snatch 'n' shove that Savini just pulled on me, it's deserved.

On my feet, I take two steps and whip my foot up between Dario's legs, smashing him in the junk. The dude doubles over with what sounds like a loud cough, and in that second I've got the big carved elephant tusk in my hand and my goggles thrown over my eyes.

"BAIL," I shout, but my friends are already on it, barreling past me as we head into the cursed city.

Immediately, things are rough. The dust and filth piled on the floor puffs up like snow, so we're all hacking and wiping at our goggles, and the jumble of rotting buildings that Dario just strolled between is totally confusing, littered with cobwebby alleys and dead ends.

Somewhere behind us, Dario shouts, "You three have made a very poor decision!"

Kendra and I share a glance as PJ comes huffing up behind us.

"What do we do?" he asks through deep breaths.

I say "Split up" just as Kendra says "Stay together," and then we both kind of look each other in the eye.

"We'll cover more ground splitting up," I tell her. "Might find O'Dea quicker and lose this whack job."

"We're in a city, Ian," says Kendra calmly. "If we split up, we'll never see each other again."

"We can follow our footsteps in the dust back—"

"Guys." PJ grabs us by the arms. Some ways behind us, Dario comes storming into view, head down and eyes angry. Kendra and I meet gazes again, and I open my mouth to agree with her—

"Split up," she says, nodding. "We meet back here in twenty minutes."

"Got it," says PJ. "On three."

THWACK. That big ol' knife we've been seeing so much of today goes flying past us, nearly taking my nose as it sinks into the side of a hut behind us, its handle wobbling rapidly. PJ nods. No three. Just go, now.

The one good thing about being lost in a huge

abandoned city—and this is important, because there aren't a lot of them—is that you can run to and hide in all sorts of places. In even the smallest cities, there are a million nooks and crannies. So as I serpentine my way between huts and longhouses that look like sleeping rhinos, I know that I can, and will, eventually lose this bozo. I don't care if he's wearing a magical cloak and has a Rambo knife, he's not going to find us each in an entire underground city. Even PJ, not the most athletic kid in the world, can find a drainage pipe or crawlspace.

But somehow, no matter how far I run, I can feel Savini at my back. Sometimes I can hear his feet, and sometimes I can hear him grunt or breathe heavy, but most of the time I just know, in the middle of me where my guts and soul are, that I need to keep moving, keep moving, don't slow down, he'll get you, all he needs is a moment of your weakness to grab you and cut your neck.

I just have to think of it like any basketball game. It's no big deal. All you have to do is stay alive. My dad would be proud of me if he didn't probably want to disown me for lying to him and running away. My poor dad, who I lied to so I could run around in the dark trying not to get caught by zombies.

A hut with its door hanging open yells out to me with its big dark mouth, so I hop two stairs in a single bound and throw myself against the inner wall, my back lined up with the doorless opening in the front of the house, the tusk clutched to my chest like it could save my life.

My heart's pounding, my breath is sharp and quick, but man, do I feel on top of this. Through the edge of the door, I watch the space where the footsteps seem to be coming from, and then around a corner appears Savini with that same walk, slow and deadly and totally ready to get down and dirty. I'm almost laughing at him for walking past me, but then I catch his drawn knife in one hand, and my laugh sort of catches in my throat, which is not good, because it makes me cough.

And then the footsteps stop.

Oh man, it's like every drop of my blood is screaming at once, like my pulse is so loud it's making the hut shake. No no no. Turn around.

Dario steps slowly backward, his eyes focused on the doorway, mouth screwed up in a sneer, and no, ah geez, he starts turning toward the hut and walking very slowly, lowering into a kind of attack stance with his knife raised at his side.

"Hey, Savini!" screams PJ's voice from off in the darkness, the sound echoing crazily off the inside of the cave and coming from everywhere at one. *"Any luck finding us yet?"*

Dario's head snaps up, his brow furrowing. Slowly, he turns around and stalks off into the spaces between huts, keeping his footfalls soft. After a few seconds, I lean my head out of the hut and watch him, slinking along with his ear cocked to the air.

"You have no clue where we are, do you," calls PJ, his voice booming through all of Kudus. He sounds like he's traveling, moving from one point to the next with screams on his lips.

"Dario, look," calls Kendra, making Savini spin on his heel with a grunt of surprise. *"Dario, I'm easily spotted. See? I'm over where the dust is."*

"Hey, Savini, has anyone ever told you your mustache makes you look like a young Sam Elliot?" calls PJ.

"I take it that when your father trained you to be a Gravedigger, Finding Loud Children was not adequately reviewed," calls Kendra.

At first, it works—Dario glances around the cave in a panic, confused by the blur of echoing voices, and I figured awesome, go Kendra and PJ, we've got him— but then, like a good Gravedigger, he lowers his head and closes his eyes and takes a deep, even breath before slowly stalking off into the city. I creep out of the hut and follow his footsteps in the ankle-high crud on the floor.

"I bet O'Dea spit in your face when you asked for her help!" shouts PJ, laughing meanly. *"She probably told you to go to h-h-HEY—"*

There's a yelp, and then I'm running, my heart

throwing me forward between houses and huts and alleys, until I reach an old town square with what looks like a fountain full of bones and cobwebs rotting in the middle of it. Next to the fountain, something makes my whole body stop short.

Savini's strolling up to PJ, who has two cave zombies creeping down the edge of a building and hissing at him. Within seconds, the zombies are split down their mushroom-covered backbones and oozing foul-smelling black foam, and Dario has PJ's throat in one hand and his knife in the other. The blade of the knife lowers slowly toward PJ's face. PJ does his best to keep his eyes shut, to look away, but really all he can do is wheeze and scratch at Dario's big, hard hands while his death comes at him.

"Stop!" I shout. "Leave him alone! You want a fight, you fight me!"

The knife just stops, man. Dario pulls his eyes off of PJ, and then lets me breathe when he tosses my friend to the floor. He turns and smiles at me like he's heard the answer to a question he's been really curious about, and then, what do you know, he drops his knife on the floor with a clatter.

"Think you can take me on, Ian?" he says. "Be my guest. I'd love to see that."

Ah, crap. I mean, what do I do? I've played sports, I can size a guy up. Dario Savini's got, what, a hundred pounds of muscle, two feet, and a lifetime of experience on me? I just watched him cut the backbone out of his zombie father, for Pete's sake.

But then again . . . then again, this guy isn't some MMA fighter, or some kind of superhero, he's a *loser*, the kind of nutcase who wants to make things bad for everyone, and those guys are never that good in a fight. Look at him, picking on kids, trying to start the zombie apocalypse—he's just a bully, and bullies always think they're tougher than they are. Besides, I'm a Grave-digger, not just a Gravedigger but the *physical* one, the fighter, and honestly, it looks like Savini only focuses on the glamour muscles. He's got those alligator arms—big biceps, little forearms.

Think I can take him? Damn right I do.

"Damn right, I do," I grumble, placing the tusk on the floor and putting my fists up in front of me before trotting over to him.

"That's the spirit," he says, raising his hands in that sort-of-open martial arts kind of way and crouching down. When I get close to him, I lower my head and begin circling him, hunched, swift, trying to remember all of the boxing stuff I've seen on TV and video games. Bob and weave, keep your hands by the side of your head, keep moving, keep moving. The guy is bigger than you so don't get too close; look for a weak spot.

He puts his left hand down a bit, and my body

responds automatically, throwing a solid haymaker right for his cheek.

That he dodges nimbly. And then he rears back his shoulder and—

WHUD!

Everything's white, and I'm going backward, my limbs fluttering after me like the tentacles of some kind of stupid jellyfish, with this sharp, almost cold feeling spreading through my nose and up into my brain, making me think, *Wow, so this is what it's like to get punched in the face.*

Then, I'm bouncing off the dusty ground and staring at the rocky ceiling of the cave some thousand feet above us, a line across the one-half of my vision telling me that I might have just gotten these really expensive night-vision goggles broken, which I guess is better than my face.

"Now, if a Gravedigger were training you and not a Warden," Savini calls out, "you would've been able to deflect that punch. Another time, I'll teach you some fighting skills."

You're not a real Gravedigger, moron, I want to call after him, but I'm too busy groaning and trying to remember how to stand to really say anything.

So there I watch, helpless, as Dario strolls past the cobwebbed-up fountain to where I laid down the seal, a look of calm satisfaction on his face. I'll give this to the guy: he's got a mean walk, the kind of walk that can freak a dude out of a fight (not me, I just go in and get my butt kicked anyway). But as he leans over, I see him overextend his knee, bending it inward, which is a bush-league move that he might recognize if he spent more time shooting hoops than thinking he was cool for being a Gravedigger. So:

My body twists, my foot snaps out, and my heel catches Savini in the knee. The dude yelps and falls over, his hands moving away from the tusk and onto his leg. Somehow, through the haze of having just gotten my face rocked, I manage to slap a hand on the big piece of carved bone, but then Savini's hand is on my wrist, and he's got that look on his face like I've stopped being a prospective Gravedigger trainee, like I'm just another zombie.

"Unwise," he says, reaching for his knife with his other hand.

Kendra's hair is the first thing I can see with my goggles, coming up behind Savini like some big puffy sun, and then I see the dusty, rotten skull held above her head. It comes down in a toothy blur, smashing on Savini's head and sending him collapsing. Skull-on-skull combat—badass.

"Thanks," I say as she yanks me to my feet. "Clutch save right there."

Her mouth flaps open and closed. "I . . . felt its memories," she babbles. "When I grabbed the skull—I could hear—there was so much *noise*—"

Yuh-oh. "Kendra, not now," I say, grabbing her shoulder and pulling her away from Savini, toward where PJ waves at us in the distance. She doesn't say anything, just nods kind of stupidly and lurches after me. I snatch up the tusk, and we begin running (more like stumbling, between my likely concussion and Kendra's crazy channeling-the-dead moment) through Kudus. Of course, now, as we're darting between huts and longhouses, my goggles begin to flicker, the punch to the face obviously having shaken some wiring loose. Stupid cheap Melee Industries brand—

Two cave zombies pop into view as we hobble around a corner, and PJ nods us in a different direction, but just as we start to move, one of them twists its head at us with this loud, gross popping noise and sniffs hard, and then its friend does the same thing. They both drop to all fours at once and start tapping their fingers loud and fast on the cave floor, the sound echoing around us in the cave.

"They're not supposed to smell us," says PJ, panic making its way into his voice. "We smeared ourselves with zombie blood—"

It's only when I feel this tickling behind my ear that I realize what's going down, and it's not good. "We're sweating," I tell him. "Bet we're giving off all sorts of human smells."

The tap-tap-tapping sound starts to grow louder

and louder, and I realize it's not just them, it's other tapping, coming from other parts of the cave, joining in with these two, and given how loud it's getting, how many fingers I can hear tapping, it might be all of them, the whole zombie horde we had to deal with before, responding to these guys. Then, it's joined by the groan, that deep, creepy rumbling that seemed to pull the zombies away before, that makes my teeth chatter and my hands go numb and makes me realize that man, something really, really bad is about to happen, and we don't want to be here for it.

"We have to book it," I say, tugging PJ and Kendra away from the noise, and thankfully, they're thinking the same thing. We barrel toward the outskirts of the city, watching as huts and houses turn smaller and smaller one by one, until only a few tiny huts and what look like small shrines are scattered throughout the streets.

A wall starts growing in front of us, all cobbled-together stones and huge square bricks with the occasional gate or window in the edge, but the openings don't go anywhere, just kind of lead into more rock heading straight up.

"What is this?" I pant as we slow down, my lungs getting a little burn around the edges.

"It's the walls," says Kendra, huffing. "Kudus was a walled city. Over time, the cave must have closed in around it and started absorbing the outer walls."

"Can that happen?" I ask. "I didn't think rocks could swallow stuff."

"Guys," says PJ softly.

She shrugs. "With how long this place has been buried underground? Anything is possible. Besides, seeing as how this place is enchanted, maybe the earth is just trying to devour it."

"That's creepy," I say. "But the real question is, can we find a way to—"

"*Guys*," says PJ, louder and harder, in that way that lets me know we should pay attention. When I look at him, he's staring the way we came with these intense sad eyes, which makes sense because when I follow his stare I nearly swallow my tongue.

The temple at the center of the city, that big spiky shadow-artichoke, looks like it's rippling, like it's made of water, only it's not rippling, it's just emptying out. From every window or doorway or balcony in the statue-covered thing there's a cave zombie crawling out, making its way into the general flood of crawling, leaping, scrambling skeleton creatures pouring off the edges of the temple and making their way toward us. There are so many of them that there's no telling one from the other, like there's just a fog made of skeletons drifting over the city, tapping a million bony fingers at once.

My eyes shoot back and forth—zombies, wall, zombies, wall, zombies, wall. A ways down from us, something catches my eye—indents in the stone, made in back-and-forth handholds that lead up to the top, where the actual city walls have made a little ledge before the straight rock wall of the whole cave system just cuts down and stops them dead.

"We gotta climb," I tell them. "There might be a way out up there, a tunnel or something that we can use to get out of here."

"We need to find O'Dea," says PJ, his eyes never leaving the zombie-lava surging toward us.

"We need to survive," I say, grabbing his arm. "I'm sorry, man, but if she's safe through this, she's safe. If not, there's not much we can do for her when this zombie horde reaches us."

PJ glares back at me, and I can feel what he's saying without words, and he's right—I'm full of it. O'Dea might not be dead, but she might be, and if we find a way out we'll probably never find her, or see her again, and she might kill herself if we don't because that's apparently the sick way Wardens work.

But you know what, I can't even think about it right now. It's like my brain understands all of these things, but it's just choosing to not look at them, the way you feel when you scrape a knee or stub a toe during a game and it doesn't start to hurt until you're sitting back down on the bench. My head's in full-on Gravedigger mode, trying to find some shelter, protect the big magical tusk in my hand, and keep me and my friends from getting overrun by hungry corpses.

"If she dies—" says PJ, his voice sounding out of tune.

"PJ, our options are decreasing by the second," says Kendra. She goes to pinch the bridge of her nose, but her hands hit her goggles, and she swears.

"Let's go," I say, brushing past PJ and slapping my hands into the dusty stone indent in the wall. Part of me feels bad, blowing off his worries like that, but then I hear bone fingers and toes clicking on cave walls, I hear that deep earth-shaking rumble, and I know that we can't be bothered by little emotions right now; we just have to go.

Staying alive: it's the only game in town.

CHAPTER FOURTEEN

Kendra

Critical thinking requires time, like sustenance. The longer a thought has to gestate, the more refined and polished it can become.

I am a thinker, but I have no time, and therefore no chance at helping us. The undead are coming. A maniac stalks the darkness. We are outnumbered, unfocused, dare I say frightened. We must climb.

It does not help that my brain still echoes with the cries of the dead. When I grabbed the skull with which I struck Savini, there was a crackle of energy before the bone spat a barrage of memories into my mind— long beautiful days, a mother's signature stew, torches bobbing in the darkness, unspeakable agony at the tip of a spear—before I brought it down with a crash. Now, the fading memories of the dead still resound in my brain, stinging less but still raw and undefined.

These newfound . . . talents, whatever they may be, are proving useful, if only they could be controlled. There must be a way to harness them.

How Ian spotted the ladder carved within the wall, I can't say—it must be part of his talents as a Gravedigger, to be able to pick up on escape routes the rest of us might not have noticed. The minute he begins scaling the wall, though, I notice the handholds, leading all the way to the ledge at the top. He is so good at automatic movement. I don't know how he does it.

"So this is it," rasps PJ, glaring at me. "We're just going to leave her."

"PJ, consider this rationally," I say to him, holding out my hands as though I were holding the answer. "If O'Dea wants us to save her, she would want—"

"Cut it out, Kendra," he snarls, glaring at me. "I get it. I know what you're trying to say. We've been over this. Just don't try to make me act like I'm okay with it."

Try not to blow up at him, Kendra. That's your fear talking, the oncoming army of mutated cadavers talking. PJ's your friend, and you're better than that.

"Well, if you want to stay here and *die*, then you're more than welcome to!" I snap.

Classic, Kendra. So much for that.

"I'm going," spits PJ back at me. "We should just admit what we're doing."

"Yo!" shouts Ian, his voice almost drowned out by the rattling of desiccated bone tapping on bedrock. Our eyes raise quickly to see him already on top of the outer barrier of Kudus, his back pressed flat against the stone toward which we climb. "What's the problem?"

"Where to begin," says PJ, flinging himself against the wall and climbing. His anger is a liability; twice, his feet slip out of the crevices that act as rungs, nearly sending him falling to his death. Finally, though, he's far up enough that I can begin my ascent.

The rock feels dusty and smooth beneath my hands, so much so that I worry at any moment I will come sliding loose of the shallow holds and I'll fly backward and hear a noise not unlike wood snapping as my tailbone shatters against the cold, hard ground of the cave. But inevitably, as my hands go numb and sweat beads on my brow and lips, and the enamel nearly chips off my gritted teeth, I scale the stone ladder. Finally, my hand reaches up to seek another hole and finds only open air on its top, a flat stone ledge on my palm. Two pairs of hands clasp me under my arms and drag me upward, until my feet touch the ledge and my weight rests comfortably thereon.

From the precipice on which we stand, our view of

Kudus is potentially breathtaking. The huts, with their simple shapes and thatch roofs, give way to great halls and longhouses with their extended bodies and horned awnings, all leading to the shape of the temple at the city's core, writhing with a swarming mass of bony limbs and hissing, eyeless skulls. The cave itself is also visible, its ceiling an endless spiked overhang of stalactites that almost seem like a reversal of the city itself, a metropolis of dangling rock stretching out before us. For this brief interval, it is as though we are merely tourists observing this strange and beautiful place, a dark oddity writhing with the dead, the seventh horror of the world.

Gravity yanks me hard, and my arms automatically windmill and grasp. On either side of me, Ian and PJ reach out and yank me back, my shoulder blades aching as they slam against the uneven natural rock at our backs.

"Careful looking out," says Ian. "We don't have much ledge to move on."

A glance down proves he's correct—though our footing is sure and our platform is even, the toes of my boots actually jut out from the ledge on which we stand. The drop beneath us, seemingly easy to master while climbing it, now confronts me—a plummet of over twenty feet, straight down.

No throwing up, Kendra. Only once every trip; twice, and you're an amateur. Suck it up. So that's a long, scary drop. You're a Gravedigger, or a Warden, or something *important.*

"Okay," I breathe out, willing my heart rate to lower and my stomach to remain subdued. "We made it. We're on top of the wall. What next?"

"That way," says Ian, pointing to his left. A few feet down, I can make out what he's directing us toward—an opening between two solid sheets of rock wall some hundred feet away, small and dark but seemingly large enough for us to fit through. Whether the cavern on the other side is a way out, a place to shelter ourselves, or simply a dead end where we'll be zombie fodder, isn't clear. But a saying about beggars and choosers comes to mind.

"All right," I say, pressing myself hard against the wall behind us, "we'll need to shuffle over and then climb in. Let's—" Within my first inch of shuffling, my foot slips and I cry out. Once again, the boys are forced to steady me, and my face burns red with overwhelming embarrassment.

"Here," says PJ softly, and I feel his small, cold hand wrap around mine and squeeze it tightly. My eyes flash over to him and catch that pained yet reassuring expression he's so good at, as though he's saying that he knows the situation is dire, that he understands, and that he's here to help me through it. In my heart, an ache of remorse at being harsh with him earlier throbs low and dull. PJ Wilson is too good a friend to be under-appreciated.

Ian catches PJ's action and switches the magically engraved tusk to his left grip before snatching up my other hand in his. His palm is huge and sweaty, but there is something nice to its feeling.

"Now look," he says, "we're going to do this slowly and carefully, got it?"

"Got it," PJ and I repeat.

"There's no reason we have to rush," he says, as though he's trying to imitate Coach Leider. "We'll just do this one foot at a time until—"

Below us, the rattling reaches a bloodcurdling crescendo, and the dead appear in the streets.

To call the mass of bony loping corpses a mob would do human mobs a severe injustice. What approaches us is more of a wave, a crawling flood of hissing arachnid cadavers. Half of them lurch into view along the ground below us, moving with slow, purposeful footsteps, while the other half creep and cling to the walls of the cave, sinking their clawed fingers into the subterranean rock and one another's leathery, fungus-pocked flesh as they rush up toward the ceiling, around the walls, worm-eaten nose holes huffing dry air, drawing them toward the ledge on which we now stand. They are all so uni-form in their blank hideousness—bodies gnarled, arms and hands distended, teeth lipless and stained, eyes long since replaced with dust and mold—that their little differences begin to stand out in my vision. Here is one still bearing a rudimentary loincloth, here is one with faded tribal tattoos inked along its membranous skull face, here is one with tattered hair, here is one with a thick green lichen growing from its neck. The main differences are, of course, the bracket mushrooms protruding from their backs and necks, some dotted in patchy outcroppings, others rising from them like solar panels made of soft white meat. But their sheer numbers soon overwhelm my vision, and their single hissing mass begins to blend and flow into something resembling a fog of elbows and knees, a pulsing invasion of the long dead and once human.

"There's no time to waste," I scream over the popping of joints, the tapping of *phalanges* (no time for that, Kendra, but yes, fine, one) against stone. "Shuffle! Shuffle like mad!"

We climb a mere ten feet closer to the cave before the first zombie reaches the wall beneath us. Before my eyes, it extends its hands and claws at the stone twice, which emanates that sickening abrasive noise we heard earlier. On the third attempt I see its fingertips sink into the rock and watch its hollow face slowly move up to stare at mine as it lifts itself off the ground.

"They're almost here," I say loudly, willing myself to stay focused, willing the zombies' hissing to *abate* (that's two, keep it up).

"We can make it before then!" cries Ian. "There's only a little—"

A sharp vibration sends us reeling, and we turn to see a cave zombie, newly dropped from the ceiling above us, crouched next to PJ. Its mouth cracks in a feline snarl, and it slashes a clawed hand out toward my friend. PJ's mouth goes wide and he leans back, lip quivering, arms bunching at his chest. Then his eyes clench shut, he exhales, and, letting go of my hand, he grabs the zombie's arm and yanks. The off-kilter creature's claws make a sickening scrape as PJ throws it into the air. The monster's arm snaps off at the shoulder joint, its remaining carcass tumbling to the ground below and taking a few of its climbing brethren with it.

"Keep moving," he pants, brandishing the arm like a club. "We'll just have to fight as we go."

"But—" Before I can form my sentence, a bony hand grips my ankle. Without thinking, my foot wrenches out of the steely grasp and my heel thrusts out, catching a withered corpse in its wrinkled nasal bridge. With a crunch and a hiss, the monster goes falling off of the wall.

Come on, Kendra. Forget everything else. You have a great and inborn skill within you. You're a Gravedigger. And Gravediggers fight zombies.

Our movement is reduced to baby steps, but

somehow we continue our death shuffle toward the black mouth in the stone wall at our backs, fending off zombies the whole time. PJ continues his strange zombie martial art, yanking the zombies from their perch and tossing them into each other or swatting at them with a severed limb when he can wrench one off, while Ian brandishes the tusk alternately like a cricket bat and sword, making the zombies rear back in terror at the conduit of pure containment magic. One leans in too close, and when Ian brings the tusk down on its head, it doesn't just die; its skull explodes in a cloud of dust and a crackle of magic.

While they fend off the horizontal climbers and ceiling descenders, I focus on the zombies below us, demolishing the face of any corpse determined enough to attempt yanking us down with them, coating my heel in black fleshy scum. I am beyond complaining. Skeletal cave zombies fall; new ones arrive. That is our current mission.

"Ian!" cries PJ. My eyes flash to my right and see him crouching, trying to stay out of reach as five different zombies—three on the cave wall, one on the ledge, one climbing up beneath him—reach out their pointed dead fingertips. "I could use that tusk for a second!"

"Here," says Ian, holding the tusk out to me.

Once again, an extra sense seems to smolder inside my head, as though something deep in my frontal cortex senses a menace behind this object. "I . . . I can't."

"What?" he says, glancing at me with disbelief and anger.

"I don't know why, but I can't—"

"*IAN!*"

"Ah, for crying out loud—CATCH!"

Before my own eyes, Ian lobs the saving grace of all Indonesia over my head (I must remember, later, to kill him for doing something so reckless). It is only the tusk's enormous size that enables scrawny, uncoordinated PJ to grab it out of the air. Instantly, as he holds it out, all five of the taloned hands reaching for him pull away with a panicked hiss; the zombies rear back, giving him a two-foot radius.

"Ian, be careful!" I scream. "If you drop that thing, we could be done for."

"Just be quiet and keep kicking zombies," he grunts, landing a sharp left jab in a corpse's throat and sending it tumbling twenty feet down.

Hear that, Kendra? Ian Buckley is being the voice of reason while you're acting the silly, fretful girl. There, with the missing teeth—kick. The one with the huge half-disc fungus bulging from its eye socket—kick. Do not plan, just think; use your swift mind to make you swift footed. There—kick.

Eventually, the hole in the wall is reachable, and Ian hooks one arm inside and cries, "Guys! We're in! Come on!"

"It might be full of zombies!" yells PJ, jabbing our

artifact at a frightening monstrosity.

"No—no," he says, glancing in quickly. "They're not here. It must be protected. Come on."

In terror, I watch Ian shuffle two more feet and then duck into the cave. Sure enough, he's right—the undead hover around the edge like hungry ants but dare not go in. As I inch closer, I catch a faint glow that likely only I can see coming from deep within.

"Oh no," rasps PJ. On my other side, I can feel him stop swinging and shoving.

"What?" I say, trying to peer farther into the opening in the rock.

"He's back," groans PJ.

My eyes meet his—wide, dark, heavy with despair—and follow his gaze to the city of Kudus, swarming with dead. There, in the midst of the forward-pressing horde of carnivorous meat scarecrows, comes a shape—brawny, cloaked, plowing through the creatures as though they were nothing. Watching Savini make his way toward us through the horde is a truly incredible sight—he crushes skulls without looking away from the wall, slices out and snaps spinal columns as though they were nothing.

You may have doubted him in the past, Kendra, but if he's not a Gravedigger, he's just pretty damn good.

The figure's hood rises, and two sparkling eyes meet mine.

"Head into the cave!" I shout, shuffling the last few feet to the stone mouth and leaping in backward past a web of snatching hands. Sure enough, a few feet down Ian sits with his back to a wall covered with faintly glowing designs, imbued with an effervescent light that dully throbs every time I exhale a breath—

"Grab PJ!" shouts Ian.

Remember PJ, Kendra?

My body spins, and my hand closes around the back of PJ's shirt. With a sharp pull, he comes flying backward into the shelter, landing on his tailbone with a thud and a sharp cry.

The tusk slips out of his hands and goes rolling toward the open mouth of the cave.

Behind me, Ian gasps; next to me, PJ scrambles, but I have the clear shot, the clear path, the perfect view of the magical seal as it skitters toward a twenty-foot drop.

It's now or never. Do or die. If O'Dea would sacrifice her life for this, it's only fitting that I would also.

Grab it, kid.

My body launches forward, and my hand closes around the patterned ivory of the seal. My hands burn, and something powerful strikes me in the chest and doesn't leave. The air leaves my lungs, my ears ring, and everything goes blindingly white.

CHAPTER FIFTEEN

PJ

For a moment, a single shining instant, I believe Kendra has saved us. It's truly beautiful—she dives, slides, and grabs the totem over which I sweatily lost control.

"You've got it!" I shout, and then everything goes downhill.

Kendra's body spasms once, hard, her arms and legs going straight out and her chest thrusting forward, her back arching painfully. It reminds me of a movie hospital when someone gets the shock paddles on their chest after their pulse drops—*beeep*, "CLEAR"—and then all at one, she goes limp, her head hitting the cave floor with a sickening thump.

"What the heck was that?" shouts Ian. "What happened to her?"

"It . . . must have been the tusk," I say, doing my best to put two and two together. "Maybe these new Warden powers . . . maybe it was too much for her. It blew out her system—"

Before I can finish the word, Kendra's body lazily slips over the edge of the cave mouth.

"NO!" scream both Ian and I, bounding to grab her boot as it slides out of sight, but we're too late. We lean over the edge just in time to catch her plummeting, limbs flailing, body bent. A scream escapes my throat and the world goes blurry as she descends toward the horde of living dead.

Savini, watching from beneath us, has a similar reaction. He puts his huge meaty arms up in front of his face and barrels forward, mowing down the frail scrawny zombies in his path. His timing is impeccable: as if on cue, he gets to the wall and throws out his arms just in time for Kendra to collapse into them with a thud.

For a moment, my heart spikes with panic, preparing myself for the cave zombie masses to pile on top of him, but it's the opposite—they rear back, hissing and gasping at the limp form cradled in Savini's arms.

It's the seal, the tusk carved with the Wardencraft sigils. Something about the sheer power of it just scares the living—unliving, whatever—daylights out of them . . . but it also almost looks like they're worshipping it.

Savini touches a finger to Kendra's throat, beneath her chin, to make sure she's alive. He glances at the tusk in her hand, then back up at us in the cave . . . then a sickening smile curls over his face. "And what do we have here," he calls out. "Why, it's a *young Warden*."

My heart deflates. Ian spits out a word we don't normally say at dinner.

As if on cue, the cave shakes with another sorrowful, earth-shattering moan. As one, every zombie around us, from the ones dangling from the ceiling to those half crushed under the feet of their brothers, turn and look to the temple at the very heart of the city, its green night-vision outlines looming and distant. Savini's gaze follows theirs, but he glances back at us one last time, eyes almost glowing beneath his hood.

"If you boys are smart and wait there," he growls, just loud enough for us to hear twenty feet above him, "I'll come back for you and help you escape before the horde arrives."

Savini pulls the tusk from Kendra's grip and tucks it into his belt. He turns and begins walking off into the city of Kudus with Kendra held in his arms like he's Boris Karloff in *Frankenstein.* The army of zombies around him slowly follow, always making sure to give him a five-foot radius. On all sides of our cave, spidery corpses descend the walls one careful handful of rock at a time, their phantom eyes pinned on the temple in the distance. For what feels like an eternity, Savini strolls along with Kendra bouncing lightly in his grip, an ocean of skeletal monsters five thousand thick scuttling next to him, crawling over huts and spilling around long-houses, until Dario seems to have disappeared into the roiling mass.

"This is not good," snaps Ian, fuming next to me.

"You can say that again," I grumble, crawling back away from the cave mouth. "What are we going to do, Ian?"

"We gotta climb back down and go after him," says my best friend, dusting off the front of his jacket and running his hands through his raggedy blond hair.

"That's impossible," I blurt out, my despair and hopelessness getting the better of me. "We're not going to *climb down* that indent ladder on the city wall, Ian. And we're not going to get through massive numbers of freakishly terrifying dead folks on all sides of Savini."

"It's the only way, PJ," he says, cracking his neck. "This isn't even about saving Kendra anymore, or O'Dea. If he's going to release these zombies, it's about saving the world."

Okay, I need to take a moment and acknowledge how cool it is that Ian just said that, and meant it. People ask me why I want to carry a camera around everywhere—it's because of things like this.

"Ian, we have no idea what he's going to do next," I say. "We don't even know if *he* knows what he's doing! How long do we think Kendra will be knocked out? Who knows if she even knows how to use whatever powers she has—"

"PJ, you're scared," he says as though it's a scientific fact. "That's okay, I get it. But this is the right thing to do. We've got a real full-on apocalypse situation on our hands, and we can't be sitting around meditating. This isn't *Night of the Living Dead* anymore, man; it's *Resident Evil*. It's time for action."

I couldn't be prouder of Ian for making that reference, but my fear is still overwhelming me. I am baffled as to what to do next. I can't get a grip, can't calm down. We were just shuffling across a cliff surrounded on all sides by vicious acrobatic zombies, after all. And . . .

And I dropped the seal. I couldn't hold onto it for more than three minutes before accidentally killing my friend.

My eyes shut, burning with tears. My teeth clench so hard I feel like they'll shoot sparks. There's got to be another way. Please, please, let there be another way.

We're being watched.

It stabs me in the chest and yanks my head up, whirling. Don't ask me how I know, but some portion of me is just aware that eyes have settled on us. Slowly, glancing from one inch of the tunnel to the next, I stare into its darkened depths and notice a rippling, a slight bit of movement.

And more. And more.

"Ian," I say, slapping behind me for my friend. "We have company."

The roaches vary in size, but the largest ones are disgustingly big, about the size of a horseshoe crab and possessing up to eighteen legs beneath their glistening shells. Where their exoskeletons should be black and shiny, like film, they are instead white and semitranslucent; ten bucks says these things were born without eyes. Unlike the zombies, they seem to moving in a single huddled mass, like a school of fish, sweeping toward us. As they click and scuttle along the floor, Ian and I steady ourselves, backs to the mouth of the cave. My throat swells up with nausea, and I can even feel Ian shudder next to me. I hope they aren't hungry—for some reason, being eaten by zombies seems far preferable to being eaten by huge, pale cockroaches that would die in light. An image from *Creepshow* pops into my head, and I force myself to swallow it.

But as they near us, the mass of many-legged creatures comes to a stop about two feet away. For a full minute, Ian and I stand there in silence, waiting for the pile of roaches to do something; for a full minute, they stay quiet and still.

"What do you think's going on?" Ian whispers, as though they could understand him.

My mind takes in the way the cockroaches sit before us, and something snaps into place. "It might be because we're Gravediggers," I say to Ian. "Remember the bats on Danny Melee's island? They treated us like gods." A strange shape, poking out from under the front of the cockroach mass, catches my eye. "There's . . . something down there. They have something. It looks like cloth."

"Pick it up," says Ian.

My mouth opens to reply, but it's dry, frozen. "I . . . can't. I can't do it."

He glances at me. "You've got to be kidding me. We're fighting undead monsters here, PJ."

"I don't like bugs," is all that comes out. There's no greater truth in the world than that. Through all of my Gravedigger training, my time spent around zombies, nothing has changed about the fact that six-legged creatures with shells that basically have acid-filled hair for mouths remain the worst thing on earth to me.

"Can't believe this," grumbles Ian, bending down toward the roaches.

"You were freaked out by the bats in Puerto Rico," I stammer.

"That's different," he says. "Bats are huge and have claws and teeth and drink blood." He tugs at the piece of fabric beneath the squirming pale creatures, sending them scuttling out of the way. Lifting it up, I take in a ripped hunk of cloth, the edges frayed and stained with dark patches. My hand reaches out and touches it, recognizing the make, the softness—

"O'Dea," I say, feeling my stomach drop into an endless pool. "It's O'Dea's clothing. They've . . ." I can't even say the words that come to my mind. The close-up shot in my head shows O'Dea, writhing in pain, before the white swarm of shells comes bulging from her mouth and nose and—

"Monsters!" I bellow, launching a foot at them. Somehow, the eyeless bugs are quicker than I am, and the horde goes crawling down into the crevice. My rational mind tells me to stay calm, but instinct overwhelms me, and I go chasing after the wave of writhing bottom-feeders, rushing headlong into the darkened tunnel. Ian's voice calls my name somewhere offscreen, but my rage at the flesh-eating insects that have devoured my friend is too powerful to ignore.

The cockroaches take a hard left into another cavern in the rock walls of Kudus, and I go after them. The minute I enter this second chamber, I freeze, my mind grappling with the sheer weirdness of what sits before me.

O'Dea is bound and gagged, tied to a stalac—stalag—a large stone spike hanging from the ceiling. Her face is a bruised mess, a little trickle of blood running from just above her right eye. Two cave zombies, crouched and sniffing the air, their black faces and gnarled claws twitching in anticipation, circle her. They seem to dance around her, making slow deliberate steps in uncomfortable-looking ways that pop and crackle their bones.

Through the sudden lump of fear that wells up in me as I draw breath, I find O'Dea's eyes, glaring at me in what looks like venomous rage.

"Oh my God," I whisper.

One of the zombies turns to us with a slow, agitated sniff and opens its mouth.

This time, when I try to close my eyes and gather my breath, I just feel a sudden blast of energy in my hand. It becomes a fist, a blazing ball of light that is ready to strike out at whatever challenges it. I take two steps forward, cock, and throw. My fist collides with the zombie's stomach, making its thin skin rupture, its tendons tear, and its upper half fall forward as its legs take a last few steps, jetting black fluid from the pelvis before they collapse in a heap.

When I turn around, Ian has finished kicking out the remaining zombie's legs and has begun stomping on the thing's back, turning it into a broken stick figure. He glances over at me, and his eyes go wide.

"Did you punch that thing in half?" he says.

"Let's get her down," I say.

It's a blur—suddenly, I'm on Ian's shoulders tugging at the rope looped between O'Dea's bound body and the ceiling spike (note to self: get that terminology down from Kendra, if she's still alive when you find her). Suddenly, the rope goes slack and O'Dea's on the floor in a pile. The minute I hop down from him, Ian yanks the handkerchief out of her mouth, and we hear the voice we've grown to love.

"You harebrained soft-witted twerps!" snarls O'Dea, writhing as we yank at the ropes on her wrists and ankles. "Are you out of your dull, half-formed little *minds*? Do you know what you *did*, going after me?"

We finally loosen her bonds and O'Dea pops free, her long spindly limbs snapping out in a sharp flourish. Then, those bony fingers go at her nose and start scratching like crazy.

"Oh, sweet mother, yes," she sighs. "Been itching for an hour."

"Are you okay?" I ask her. "O'Dea, your face— what'd he do to you?"

"Never mind that," she snaps, sticking a finger at me like the Ghost of Christmas Yet to Come. "I've taken a cheap punch or two in my day. What were you *thinking*, you two—" Her face goes slack and terrified. "Where's Kendra?"

"Savini's got her," says Ian. "He's going to use her to unlock the city and let out the crazy crawling zombies."

"What are you babbling about, Ian?" she snaps. "He needs me. He needs a Warden. Ugh." O'Dea gets to her feet and brushes herself down.

"Kendra's a Warden," says Ian.

O'Dea freezes, arching an eyebrow hard at Ian. "No. Kendra's a Gravedigger."

"She's seeing sigils," I say to her. "She's reading the walls by touching them. Grabbing the seal of this place knocked her unconscious."

"Gravediggers and Wardens are separate breeds," says O'Dea, turning to me with a glare of pure contempt. "Those aren't the kind of skills Gravediggers learn. They don't learn anything; they just happen. Wardens have to be trained." She shakes her head. "You're obviously not thinking straight, and you're not *listening*. I told you to *leave me*."

"We came to save you," I say, now doing my best to keep calm, breathe slowly, not look away from her, not grab her by the collar. "We just *did*."

"I didn't need *saving*."

"All right, guys," says Ian, holding up his hands.

"You have to be kidding me," I say. "Killing yourself? Letting him *beat you to a pulp*?"

"It's our *way*, PJ," she yells, so hard her lousy breath blows into my face. "We protect the secrets and dark karma. And *this is why*. Every second I'm still alive down here, it's bad news for everyone on Earth. *Look* at these zombies. You let these mutated freaks out, it's history for everyone."

"They die in the light," I tell her. "Even if Savini let

them out, they wouldn't get far."

"All it takes is one night," spits O'Dea. "PJ, what were you thinking? You, of all people. This is a scary business. Scary things happen sometimes, but you've got to let them happen."

"Wait, so I was supposed to sit there and let you die?" I say, torn up by equal parts shock and heartbreak.

"Let's keep it polite, guys," says Ian.

"You should've done what I told you!" she keeps shouting. "I'm sorry if that's hard, but something like *this* gets avoided! That's worth it! Containment is maintained! *Now*"—she swings the finger out toward where we came from—"you have two options! One is that Kendra isn't a Warden—which, I gotta tell you, I don't think she is; I'd know—and Savini kills her and comes after us, and we all die. The other is that she somehow *does* unlock the seal—and *everyone dies*!" By now, she's screaming, curling her hands into claws in front of my face. "Do you hear me, PJ? Do you know what will happen if a bunch of weird, twisted zombies get loose in Indonesia?"

" . . . I wanted to help you," I say hoarsely over the lump in my throat. "He . . . he would've hurt you to be able to unlock this place. I had to help."

She looks even angrier, witchier, than before, but then she softens her face and looks at me matter-of-factly. "PJ, Kudus is our atom bomb," she says. "This place is our Pandora's box. It's the one thing every Warden has always been afraid someone will accidentally find and unlock. And when you came after me, you led the wrong person right to it."

Her expression bores into me and hollows me out. There is not simply anger, or irritation; there is blame in it. There is total hopelessness. Something heartbreaking has been awakened within her, and it's our fault. Before I can try to stop them, two fat tears bunch in the corners of my eyes and rush down my cheeks.

"Look," says Ian in his best imitation of someone doing all right, "let's calm down. There's still some time. Savini seemed like he was bringing Kendra into the city."

"He's taking her to the temple," sighs O'Dea. "It was the magical center of the city. With any luck, they—"

Her voice cuts out with a loud cry.

The upper torso of the zombie I punched down the middle is hauling itself along the ground, a slime-caked tail of spinal column with a big hunk of pelvis attached trailing from behind it. Its bony fingers wrap around O'Dea's leg, its pointed fingertips pressing hard against the denim of her jeans.

My rage at my Warden friend, my sinking feeling of doom and inadequacy all crashes together, and I grab the zombie by the shoulders, lift its half body from the ground, and slam it up against a wall. The creature writhes in my arms, hissing and swiping its bony claws out into the air behind me. Its skull snaps out, teeth clicking together, and its kite tail of sinews and organs flaps violently, spraying my pants with zombie fluid.

I snap my lamp on and the wretched monster cries out, twitching. It turns away from the glare of my light, but I clamp my hand onto its face and twist it forward, forcing it to stare me dead on as I fill those hollow sockets with burning, torturous agony. With any luck, the monster's pain is nowhere near the anger I feel inside. Kendra falling to her death, O'Dea chewing me out—I channel it through my headlamp until I am totally numb with hate.

I don't even see how close the zombie's teeth are to my hand until it twists its neck sharply and sinks them into my palm.

CHAPTER SIXTEEN

Ian

PJ's scream makes me jump, 'cause it's not a little shriek—it's loud, it's deep in his throat, it's that kind of scream that's uncontrollable, that comes from pain. Then, he stumbles away, letting the zombie torso drop with this splattery thump, and he holds up his hand in the light of his helmet lamp, and I see the wound, that curve of little tiny lines with blood running from them that now marks the webbed part between his thumb and his index finger.

And it takes me a moment, just a moment, where I'm wondering what happened.

And then it hits me. Slams me in the chest and sinks

down into every inch of me, like a sickness I can feel coming on.

He's bit.

PJ got bit.

No, nah, nah man, oh no, oh no.

It's the end of the world. It's—

Oh my God, PJ got bit.

PJ stumbles away from the upper half of a cave zombie, which lies there sucking the blood from its teeth in hissing gulps of air.

Next thing I know, I'm standing over it and my foot has crushed a Nike-printed opening in its skull, but it doesn't stop, just keeps sucking at the blood until my foot has gone through it over and over, finding the sweet spot and smashing its feeble brain back into whatever horrible mossy stench hole it came crawling out of.

When it's a foaming pile of dead, I turn back to PJ. O'Dea's got his hand in hers and is saying . . . something.

She's not really talking. It's more like she moves her mouth and something huge, and deep, and old, is speaking out of her mouth, like she's someone's magical . . . kazoo. Her fingers seem to stand out in the darkness, like they've been heated red in a fire, and she shakes his hand with a soft, steady rhythm. Tears course down PJ's cheek, but he doesn't sob, just grits his teeth and glares at his hand, probably feeling some kind of crazy magic current running through it.

A cockroach skitters past her, and before I know what's going on, she snatches it off of the floor and jams it into her mouth, chewing loudly. Without meaning to, I let out a pained "*AWWWW.*" After a bunch of crunches, she spits the mess of bug in her palm and claps it on PJ's bite. Then she goes back to chanting. It's truly the most disgusting thing I've ever seen. I try to talk, but my mouth is dry as a desert, and my stomach is just swimming with acid-covered butterflies. I try to move, and it's like I've grown roots. What this means—what's going to happen now—doesn't stop hitting me; it just slams into me in slow, steady waves that drive me back against the cave wall, feeling like I'm going to yak everywhere.

"O'Dea," says PJ in a slow, shaking voice. "O'Dea, look at me." She closes her eyes and looks away, still chanting. Slowly, PJ's face turns to mine, his voice coming out in these quick little sobs, and he's like, "Ian."

"Yeah, man. Yeah." I try to take a step toward him, but can't. "I'm here."

"You know what you have to do, man," he says, trying to sound calm. He switches to these deep, slow breaths. "Ian, I don't want to walk around after I'm dead."

Aw. Aw, no. "Shut up, PJ, you're going to be fine," I babble, trying to push the thought out of my head.

"I don't want to crawl around some cave for hundreds of years until my eyes rot out," he says, reaching his free hand out to me.

"PJ, *be quiet*," I snap at him. "Just calm down and hold on. O'Dea's helping you. You'll be okay. You'll—"

"There's no help," he says. "There's never any help. The bite's the thing, Ian."

"PJ—"

"Do you still have your machete? Can you—"

And then I'm outside of the cave, running down the tunnel, finding a spot and curling into a ball, clapping my hands over my head, trying to block out the image of PJ's face as he asked me what he just asked me. Around me, the cockroaches sit, staring, as I slide to the floor and gasp for air, clenching my eyes, trying not to think about it.

Because I can hear it in his voice, man—he believes it. There's not an ounce of doubt in his mind. PJ, who's stood up to me when I've tried to run headfirst into a zombie horde. Who did everything he could to keep his friends safe. Poor scared PJ, who has to meditate just to not be a nutcase the whole time. That guy, my friend from toddler days, wanted me to do it. He was asking nicely in the hopes that I would do him a favor and effectively ruin my life forever.

This wasn't supposed to happen. Why is this happening?

But I know, and it feels like maybe I've known the whole time we've been down here, slogging through the pitch-blackness. We've been lucky so far. O'Dea, Danny Melee, even Kendra's crazy new Warden powers—they've all worked in our favor. But down here, in maybe the most awful place on the planet with air that feels like a massage from a dead fish, there's no room to pivot around the curse. The whole place is soaked in it. So when the terrible thing goes down, which it definitely will, because look at where we are, it goes down hard. It's not a bad time; it's the big one.

The droning of O'Dea's amplified voice and PJ's pleas go on for a while, all just a bunch of background noise behind my lungs gasping for breath and my blood rushing like crazy through my ears. After a while, PJ goes quiet, and then, gradually, O'Dea's voice sinks to a low rumble, then stops altogether. Once again, it's just us, alone, floating in this black space that we can feel stretching off around us for miles.

A while later—I can't really remember how long I stay curled there—footsteps ring out in the cave, louder and louder, until they reach me. There's a thud as a body flops down next to mine.

"I put him out for a bit," says O'Dea in that gruff, low voice. "His hand is stable. Stopped the bleeding, dulled the pain."

When I uncurl out of my ball position, I glance up

at O'Dea, and man, the woman must've taken a couple hard ones on the jaw. Her one eye is swollen up, and her cheeks and lips look just a bit puffy and dry, and there's this tiny scratch on her brow all smudged and running blood. She's got a look of straight-up hit-the-wall exhaustion, face all bunched up and mouth curled down. That doesn't make me feel good—heck, when she was yelling at PJ before, that at least was normal tough-ass O'Dea. This look, tired and beat, is not good.

"Sorry about that thing with the cockroach," she says. "I bet you didn't want to see that."

"It's okay," is all I can say. "You had to make a . . . a poultice." The word stings the back of my eyes. It rushes back to me—the first zombie horde, on the mountain where we met O'Dea. It's a Kendra word. Remember how much we fought, she and I? And now she's gone. She's somewhere in this giant death trap. And I never got to tell her. I never got to tell either of them.

"Exactly," she said. "Bugs aren't normally friends to magic, but I guess the ones down here are the only forms of life left, so they—are you all right?" She reaches out a hand, but doesn't quite touch me. "Ian?"

"How bad is he?" I ask.

She exhales through her nose. "We've bought him some time," she says. "That thing had all the jaw strength of a jellyfish, so it didn't get that deep. But it definitely broke the skin."

"But . . . is he going to be okay?" I ask.

O'Dea just swallows and half shrugs. "We need to get him out of this place," she says out into the black all around us. "It's crawling with the evil. I can smell it everywhere. These zombies . . . they're something new. No wonder the Wardens are so protective of this spot. It's nothing like we've ever seen before. The longer his cut's down here, the quicker it'll become infected."

All I can think is that it's not a cut, it's a *bite*, a freakin' *zombie bite*, but I refuse to say it. "And how do we do that?" I ask, trying to make sense of everything.

"Preferably," she says, "we do it by you three listening to me and not coming here in the first place." I shoot her a look that she understands, holding up a hand and nodding. "But! Given the circumstances, the best bet would be for you two to go find Kendra. If Savini's as crazy as I think he is, he'll probably convince himself she's a Warden, too. Did you tell him that little chestnut?"

"O'Dea, she's . . . got some kind of powers," I babble. Dang, PJ can talk to her so easily. For me, it's like chatting with a teacher. "She used them to fend off the zombies earlier. And she's been reading things off the sigils in the walls. When she touched the seal for this dump, it fried her brain or something. Trust me, we're not making this up."

"Ian, I'm telling you—"

"Remember on the island?" I say. A memory clicks into place—PJ, Josefina, and I, surrounded by soggy hungry corpses, a hypnotic noise filling the air. "She played those drums to draw the zombies away from us. Josefina said only a Warden could do that. You were *there*."

O'Dea's eyes are wide and hard like plates, but there's that little bit of recognition in them that lets me know I'm right. She stares straight ahead for a few moments and then, in a real quiet voice, says, "That shouldn't happen. None of this should be happening. Strange things going on down here in this hellhole, Ian, things I've never seen before. And when the rules change . . . it usually means we're taking part in something big."

Great, fantastic, *no one* has any idea how to fix this mess. Right as we're getting a handle on what it is to be a Gravedigger, the game changes. For a minute, we go silent, staring straight ahead. It's weird, being just us, 'cause O'Dea and I were just never tight the way she was with the other two. PJ and her had some kind of weird deep friendship, and Kendra was always asking questions and figuring out secrets with her. Me, I feel like I got a lot of my physical smarts from Coach Leider and my dad. O'Dea's just been teaching me how to make it work against zombies.

"I'm sorry we came after you if you didn't want us to," I say, finally, because what else is there to say?

231

"Ah, it's all right," she says, waving me away with a skinny knobbed hand. "I appreciate the thought. Besides, maybe that psychopath Savini is onto something. This place has sat around rotting in this cave for nearly a thousand years. Someone was bound to find out about it. It was just about when, and if they could unlock the magic holding it down."

"You really think these crazy mutated zombies could take over the earth?" I ask her.

She nods, slowly and calmly. "Don't get me wrong, they seem about as dumb as your average corpse, and like you said, daylight won't be their strong point. But all of this climbing? The whole stepping-around-sigils routine? Yeah, I saw that, too. And the mushrooms growing out of their spines . . . it's not natural." And she hasn't even seen what's living in the sewers of the city. "If these things get out, it could mean a lot of trouble for a lot of people."

"Then what are we sitting around for?"

PJ comes calmly down the cave tunnel, his one hand clenched tight and smeared with gray cockroach guts. At first, I'm worried I'll see him bleeding all over the place, and then I see that there's, like, no blood at all. The wound has basically scabbed over. And you know what, that's almost worse.

"How are you feeling?" I ask him.

"Like time's wasting," he says, nodding toward the

mouth of the cave, the city of the dead beyond it. "If we hurry, I bet we can catch them and stop Savini's weird apocalypse plan before it's too late."

"That's not what you were saying a few minutes ago," I tell him, feeling something like real anger as I look at this scrawny little madman who tried to get me to do the worst thing on earth one second and then starts ordering me to get out there and sink a three-pointer for him. "You were asking me—"

"I remember," he snaps. "I was there. I—" He goes quiet and lowers his head, then exhales real hard and sharp. "What happened back there scared me. I wasn't thinking straight."

"I'll say," says O'Dea.

"But it doesn't change the fact that we're on borrowed time now," he says, raising his hand up as though we didn't see it in the first place. "The longer we wait, the worse this is getting. Let's just get out there, find Kendra, and leave before anything else happens. That way, this didn't happen for no reason."

"Maybe you should sit this one out," I say, holding a hand out to him. "You seemed pretty shook earlier."

"Not a chance," he says, closing his eyes and grimacing. "It's Savini's fault we're in this mess. Besides, you guys are going to need all the help you can get."

I trade a look with O'Dea, and she nods halfheartedly. I guess when you've been dealing with hordes of hungry, cursed dead people your whole life like she has, you get over any ego pretty quickly.

"All right," I say. "So, what's the plan?"

Like I needed to ask—a quick back-and-forth look from O'Dea and PJ, and I realize who's leading the way here.

"You just . . . play sports," says PJ, trying to explain rationally as my feet touch down on the ledge overlooking the city.

"Yeah, yeah," I grumble, edging out to my right with my back pressed against the uneven rock wall. Bit by bit, I shimmy over toward the indent ladder that we used to climb up into the cave. Out before me, the cluttered skyline of Kudus is what I focus on, trying not to look down as I side wind out to the ladder, which is a lot easier when you don't have a couple thousand angry wall-climbing corpses coming at you in a steady wave.

It's funny how, climbing up this thing, getting onto the ledge of the city wall and turning around to face the oncoming hordes was easy, but here, trying to mentally plan out how I'm going to do this, I have no idea. Slowly but surely, though, I manage to turn to one side, sort of walking like an Egyptian, and then swing my foot around so I'm facing the sheer rock face of the cave itself. Slowly, suuuper carefully, I lower myself to one knee, trying to ignore the drop of sweat creeping down the back of my neck, and prod around the wall below me, looking for a foothold.

My first couple of kicks at the wall don't give me anything, and I'm beginning to wonder if I've totally screwed this whole thing up, when my foot presses into a huge hole in the wall. Reaching out with my other foot, I find the next one, then the next, and inch by inch I lower myself down the ladder and onto the ground.

PJ and O'Dea follow after me; PJ takes a while, and turning around on the rock ledge puts that old stark PJ Wilson fear in his eyes, but he breathes deeply through each slow motion and somehow manages to climb down the wall. O'Dea does the whole thing like it's nothing. The woman's made of stone.

"We need to fix something," she says, clapping her hands together to dust them off.

"What's up?" asks PJ. "Let's hurry, what is it?"

Her bony hand snaps out at my face, and suddenly my goggles go over my head, sending me into total and complete blackness, and man, oh *man*, there's never been anything as black and dark as this. My body goes prickly with goose bumps as my eyes just stare off into forever and see nothing but pure, endless blackness. By the sounds of PJ's cries, she's done it to him, too.

Her calloused hand clamps on my head and a damp thumb draws something like a cross on my forehead. O'Dea grumbles a deep, guttural word, and with each blink, I feel a cold sort of buzzing spread up through my sinuses and move behind my eyes. It's like the skin of O'Dea's hand and the top of my head kind of melt into each other and there's this flood of energy moving between us, going all the way from my eyes to O'Dea's and back again, and man, I didn't know my eyes could feel cold, that they could feel this kind of sensation this deep in them. All my years doing sports, it never felt like my eyes were muscles.

The coldness sends ripples of light through my sight, making shapes out of various big black lumps that surround us. Everything around me begins to stand out—it's still dark, still shadowy as it can be, but now it's like shapes float on top of the darkness, standing out against the shadow as though they were floating on top of it and entirely visible to the naked eye.

"Whoa," I say, stepping back and trying to hold on to my balance. "O'Dea, is this some kind of . . . spell?"

"Pretty simple one," she says, sneering, and holy crap, I can see her sneer, I'm seeing in the dark over here. "Those goggles just get in the way. You see in the dark, you're part of the dark. Makes it easier to move around in the dark."

"Well, come on," says PJ, pointing toward the city and starting to trot out into its streets. "They're waiting for us. We have to get Kendra and stop Savini."

O'Dea and I trail after PJ, who jogs along like we have no clue what he's doing, when it's actually so obvious. Because PJ's bit. And he wants us to think it's fine, that it's all going to be okay once we save Kendra, but it's not.

I can see it in the way O'Dea jogs after us, her head down and her eyes all squinched up.

He's not going to make it.

CHAPTER SEVENTEEN

Kendra

Darkness. My eyelids feel dense, impossibly heavy.

Around me, there are footsteps, surrounded by an endless sea of scratching and bony popping. My stomach cramps. My whole body feels sore, slumped over a hard, jostling surface.

Where are you, Kendra? Can you open your eyes any farther?

My mind is a blur of images and emotions. These are fleeting glimpses of a life I did not lead, pieces of a story that seemed to hit me all at once and now unfold slowly, like a sophisticated aftertaste.

My mind is that of a mother, fleeing through

pounded dirt streets, tugging her child away from the rushing hordes of laughing attackers behind her. Then I am the child, struggling along after her mother, a man in full war paint and wearing a complicated feathered headdress rushing toward me with a wicked grin lining his pierced lips. Then I am the man, my spear held high, the smell of smoke and the sound of screams accompaniment to my battle cry . . . and then I am that same man, my spear and headdress falling as I try to outrace my brothers. My foot catches, and I stumble to the bloodstained ground. When I turn, the mother and her daughter are there, only their faces are pale and lifeless, their eyes blank and full of hunger, followed slowly by their fathers and mothers and friends, the people I slaughtered, now closing in on me. Finally, I am a woman, standing on the shaking earth as a great crack splits open down the middle of the city in which I was raised. The dirt suddenly gapes wide in a gash, and the whole city—the grand temple, the glorious longhouses, and finally the walls themselves—are eaten up by the hungry grimace of clay beneath it.

As my consciousness returns fully to my own mind, my eyelids crack open. The night-vision goggles no longer bite into my face, and so I expect impenetrable darkness . . . which is why I'm surprised when I see light, faint and green, coloring the reconstituting world around me.

A cold breeze hits my back, and the person carrying me stops. In one swift motion, he flings me off his
shoulder, my body landing with a resounding *thump* on
a dusty stone floor.

*Well, Kendra, you're definitely awake now. Get your
head together. Something's wrong here—grossly wrong.
Can't you feel it in your bones? Can't you feel it in the
way the cool air prickles against your skin like a fine mist
of acid rain?*

As my eyes adjust, I see Savini standing before me,
his face and body bathed in eerie green light. He says
nothing, his eyes are cast upward, caught on something
behind me, and his mouth hangs open.

"Where are we?" I croak, my throat impossibly dry.

Savini's lower lip quivers oddly, and then he whispers, "Look, Kendra. Look at what they've created."

When I turn and look over my shoulder, my first
instinct is to scream, but the sheer revulsion stops the
sound in my throat and refuses to let go. Instinctively,
I crawl backward, until I collide with the shin of Savini.
Before I can rise of my own accord, his massive hands
clamp on the sides of my skull and force me to stare
straight ahead.

"No looking away," he says. "Behold."

The pale, bulbous thing that fills the center of the
temple's main chamber nearly reaches the ceiling; I
would guess it to be approximately forty feet tall. Its

repulsive upper section is a bulging tumescence the pale, semitranslucent hue of a zombie's flesh; indeed, peering at it, I can see blue and green veins running beneath its slowly pulsating surface. The light emanates from the flat portion beneath its top mass, a circle of fluttering gills that glow a bright toxic green as they shudder and sway around a stalk as thick as me that pushes into the stone floor, sending thick, rubbery roots splitting through portions of the rock around us. With a deep creaking noise, the mass sways back and forth, throwing emerald shadows across the room.

A few blinks on my part are required to fully understand: a mushroom.

A forty-foot, pulsating, glowing mushroom that appears to be made out of dead flesh.

Well. I mean. We thought it could be a lot of things, Kendra, whatever was making all that noise within this temple. But let's be honest—this was not one of them.

Slowly, I realize my surroundings—every inch of the temple walls, of the floors around us—are occupied by some few thousand zombies. They don't move an inch, but instead simply stand or hang, their eyeless faces raised to peer out at the mushroom. Some even sit perched on pale fungus brackets that grow off the walls, dozens of them cluttering on each half disk of vile blubbery matter. And though I know they have nothing on which the fungus's eerie bioluminescence could reflect, it is almost as if green orbs hang in those long-empty ocular cavities, as though the light gives them eyes enough to see it.

"W-what is th-that?" I somehow stammer.

"The result of their containment," whispers Dario, his hands tightening on my head. "The mutation of the cursed, left down within the belly of the earth for so long. This, Kendra, is their great achievement. This is their god." His voice quivers, his fear almost a fragrance drifting off him. "Have you ever seen a horror so great?"

As though it heard him, the mushroom seems to quiver and then lets out the deep, rumbling groan that we've heard all through the endless night of our journey down into the cave. Its lamella—the flaplike gills on its underside—make a wet slushing sound as they ripple in unison, and from them and a few other gill-like fissures that tear open in its disgusting head, a cloud of faintly glowing green particles blow out, drifting over the cave zombies. Dario and I yank our shirts over our mouths, hoping to block out the cloud, while the cave zombies suck deeply at the air through their nose-less trunks and lipless mouths. With each inhalation, they let out a faint, almost contented hiss.

Immediately, different aspects of our unspeakable journey click together, and a bridge forms in my mind connecting one fact to the other. The cave zombies, the climbers, did not attempt to devour us, only drag us along—because they didn't need to eat us. It is just as Danny Melee told me on the island: eating the flesh is an act of spreading the deadly zombie spore. These zombies need no new matter to spread their life stuff to because they receive it directly from the source. That's why the zombie mass within the sewer tried to devour us, and why it ate another zombie. It needs more matter, more food for the spore.

As the cave zombies inhale the last of their sustenance, the great mushroom quivers, making another rumbling noise deep within its fungal innards, one not quite as loud and despairing as the last, but enough to send a ripple of movement through the cave zombies, crouching and hissing.

Slowly, with the grace of a bat spreading its wings before taking flight, a fissure in the side of the mushroom's head opens, revealing a moist, gaping hole from which blasts a beam of green light.

Hands—two, then four, then a preponderance of them—reach out and grasp the edges of the pathway into the mushroom. Slowly, accompanied by a symphony of wet slapping and carnal popping, a shape emerges from the crack in the mushroom's flesh and begins lowering toward us, bringing with it a stench of mildew that makes my eyes water and windpipe tighten.

The creature coming out of the mushroom is somewhat like the sewer zombies—an extended mass of many different zombies that have fused together into a single organism, the brain at the center of the mushroom. Its body is like that of a centipede, impossibly long and flanked with row after row of feet and hands, half suspended in air by thick, pulsating tendrils of fungus attaching it to the gaping stoma in the mushroom.

Its face, a many-eyed terror made of at least five fused and warped skulls, leans a foot away from ours, bathing us in a foul green light that seems to sting my skin. For a moment, nothing happens, and then it opens its wide, toadlike mouth, and in a deep, sonorous voice that resonates in the back of my head, it speaks.

"You have come," it says in a disjointed, buzzing tone like that of a haunted radio.

"I have," says Savini. "My time to retake the earth has led me to your abominable home—"

"You must be silent," says the mutant zombie lord, holding up three hands full of gnarled *phalanges* (two, but now's not the time) to Savini. "We will speak with her. She is keeper and destroyer. She is teller of secrets and slayer of us all."

My mouth opens, sucking in mold-laced air, and I want to scream, to protest this hideous violation. Instead, I can only find myself stammering, "You . . . speak English."

The creature's seven eye sockets seem to squint at me. "We see your brain," it growls. "We read your speech, and use it. There is so much power there. You will use it to destroy the tooth. The power totem. You will destroy it for us. Release us."

"No," I say, softly but sternly. This may be a giant horrible zombie mushroom I'm speaking to, but I have to be firm in my commitment to the cause. I will not be bullied by fungus.

"Yes," says the zombie god in a hollow and empty voice. "You will release us. We will fill the sky and earth. We are the great shadow that will cover all. You will do it."

Wait. Hold off on the "No" responses, Kendra. The longer this horrific being is talking to you, the longer it isn't killing you. There must be rules to this game; maybe you'd always imagined it with a Sphinx and not a dead plant with a mouth made of ancient corpses, but it's still a process you're familiar with.

"What are you?" I can't help but ask.

"We are the great shadow," repeats the zombie thing, its voice taking an almost proud tone. "We are the eater of all things. We will choke the growth and swallow the garden. We will control your dead until all are like us. When the keepers imprisoned us down here, we began. This body was once one of us, but it has grown. Our core collected and brought it more. It intensified in that shell, and we are now it, and it is us."

A nauseating undulation troubles my guts. My

zombie mold—ese is a little rusty, but I think it's saying: "You used to be a zombie? A—" I point to the hordes standing around us. "A shell?"

"All shells are us, and all are shells," says the creature from the mushroom. The thousands of zombies around me bow their heads. "Each shell has within it great shadow. I am the first great shadow. Each is more. You will break the totem. You will release us, and each will lay roots, and spread, and reach out to the dead so that we may spread and devour."

My mind wraps around what it's saying, convoluted though it may be. Each of these zombies, if the fungal outgrowth is right, can grow into the towering mold mountain before me. And let's presume that I am currently surrounded by some five thousand zombies, the citizens of Kudus who somehow mutated enough or didn't descend into the sewer systems. My mind paints an image: a cave zombie creeping into someone's basement, or an abandoned well, laying down roots and then swelling, reaching upward and becoming a thick stalk of mold. Then, I picture our hometown, the town hall at its center replaced with a towering heart of fungus, throbbing out spore-filled vapors and turning every dead body within a five-mile radius into a staggering death machine. I see the skies going gray, the rivers clogging with corpses, a great and ponderous shadow thrown over all.

"And if I unlocked the seal," I mumble, only out of curiosity, "would you spare my friends?"

"No," booms the corpse being. "None will be spared. We will devour all. All land and sea and sky will be ours. You will be devoured when you have unraveled the seal. They will be devoured. We will take all. You will do it and release us."

"No," I say again, almost offended. "I will never—"

"We will make you," it says.

It is with unbelievable dread that I watch as, with the leathery sound of colliding flesh and an explosion of cracked bones, all five thousand undead faces in the room turn at once. Every single zombie, its eyes long gone, its face an almost expressionless skull, looks at me in unison.

"We feel no pain," intones the corpse. "But you feel pain. We will give you great pain if you do not unlock the great seal. We know the ways of agony. Unlock the seal, and you will join us in the great mass. Your mind will become one with us, and give us power to make our way out of this place. We can feel the world over us, alive, full of noise and rushing blood. We will bring it silence and darkness." The zombie's teeth click together loudly as he finishes this sentence; flecks of gray foam spatter from its mouth.

It's salivating, Kendra. Its mouth is watering at the end of the world.

247

"Either you will unlock the seal and join us swiftly," it says, "or we give you pain until we get the answer from you. You will be ours now, or you will be ours then. But we will know your secrets."

Well, there it is, Kendra. Your options are limited to either being eaten by a mushroom the size of a moderately priced house after unleashing certain death on the entire planet, or that same thing after some hours of excruciating torture ("hours" assuming, of course, you don't use your new Warden powers to unlock the magical seal on this place within the first three minutes of undead torment). What do you think—attempt nobility and go with the torture, or say "screw it" and not suffer before dying?

The ornately carved tusk falls to the soft earth in front of me, tossed from a gloved hand. The superior zombie rears himself back, wary of it; the mushroom's pale, fleshy surface quivers and ripples at the sound of it hitting the floor. In its surface, I can not only see the dull throb of elemental energy, but I can actually feel it, pulsing at the same rate as some kind of power deep in my veins, burning and throbbing and begging for release.

"Do it," grunts Savini. There's the sound of metal on leather as his knife comes unsheathed. "Unlock the seal, and then make a run for it. I will hold them off and come soon afterward. Then, we'll make our escape, and the world will know who is in charge."

This was his plan? To outrun a horde of mutated corpses? "I don't know *how*," I whine, staring down at the totem before me. "Wardens need to *learn* magic!"

"And Gravediggers do not," he snaps. "Though you may have the blood of a Warden, you act as a Gravedigger. You are above their simple laws."

And sadly, I recognize his words as the truth. Though I am unlearned in the ways of Warden enchantment, it is increasingly obvious to me that I can, somehow, inherently, tear asunder the magic guarding this seal. The zombie mushroom sees it, Dario knows it, and I know it. It's aware that, though unpracticed, I am capable.

If you wanted to, Kendra, you could set them all free. It's like Dario says—learning or not, you act as a Gravedigger.

A spark of internal power speeds my pulse and furrows my brow.

Then choose not to be Warden, Kendra. Act as a Gravedigger.

My hands snatch up the tusk, feeling its enchanted power burn against my hands. The pain is nothing, lost in the scream that rakes its way out of my throat; I am already in motion. With one deft swing, I bring the tusk's point up under the zombie god's head. At the touch of the magical seal, there is a crackle of green light as the creature's face splits down the middle in a splash of foul-smelling fluid.

"NO!" bellows Dario. "WHAT HAVE YOU DONE?"

The super zombie rears back with an ear-piercing shriek, its body bisecting laterally and revealing a twisting mass of green-lit bones, sinews, and teeth, countless teeth. As it vanishes back into the gaping hole in the mushroom, the cave zombies attack.

The zombies begin dropping from the ceiling and leaping at us from the cave walls, hissing and clawing at our faces with talons of bone. The tusk burning in my hands fends plenty of them away from me, but Dario bears the brunt of their assault. He goes into full combat mode, a sight to behold as his knife wheels, his fists swing, his mouth foams in rage. Zombie parts fly every which way as he slices and dices the thousands of bony assailants, grunting and growling with each undead monster he takes down. For a moment, I see how strong his training is. He would have made a good mentor.

Soon, however, even Dario's massive shape is overwhelmed, writhing and bellowing as the swarm of bony assaulters seizes him and drags him in the direction of the towering mushroom.

"NO!" shrieks Dario Savini, wild and girlish, as the cave zombies raise him up. "I AM A GRAVEDIGGER! I AM CHOSEN!" Between their frantic limbs, I catch one eye, wide and streaming tears, that latches onto my own. "KENDRA, SAVE ME! DON'T LET THIS HAPPEN—"

But there are too many of them between us, and try as I may to clear a path and reach him by using the tusk as a sort of battering ram, I have no chance of reaching him . . . and at heart, thinking of O'Dea, of this grueling ordeal I have somehow survived, I simply don't have the desire to rescue him. It is a damning thing to know, but I cannot help it.

Admit it, Kendra: he deserves this.

His feet vanish into the opening in the mushroom, and its edges pull greedily at Savini while the zombies push his body deeper into their fetid master. His pleas for help become a feral scream that fills my mind and the contours of the temple's chamber.

Through it all, I am suddenly aware that someone is speaking my name.

CHAPTER EIGHTEEN

PJ

"Kendra!" calls my voice in the darkness.

Food, calls the bite.

Through the shadows, we climb up the walls of the temple, pulling ourselves up the edges hand over fist. With every movement, with each inch we cover, it grows a little louder. Back at the wall, it was a dull, throbbing ache, more pain than message. Now, it is a voice as loud as my own in my head, ringing out over and over again.

Food. You are food. You die. Then, more food is needed.

Ian grabs my hand to pull me over a ledge, and his

finger touches the bite. He pulls away with a gasp, but I barely feel a thing. There's just the call over and over again, a steady command.

Food. Die. Food.

The central chamber of the temple is tear drop–shaped, and so after a few perilous swings and yanks from Ian or O'Dea, we're on an incline, pulling ourselves up by the posed hands of stone Buddhas and the jutting jaws of ancient carved demons. With our new magically corrected night vision, their twisted grimaces and petrified smiles send shivers down my spine. With the goggles, everything seemed sort of . . . scientific. Like we were examining it with a special camera. Heck, the goggles were like their own set of cameras, like this was all a scene from a weird nature documentary and I was making some kind of strange investigative masterpiece.

Now, these jagged, ancestral shapes floating in front of the shadowy blackness around us are like silent observers, judging us, mumbling, *Go, go, time is of the essence, she could be dead, you could all be dead.*

You are dead. Soon, anyway. Die.

Food.

"You okay?" asks Ian softly as I climb up next to him with a grunt.

O'Dea hops up beside us in the lap of a cobweb-veiled Buddha, and says, "He's fine. Right, PJ? You're fine."

Her blank look and matter-of-fact tone drive home my purpose, making me nod and reply through the tireless commands that yeah, I'm just fine. Ian's worried, which I appreciate, but O'Dea understands me. She knows I can't let that despair overwhelm me. We have to focus on saving Kendra. Don't let the hate and fear sit; make them work for you. The fear is a part of me, and I can use it. Throw it at something.

"Up there," mumbles O'Dea, pointing to a section of the temple ceiling that has either been destroyed or caved in long ago. From it, I can make out a sickly green glow, faint but persistent. The sight of it makes the sigil on my forehead itch . . . and the bite on my hand pulsate faster and faster.

We climb—well, we climb; Ian bounds—to the edge of the hole in the roof, my hands feeling solid on the jagged stone edge of the opening. For a moment, I wonder how we're going to get down into the temple from here, and whether or not Kendra will actually be contained inside of this central area.

Then something starts screaming deep in the temple. Something not human, something whose voice bores deep into my chest and sends blinding pain through my bitten hand.

When I yank my face over the edge of the cavernous opening in the temple roof, it takes a few minutes for my eyes to adjust to what's going on in front of me.

After blinking a few times and putting some sense to the shapes moving fifty feet below me, I finally open my mouth and say between dry lips:

"Guys . . . you're seeing this too, right?"

"I . . . don't even know, man," whispers Ian.

There's some kind of giant shuddering mound of what looks like human meat, skin and all, occupying most of the inner chamber of the temple. The sickening green light seems to be coming from this bleeding . . . radioactive . . . bug zombie that's coming out of it (this is truly the best description I can think of). On the walls and floor around it are the cave zombies—all of them, thousands and thousands, pressed together into a single mass of crawling, swaying skeletal death that ripples and shakes like a school of minnows on *Planet Earth*. One or two even cling to the walls right by where we're peering into the cave, but their bony heads don't even twitch in our direction, instead focusing on the giant tumor that fills the room.

And all of it seems to reach out and touch my bite. The voice becomes solid, powerful.

FOOD. DIE. DIE. FOOD. DIE.

On the floor, Kendra stands crouched, the tusk gripped in both her hands. Meanwhile, the zombies surge as one, raising up the screaming form of—

"Savini," growls O'Dea. "Sweet mother, they're feeding him to it."

"To . . . what?" asks Ian, his voice still awash with total incomprehension.

My mind spins, going through every horror movie I've ever stayed up late to watch, but every alien or undead or mutant just turns into the word *food* or an image of me flinging myself over the roof's edge. This monster is different—ugly, giant, but in my mind, too, deeply rooted. There's a power coming off it, and every so often it moves or quivers, so it's definitely alive. But this thing knows only the cursed un-life of the zombie, a living death. The sensation in my festering bite tells me that much—this undead blob is wrong beyond wrong.

Without a moment's pause, the caves zombies press Savini's thrashing body into the side of the pale, jelly-like mound, and his feet disappear into the flesh. Soon, only his head and hand sprout from its side, still gasping and clawing at the rotten air.

"KENDRA, PLEASE!" he cries. "DON'T LET THIS HAPPEN!" Then, his mouth is absorbed, eaten by the flesh pile, and his screams go muffled and then stop. His hand soon goes limp. Then, a hissing sound fills the air, and the hand falls to the floor, its wrist eaten away by green fluid and sizzling.

My mouth clenches shut, and stomach acid burns the inside of my throat. My head swims, my hand pulses and throbs beneath O'Dea's roach-goop bandage. Whatever's going on here, no one should ever have to see it.

And yet, the bite in my hand reacts as though it were

a beautiful sight to behold. It seems to swell, to tingle with cold pricks of pleasure. The bite is rooting for the monster.

Finally, I pull my eyes away from Dario Savini being eaten alive by some kind of gigantic undead wart and focus on Kendra. The cave zombies have cleared a circle off to one side of the temple floor, and they all stare eyelessly down at a figure, frozen, a halo of ratty black hair surrounding her head. Steam or smoke pours from her hands where they touch the seal.

"Great," I say. "How do we get to her?"

"Here's what we have to do," says Ian, nodding slightly to himself. "We're going to jump down on top of this . . . zombie monster here. O'Dea, you cast a spell around me while I distract the zombies so that I'm kept from getting hurt, while PJ, you slide over the edge of this weird creature and grab Kendra."

I glance back at O'Dea, who looks at our friend like she pities him. It's not his fault—he's the physical Gravedigger, the action hero, so of course he thinks that pulling a Jason Bourne is the way to win in this situation. He doesn't see a putrid mass that eats people alive, just an enemy.

"There has to be another way," O'Dea says. "There are too many of them."

Ian and O'Dea look at me expectantly, and I realize I'm supposed to have an idea.

DIE. FOOD. FOOD.

Then again, I have no idea what this giant evil meat being is—but, hold on. I do know zombies. I know *monsters*. So I might be able to help us out.

". . . there has to be a weakness," I tell them. "All of the zombies have had it so far. The mountain zombies were dry, so water hurt them. The water zombies were soft, so solid weapons hurt them."

"And the cave zombies don't like light," finishes Ian. "We've been using light on them already. We don't have enough lights to stop all of these things, man."

"Maybe . . ." I say, pushing my imagination harder, trying to remember every horror movie I've ever seen at once, "if there was some way to . . . reflect the light . . ."

"Come on, PJ," groans Ian. "It's not like they made mirrors in ancient Indonesia, man. We need to take action."

"Look, man, we can't—"

"Got it," snaps O'Dea. Our heads turn to her, the swiftness of her reply and sharpness of her tone nearly making me jump. "I think I got it. Ho boy."

"What are you thinking?" I ask.

"That seal," she says, nodding at the white shape in Kendra's hands. "It's bejeweled, isn't it? Covered with precious stones?"

"Yeah," I say, the sense memory of its bumpy surface running through my fingertips. "It's pretty thick with them. Why?"

O'Dea nods to herself and rubs her chin. "We need to get Kendra to hold it up over her head," she says. "The minute she has it up in the air, you two are going to turn those hard hat lights on and shine them directly at the seal."

"You think it'll act like some kind of . . . disco ball?" asks Ian.

O'Dea shrugs. "It's a long shot. But it might just do the trick. Heard about it working once. Seal was an urn in India, covered in jewels."

Here we are again, low on options, relying on folklore. Every time, it's like this. Does O'Dea's plan have any real legs to stand on? It's hopeless. I'm dead already, aren't I?

JUMP. IT WON'T WORK. JUMP. DIE.

No.

That voice has been with me my whole life. Even before the zombies, it has plagued me, made me hate my life, hate myself. Just because the poison pumping through my veins is making it stronger, making it real, doesn't mean it's allowed to win. It's just fear again. This time, it's just the ultimate fear.

You're going to die from this bite, PJ. Accept it. Now, help your friends. Let you be the only one.

"Kendra!" I hiss at her, trying not to be so loud as to make the cave zombies aware of us. "Kendra!" Her head twitches, rising up and glancing to her left, then her right. Ian and O'Dea join in.

"Kendra! Up here! The ceiling!"

"Farther! Kendra, follow my voice!"

"Hey, Queen Brain! Look alive!"

Finally, her eyes flutter up past the hordes of clinging zombies on the ceiling over her and land on us. They are barely open, basically slits. Her body shakes and shudders, her teeth grit hard. Something dark runs out from under her nose. It's like she's having a standing seizure.

"Kendra, hold it up!" shouts Ian, mimicking the motion over his head. "Come on, you can do it!"

Kendra stares at the zombies huddled on all sides of her, then back at the tusk electrifying her as we speak. In a flash, she thrusts it upward with a cry, just as a crowd of bone-clawed zombie hands lean in toward her.

"NOW!" shouts O'Dea.

Ian and I flick on our helmet lamps and point the light directly at the tusk. In my heart, a prayer—*Let this work, please let this work*—runs over and over again.

For once, my prayers are answered.

The tusk explodes with light, each gem and stone studding its white surface illuminating and sending colored beams blasting throughout the room. The zombies recoil as one, holding their gnarled claws up to their faces to shield their invisible eyes from the blinding light. It's no use, though—the light reflecting from the seal must magnify its magic, because those zombies it illuminates begin sizzling, their meager flesh peeling away and their black gummy viscera turning to gray, sandlike ash beneath the glow. The giant mound of flesh in the center of the temple shakes and twists, letting loose the deep, vibrating rumble we've heard all day; its surface throbs and bubbles where the light glances it.

Kendra moves the tusk slightly, and a gem reflects a beam directly into my eyes.

The pain starting at my palm stabs me in the face, sends me screaming. My hands bat at the stone beneath me, the people around me. My whole body tenses up, shocked, and suddenly I am leaning away from the opening, falling backward, spinning out of pain's reach and into the darkness.

"PJ, no—" shouts Ian, but my body is tumbling, crashing into statues and knocking off heavy stone demons with loud, booming crashes. Part of me wants to apologize every time I accidentally knock over an intricate gargoyle or leave a crumbling statue cracked and rotten after using it to jump from, but there's just no time, and my head's a blur. My body bends in ways it shouldn't and slaps against hard stone over and over again, until I hit the dusty ground with a solid *whud*.

O'Dea and Ian call my name, their voices getting louder and louder until I hear them right above me. Then, Ian's crouched at my side, peering into my eyes.

"PJ, man, are you okay?"

My mind roams my body, taking inventory. "... Uh-huh."

"Is anything broken?" he asks.

I shake my head and push myself up with one hand, surprised that nothing hurts, nothing even feels that bad—especially when I try to use my other arm. Ian and O'Dea gasp.

"PJ, your shoulder's dislocated," says Ian. He's right—my left arm, my bitten arm, hangs six inches lower than it should, and swings limply. But it doesn't hurt. Honestly, I can't feel a thing. Ian reaches out carefully, mumbling about popping it back in, and before I know it I give it a hard yank and Ian backs off with a gasp as it pops back into its socket.

As I flex my left fingers, I marvel at the bite. It's like it kept me from hurting, like it took away that deep, terrible fear—

A powerful vibration cuts my inner monologue short. On the edge of the temple, a section of ceiling breaks off and goes falling, sending up a storm cloud of dust with a deafening crash. A gray blast of filth comes raging out of the front door, covering us with soot and cobwebs. . . .

And suddenly, there's Kendra, charging out of the smoke like someone in an adventure movie, the tusk jutting gracelessly from her belt. We scream her name, and her head darts back and forth, blinded by panic and dust. When it's obvious she can't see us, we go running to intercept her. My hands reach out and grab her arm—and there's a pop, the same sharp pain that I felt when getting struck by the light reflecting off the seal. Kendra feels it, too, because she ducks backward, fists raised, ready to fight. Our eyes meet, hers baffled, mine widened with a sick realization.

Touching her is painful for me, because she's both a Gravedigger and a Warden—

Witch, moans the bite, *devil, captor, keeper, ruler, hag.*

And I'm a—a—

Before the word can be born in my mind, Ian and O'Dea are grabbing us and pulling us along. The urgency retakes me and I push ahead, making my way through the darkened city as the temple crashes down and the bite on my hand screams in rage and hunger.

It may be small by modern American standards, but Kudus is still a city, and we easily run for a mile through its streets. Before long, my lungs feel seared around the edges, and sweat stings my magically enhanced eyes. Somehow, though, my feet refuse to stop pumping, and the pain blends in with the fear. In my peripheral vision, I can see bits of rubble and wisps of dust go crashing around my feet, the white noise of the temple coming down filling the space behind us. The bite on my hand throbs, itches, burns with a horrible infected pain.

Wait.

Something in the bite stops me dead in my tracks. My friends keep running, unnoticing.

A voice, deep and beautiful and full of calm, speaks in my head. It feels like when I have a camera in my hands. Like when I close my eyes and meditate. It is peace, vast and transcendental.

Slowly, I turn around, and my eyes drink in the unthinkable.

From the cloud of dust and rubble billowing out at us, the mushroom emerges, like a sickly pale whale breaking an ocean of smoke. It leads with its top, surging forward nose first and crawling along the ground with a series of grasping, yanking roots that look somewhere between albino arms and bloodless veins. From its horrible flapping underside comes a jet of glowing green spores that pull with it the few remaining cave zombies, skittering through the cloud with their faces pointed skyward. Its giant body makes the ground shake, its mass topples longhouses and huts on their sides in crunching bursts of clay and wood; on its pale and revolting skin I can see the burn marks from where the seal-reflected light assaulted its flesh. As it nears me, the ground cracks beneath its weight, the ruptures in the earth reaching my sneakers and making the ground I stand upon bounce.

My body freezes, unable to digest what my eyes are absorbing. This—this would be the greatest shot my camera could ever catch: a crawling, hungry fungus emerging from a destroyed temple, making the ground beneath our feet shake as it hauls itself along.

This is what Josefina spoke of when she warned me about coming to this place. This is pure horror; this is clumsy, shambling death incarnate.

Yet I can't look away. The bite won't let me. Through it, I feel the cold and flawless song of the mushroom, the promise of eternal peace, of a purpose. As an eyelid of flesh opens on its head and that green glowing creature emerges, I feel bathed in a wondrous, healing light. As the being stretches its many hands and its singed, misshapen mouth toward me, the bite shushes my fear and worry and tells me to simply stare deeply into the eye sockets of God.

"PJ, NO!"

Ian's voice, from far away, reaches out and shakes me from my reverie, just as the glowing zombie deity comes close to my face and splits in half, becoming all mouth.

Hold still, says the bite.

No, I tell it.

When I click on my headlamp, the beam of light blasts directly into the mushroom zombie's maw, and its insides blacken and crackle, sending up a gust of foul-smelling smoke. The creature rears back, raising its many hands and legs and jaws and screaming deeply. My bite screams with it, bringing me down to my knees.

As the creature screams, the mushroom's gigantic mass shakes and writhes, making the stones beneath it shatter even more. With a great *galumph*, a section of the floor collapses, giving way to blackness. The mushroom lowers halfway, threatening to slip into the dark.

But then the fused zombies of the sewers rise up as one. In a rotting green tidal wave, the merged bodies of the waterlogged dead surge out of tunnels beneath Kudus, hungry for the spore-filled flesh of their God. With their many decaying hands, they begin wrenching great hunks of bulbous fungal meat out of the mushroom, revealing glowing green insides heavy with organs, bones, and wriggling flaps. The cave zombies around it claw at the collapsing floor with their bony hands, but they, too, slip into the sewers, hissing as they go.

As the last of the skyscraper-sized mushroom goes sinking into the sewers, the whole cave begins to shake. The hands of my friends grab me from all sides, pulling me to the walls of the city, and before I know it we're climbing up the ladder carved into the stone, inching along the thin ledge, and barreling into the narrow opening in the rock just as the stalactites over the city come shuddering out of place and bury the dead of Kudus once and for all.

NINETEEN

Ian

For a while, my whole life is noise. The ground, the sky, my friends, my body, everything's screaming at once.

After a moment, though, it lets up. The rocks settle into place, the dust stops blowing around the tunnel, everyone's yell turns into a squeak, my aching joints have a moment to work through the pain stored up in them, and there's just the big, tight black of the cave. Everything hangs there in stupid campfire shadow because PJ's headlamp is still turned on.

When I peek outside, I'm freaked out. It's like Kudus was never there, or no, it was there, but it got eaten alive. There are bits of wood and hunks of statues sticking out this way and that, but it looks nothing like the big dead sprawl we hunkered through before. Mostly it's just jagged crags of fresh rock jutting out of the ground and forming a new layer. Like the cave was a mouth, and it finally decided to chomp down on the place.

Back in our tunnel, things are still tense.

O'Dea's on her hands and knees with her palms and forehead flat on the ground. After a few more moments, she sits back on her haunches and takes a slow deep breath. On the floor are two handprint-shaped burn marks, blackened onto the stone itself. And she's not looking her best, man—her eyes are all sunken and her face is pale, and there's this twitch going on with her upper lip, kind of pulling it at the corner, like she's snarling.

"Guys," I say. "Guys, help me out here. I think O'Dea might have pulled something."

Kendra and PJ groan as they climb to their feet, but they snap into action when they see O'Dea looking half dead.

"O'Dea?" asks Kendra. "Are you conscious?"

"Uh," she responds.

"Are you okay?" asks PJ.

"Yeah," she says softly. "I might just need . . . glass of water." And then the Warden's eyes roll back into her head, and she falls forward and hits the ground with a hard *whack*.

The three of us crowd around her and do everything we can think of to wake her up—we shake her, we yell her name, Kendra even gives her a light slap on the cheek—but it's no hope, she's out, gone, lost to us. When I put my ear to her chest, I can still hear breathing and a heartbeat, so at least we know she's alive, a fact that makes PJ sort of grunt, which is weird; he's normally super-concerned about O'Dea. But as much as we try to get her awake, she won't budge.

"Great," he finally says, running a hand nervously through his hair. "What do we do now?"

"We have to get her out of this cave," I say. I mean, what else are we supposed to do? "It can't be good for her to be down here, what with all the cave-ins and the giant monster mushrooms and the zombies that eat other zombies."

"We have no clue what's wrong with her," says Kendra, peeling open one of her eyes and squinting into her pupil. "If we move her, it may be detrimental to her state. It might even kill her."

"Yeah, but a falling hunk of cave ceiling will *definitely* kill her," I say.

"That logic is certainly sound," sighs Kendra. She's blinking hard in that way she does when she's working something out in her head, but then her eyes light up and she snaps her fingers. "Wait. I have an idea."

Ho boy.

"What's the deal?" I ask.

"PJ, hand me the tusk," she says, pointing.

A little ways back in the tunnel lies the magic seal, the carved-up tusk that Kendra somehow managed to keep her grip on the whole trip up here. PJ leans back and reaches out for it, but his hand stops a few inches away. He furrows his brow, and then he sits back, staring hatefully at the tusk.

". . . No," he says.

"What?" I ask. He shakes his head and mumbles something. *Food* or something.

And then I see PJ hiding his one hand in his armpit, and *bam*, I'm the world's biggest jerk, it all comes back to me in an instant, grabbing me by the throat and slamming me into a wall. The more I focus on him, the more I can see just how crappy he looks, how pale and tired and sweaty, how much his whole body rises and falls with every breath.

The zombies, people with the whole reanimated-dead-guy thing, can't touch any of the objects with good karmic sigils carved into them.

They can also probably pop their shoulders back in place without even *wincing*.

And here's PJ. Mumbling about food.

"Why not?" asks Kendra with a frown.

PJ looks at me, and his eyes are sad, tired, uncomfortable, and he doesn't say the word, but his stare explains, crystal clear, what he's thinking, which comes over me in this awful, heavy wave:

Kendra doesn't know. PJ got bitten after Dario carted her off, and we haven't really had a chance to chat, what with all the cave corpses and zombie fungus and flesh-eating disco lights.

PJ opens his mouth to say something, but some automatic instinct in me kicks in, and I grab the tusk and hand it to her with a "Here you go." My eyes shoot back to PJ, and I shake my head, saying no, don't mention it, don't say a word about it, I don't even want to hear it.

Because . . . because, even though Kendra's one of my best friends, and is so much smarter than I am, she's all logic, and I don't want to, *can't*, deal with that right now.

Because with PJ's bite, we all know there's one logical answer.

"Hold it to O'Dea's forehead," she says. "I have a hypothesis."

Slowly, I touch the tip of the seal to O'Dea's head. Nothing happens; she still just lays there. "Am I doing something wrong?" I ask.

Kendra scratches her chin and blinks some more, and then, carefully, she sticks out her index finger and touches it to the other end of the tusk—

There's this sharp, cold shock that zaps my hand and

makes me drop the tusk and forces Kendra to yank her hand back and hiss, but man, it works—O'Dea gasps loudly, and her whole body twists and her chest rises up, and her lips pull back like she's trying to scream but no air is coming out. Then, she starts coughing and finally sits up. Finally, she whacks her chest with a fist and hocks a loogie blacker than an eight ball.

"O'Dea, you okay?" I ask.

She nods hard. "Yeah," she coughs. "Geez Louise, what a rush. Yeah. I'm okay."

"Thank God," mumbles PJ.

"What Warden spell was that?" I ask her, basically stuffing the whole *What happened, where am I* routine that I'm pretty sure we're headed for. "Cave-in spell?"

"Protection," she coughs, giving me the stink eye. "Figured anything I could do to keep a big piece of rock from busting through that window and impaling your scrawny butt was the least I could do."

"Do you feel well enough to move?" asks Kendra.

"Sure," says O'Dea, climbing weakly to her feet. She spies the tusk and starts. "First, though, we have to do something about that seal. Keep it from ever getting found again."

"What do you figure?" I say, picking up the jewel-covered tusk.

"Why not bring it with us?" says Kendra. "You don't think a museum—or a Warden could look after it—"

She shakes her head. "That's how this happened," she says. "We Wardens are just a bunch of old folks. We can be easy pickings to the right guy. This needs to go unfound . . . wait. Come with me."

Slowly, O'Dea hobbles deeper into the cave mouth, the three of us slowly trailing her. We eventually reach the side cave, the one where she was tied to the stalagmite about to get eaten by sigil-avoiding cave zombies, where those big white disgusting cave roaches are still milling around the floor. She points to a gaping black hole at one end of the cave, which sparkles as we get near it—an underground pool.

"There," says O'Dea, pointing to the hole. It doesn't look big enough from far away, but close up it's huge, a glittering piece of water, looking black as ink and super cold. A shine of one of our headlamps shows it stretching deep down into the ground and sends a horde of tiny white fish shooting through the water frantically.

"You're positive this is a good idea?" asks Kendra.

"If it's at the bottom of some deep pool, no one can get to it," says O'Dea. "No one can get to it, no one can mess with it. Ian, go ahead; drop it down there."

She doesn't have to tell me twice—this thing has been nothing but trouble since we found it. When I toss the tusk into the underground pond, it splashes, and we watch as it drifts deeper and deeper down and then nothing, gone, like it never existed.

"Done," says O'Dea with a sigh. "All right. Now, we get out of this damn hole in the ground."

Just like that, the end of the world is gone.

Except, I think, looking at PJ aggressively keeping his hand jammed in his pocket, it's not.

Leaving the Kudus cave isn't nearly as easy as I'm hoping it'll be. We follow the path O'Dea and Dario took, a different set of tunnels than we used (as in not through a crack in the wall—O'Dea's hair was on the edge only because a zombie tried to yank her into it before Dario saved her).

Kendra and O'Dea keep reading sigils on the walls, finding new tunnels carved in the stone. Kendra's Warden abilities keep shocking O'Dea—she'll read something off a wall by putting her hand to it, and O'Dea will just nod along and kind of peer at Kendra, like she's beginning to actually consider what we told her earlier. Kendra doesn't even ask how we can see in the dark—she just *knows*.

What's especially weird is how Kendra's reacting toward PJ. Just like with her new Warden abilities, she doesn't seem to realize it's happening, but I can see it from miles away. Every time PJ speaks to her or offers some advice on the directions, she screws up her face like the sound of his voice is nails on a chalkboard, like he smells bad. Even O'Dea has to jump in here and there when Kendra begins to peer at PJ like he's a specimen in a glass cage or something; for all we know, she's seeing the change in PJ, watching black mud spread through his veins or whatever. Some part of me wants to tell her, but I keep coming back to the same worry—that she'll have a "solution to the problem."

It's tough, 'cause most of the time, I'm the harsh truth guy, saying the stuff no one else wants to mention 'cause they're too chicken. But I guess this truth is just too harsh for any of us, especially me.

Finally, we come upon a narrow tunnel in the rock through which we see something, something weird and unusual and a little painful on the eyes after all this time.

"Light," says O'Dea, nodding to the pool of dim white on the floor at our feet.

"It's narrow," says PJ. "We'll have to crawl single file up to the surface."

"Obviously," says Kendra, snapping. "How else would we do it?"

O'Dea and I share a look. Getting worse by the minute.

Of course, no one else wants to go first, so it's up to good old Ian Buckley to go shimmying up this tube of stone. The tunnel's so narrow I have to bunch my arms in front of my chest and use my elbows and sweaty palms to push me up, one little shuffle of dusty cavern after the next. At first, I'm doing all right, just a little

275

annoyed at how tight a squeeze it is, and then I think about getting stuck in here, or about a cave zombie's cold bony hands scratching at my ankles and calves, and I almost freak out and lose it. It's only Kendra's hand, warm and sure, gripping my ankle, that calms me down, gets my heart to stop uppercutting my ribs, and gets me back to shimmying.

As the circle of light fills up my whole vision and opens up over me, I expect to see some blinding blast of daylight, but instead there's the sunset, all orange and red and peachy as it goes down behind the mountains around us. The fresh air is the most delicious thing I've ever tasted in all twelve years I've been around on this planet. My eyes spin around, and I take in our scene—the hole is actually a few yards away from the cave itself, the ticket booth, our Danny Melee–provided car and driver . . . and the two police cars parked next to them, their lights flashing. Indonesian cops.

Oh, crap.

As Kendra comes sliding out of the hole, taking deep, loud breaths, I pull her aside and start yanking PJ out. "Come on, we've got to go," I say.

"What's the hurry?" he says, wincing as I tug at his wounded hand.

"There are cops here," I tell him, reaching for O'Dea the minute he's clear of the hole. "We've got to bail before they want to ask us some questions."

One look at my friends tells me it's worse than I

thought. PJ and Kendra are covered in dirt and scratches, and O'Dea's bruises are mad purple and yellow and puffy, and great, we're going to end up in Indonesian juvie playing some kind of dice game we don't understand where we're betting fingers, all because we had to go and save the world—

"The police are of no concern to you."

The deep, smooth voice gets us all turning at once, pointing and yelling and scooting back. The old woman is wrapped in what looks like some kind of huge colorful shawl and rocking one of those dots, what's it called, a bindi on her forehead. Beside her stand two other women, similarly dressed but much younger, glaring at us like we're the away team. The old lady, though, she's smiling, cool as a cucumber.

"What?" asks Kendra, squinting at the three weird ladies.

"We have pacified the authorities," says the old woman calmly. "Our magic is strong, and they are easily fooled. I am Ratna Furani. I am Warden of area eighteen, near Jakarta. I have come to Borneo to help you." She does a little half bow and says, "Greetings, sister."

"Greetings," say both Kendra and O'Dea, and then they give each other this little look, like, *Oh yeah.*

"We were on our way to lend assistance at the instruction of the Wardens' Council when you arrived," she says.

"Is that right," says O'Dea, sneering. "Guess

you're a little too late, huh?"

Ratna Furani nods and smiles even wider, but it's a smile I know, the kind of smile Kendra's given me one too many times. "Too late for many things," she says. "We heard the noise from within the earth, and felt the karma of this place change. If we'd been here in time, these unorganized imitators would not have destroyed this ancient and hallowed city."

More than anything, it's that one word, *imitators*, that gets me. All the other stuff, the hours of fighting cave zombies and getting punched by some nut-bar world-ending psycho and fending off a big meat-eating mushroom, it's like that's all stored up in a pile, and that word, *imitators*, strikes the match in my head and tosses it onto that heap of trouble, until I can't take it anymore and I open up my mouth and let the fire out.

"I'm not imitating anything!" I say, jabbing a finger at the old woman. "You hear me, lady? I'm the real deal. I am Gravedigger numero uno. And I just *saved your butt*, so I wouldn't mind a thank you."

Her smile goes down about two notches. The women on either side of her look at me like I've got a tattoo of a pony on my face.

"Containment would have prevailed," says Ratna in an intense tone. "It always has."

"Ms. Furani, *ma'am*, today containment *failed*," I say with a chuckle, because let's face it, I want to get at this woman, and nothing gets at a person more than someone laughing in their face. "Five people *waltzed* into this sunken zombie city, and one of them nearly busted the whole thing wide open and killed everyone on earth. And he did it just. To show you. That he could. So in some kind of way, he was right. You guys came up short today. And thankfully, me and my friends"—I motion to PJ and Kendra—"were here to clean up your mess. We went down into the place you guys have been guarding for years like a bunch of scared little kids, and we wiped out the threat of anyone else using it to hurt you. So, before you go making accusations, remember that you *need us*. That we're here for a reason. And honestly, it'd be best to stay out of our way."

"You dare speak to me in such a way?" she says, looking deeply offended even though *I'm* the one who just fought the God mushroom. The Wardens on either side of her look down at me, like cobras ready to strike. "Such insolence! Such—such—"

"Flippancy?" croaks Kendra, softly. "That's a good word. I did that one."

"Miss, I'm twelve," I tell her. "Insolence is the name of the game. I beg your esteemed pardon, but seriously." I point to my bruised body, my filth-caked clothes, my split lip from a punch to the face. "You don't know where I've been today."

Silence. Behind me, I can *feel* O'Dea face palming

and shaking her head, but I couldn't care less. I feel great, I feel in control and full of energy and just Gravediggered out from head to toe.

And then one of Ratna's attendant Wardens whispers to her, and her smile's back, but in a bad way.

"You call yourselves Gravediggers," she says, pointing over my shoulder. "And yet you shirk your duty."

"What?" I ask.

"That one is cursed," she says. "He bears the bite of the demons. He must be either contained or destroyed."

Aw, no.

My head moves slow, because I know what's coming, and there, over my shoulder, I follow her finger to PJ, back by the cave entrance, staring straight at the ground. Even if he didn't have his bit hand clasped in the other one, you can see it on him in the fading sunlight. His skin's all pale and waxy with deep dark spots under his eyes and cheekbones. There's a slight weakness about him, and a whole ton of agitation.

"PJ?" says Kendra, blinking hard and fast. "You're— you—one of them, a . . . a zombie, managed to—" She chokes on the last words, putting her hands to her mouth.

"I will handle this, sisters," says O'Dea, her voice as cold and scary as I've ever heard it. "He is one of my team. He will receive the proper attention."

"You cannot be serious," gasps the Indonesian

Warden. "You think we will let you take the very *curse of Kudus* out into the open world? He must be dealt with immediately!"

O'Dea gulps. Her eyes hit us, then them, then us. Then she steps in front of PJ and grimaces at the other Wardens. "Then you're going through me, sister," she says, hard as hell.

Ratna gets a little pale, and the Wardens she brought with her share a look like they're wondering who has the guts to go to war with O'Dea. But with Kendra and I there as well, it doesn't feel uneven. They channel all the karma of the planet, but I can shoulder check someone really, really hard.

"You also forsake your calling," sighs Ratna. "You release the curse into the world."

"Make no mistake, Sister Furani," says O'Dea, lowering her head a little, "I will take care of this."

Nothing else is said. The wind blows; we glare at one another. The four of us walk away slowly, and the Wardens watch us go.

CHAPTER TWENTY

Kendra

"Kendra?"

The voice snaps me out of my vacant stare at the lined paper on my desk. In less than a second, I have been transported from the Indonesian cave in my mental vision to the brightly lit classroom, hung with black and orange streamers and construction paper pumpkin visages in honor of tomorrow's holiday. Jenny Dylan stands by my desk, clutching a sheath of papers and looking down on me with a bright and poised expression of wariness and pity.

"Yes?" I manage.

"I have PJ Wilson's homework for you," she says,

making sure to add, "again."

As though you have not noticed the pattern, Kendra. As though she couldn't lay the papers on your desk and leave. "Again." Who the heck does Jenny Dylan think she—

"Right," I say, reaching out and taking the packet of assignments from her. "I'll see that he gets them. Thank you."

Jenny nods, yet she doesn't budge. There were times, months ago, when I might have been intrigued and excited by the attention of one of the kids in my class—back when I was friendless, when I had only a smartphone and a web forum to keep me company.

A life you might be returning to, Kendra.

"What does PJ even have?" she asks, looking quizzical and almost slightly annoyed. "I mean . . . is it serious?"

"They really don't know," I lie.

"But, like, he's getting treated, right?" she asks. "He's not going to die or whatever?"

For a moment, some Gravedigger instinct flares up in me and I imagine slamming my fist into Jenny Dylan's stomach and asking her if *she's* going to "die or whatever." Good Lord, no wonder the Wardens had us disbanded.

Before this conversation can continue, Ms. Alexander calls Jenny's name, and she waves and backpedals for the door. A glance shows that I am the only remaining student in our homeroom, a departing flash of Jenny's chestnut ponytail the last vestige of another person my age. As I hoist my backpack onto my shoulder and begin to leave, Ms. Alexander, our new homeroom teacher, says, "Kendra?"

"Yes?" I sigh, turning to her.

"I'm sorry to hear that your friend is so sick," she says. "He seemed like a sweet boy. If you ever need anyone to talk to, I'm here."

What do you say to that, Kendra? "The sweetest I've ever known"? "It's okay; this is our job"? "There is no known cure for what he has"? Her intentions are kind, but her tone is simply too much like those of your parents during the divorce—concertedly sensitive, ready to Be There for Me at a moment's notice.

"Thank you," I settle on, and make my way out into the hallway.

The blue linoleum hallways of our school are drenched in playful morbidity—ghosts and skeletons, noble vampires and scientific revenants (PJ would probably call them "Draculas" and "Frankensteins"), even the occasional proper zombie. My mind does its best to block it out, not because it references death, but because I am inherently aware of how much PJ loves Halloween, the lighthearted exaltation of fear and darkness. He might not even know it's tomorrow.

Unconsciously, my feet bring me to the school exit

closest to the gym. The sound of rubber slapping polished wood fills my ears to the point of being deafening.
Against my better judgment, I turn in to the double
doors and observe the basketball court, the tall windows throughout it filtering in afternoon light. A whiff
of foam padding and sweat fills my nostrils.

Boys' JV runs exercises, each boy running alongside
the basket and performing a layup. Coach Leider claps
and shouts, the echo of his deep baritone voice seeming
to emanate from his square chin rather than the vast,
cathedral-like space of the gym around him.

A few of the eighth grade boys file past the basket,
tossing their balls. When Ian arrives at the basket, his
eyes are cold and set, his movements mechanical. He
makes the shot, but even Coach Leider can see his lack
of motivation and stops him as he runs back to half-
court, crouching down and whispering into his face.
The words are too far off and overpowered by the noises
of practice to reach my ears, but Coach's stare and hand
motions make his message clear: something is wrong.
It's Ian's job to find out what. Ian nods, but his gaze is
miles away.

As he turns away from Coach, his eyes find me,
and a swift shock shoots through my system. My hand
raises in a wave, and I instinctively smile—

Ian's eyes dart away, and he jogs off after a loose
basketball.

A gust of disappointment carries me out of the doors

to school, down the stone steps, through the crisp chill and smoke scent of the October air.

Logic must be respected here. It's not his fault. His parents went berserk. This time, Vince and Emily Buckley had looked into our story, called the hotels we were listed at in New York, screamed at our parents. (The Banjarmasin police are apparently searching for us as we speak due to our "disappearance" within the cave, a thought that is both terribly sad and somewhat exciting.) And when we got back, they put Ian on lockdown. He's never to speak to either one of us again; if they catch him spending time with us, my parents told me, the Buckleys will move. They will literally pick up and disappear.

You've all been lying to the people you love too much, Kendra. It's time you took your medicine. Besides, why so eager for him to notice you?

My mother waits for me outside of her car and gives me a quick wave as I reach it. Before I disappeared for a weekend, she might have smiled and inquired about my day. Now, there is a cold reception and a stony tone of voice. I am not the obedient daughter she believed herself to have raised.

"Samantha Wilson called me at work," she says as we speed away from school. "She was hoping you would visit Peter Jacob this evening. He appears to be progressing, in her mind. Would you like to go see him?"

"Is that all right with you?" I ask. A question to answer a question is a tactic my mother loves to employ. She almost smiles.

"It is."

"All right. Once I've dropped my backpack off, I'll—"

"And after you've finished your homework," she says, as though I'd forgotten such a thing. "And had dinner, and finished that workbook lesson your father gave you."

"My friend is sick."

She purses her lips and sighs sharply. "Kendra, consistency is important in life. You must be prepared to maintain normalcy, contain your passions. Containment is key."

The phrase sends my eyes snapping back to my mother, shock replacing my sadness. "What?"

"Something your grandmother used to say," she says. "It was about maintaining a personal standard, not letting your emotions overwhelm you."

Come on, Kendra—was that what it really meant?

"Mom, did Grandma ever mention a . . . 'Warden' to you?" I ask.

My mother frowns. "Not that I remember. Like a prison warden? Why?"

"No reason," I say, making a mental note to take an in-depth look into my family tree in the near future.

Homework is, as always, a breeze. Dinner, meanwhile, is interminable. Herman, my mother's boyfriend, tells a seemingly endless story about a lunch mix-up at work that I'm expected to laugh at. He even has the nerve to ask me what I'm "being" for Halloween, and I glare at him like he's a noisy toddler until my mother butts in, saying that I am "too old for that kind of thing."

Finally, I am excused and run up to my room to get suited up for visiting PJ—my bike helmet, my jacket, and a copy of Vincent Price's *The Last Man on Earth*, a film I have never seen but believe, according to Wikipedia, will be right up PJ's alley.

Just as I'm about to venture out, a clatter draws my attention to my bedroom window. At first, I wonder if it's a tree branch or some sort of imagined phantom noise, but then a pebble strikes the glass near my face. A scrawny silhouette stands in the shadows of our backyard, hooded, staring up at me.

"Yo," says Ian as I emerge from our house. Hearing his voice for the first time in a week immediately sparks a visceral reaction in me, but his complete aversion to me for these past few days keeps me guarded, bitter.

"What is it, Ian?" I ask, doing my best to sound stable and sure. "I'm on my way out."

"Are you going to see PJ?" he asks. "His mom

contacted my parents and said he wanted to see me, and I thought they might have . . ."

A pause, the silence between us thick. This seems like a foolish question to be unresponsive to, and yet here I am.

Stay tough, Kendra. He wouldn't even look at you today.

"Well," I tell him, "I suppose I should be grateful you'll even deign to speak to me again. Shall we?"

His face softens considerably. "Aw, come on, Kendra, you know that's—my parents don't—"

"Forget it, Ian," I tell him in a casual tone. "I understand. We had a rough time, and you decided that—" *Do not break down, Kendra.* "—that this, our, uh, *partnership*, was a little much for you. It's no loss on my part; it just means I have to take care of your dying friend. Alone." That one gets him. He nearly crumbles, and it hurts me to do it, but it's what I want to say. "Shall we go?"

He doesn't say anything, so I turn my back to him, blinking the stinging sensation out of my eyes and attempting to find the outline of my bike against our house in the gloom—

"No. Wait. Look."

When I turn back to him, Ian has his hands held out in front of him, and he observes them as though baffled, like they did something he didn't command. His mouth opens and closes repeatedly, but he makes no sound.

"Ian, what is it? It's getting late—"

"I'm such a *part*, okay?!" he practically shouts. His eyes, wide and frightening, land on me. "I'm just some . . . like, an *arm*!"

Oh no. All right, Kendra, Ian is having a seizure. The first thing you'll want to do is find something to wedge in his mouth so he doesn't swallow his tongue.

"Like, I just do these actions that come to me, over and over!" he says, pumping his arm for emphasis. "Like a limb. But I'm just that! Just some arms and legs and a . . . a bunch of organs. But you're, just, so many things! PJ, too, but PJ I can almost get, all feelings all the time, that makes sense more, but you're . . . so *on top*!" He steps toward me, hands held out. His eyes have gone red, and tears cling in the corners, but he's doing a good job of keeping from breaking down. "And I really dig that. I'm so *into* how smart you are, Kendra. And how weird, and crazy you are, and all your Latin animal names, and how you have to blink hard before you say anything you already *know*. It's so cool to just . . . just . . . to *be around* you. That's what this week taught me. I can't do this, I can't do anything, just being alone, like I was before. Before the mountain. Remember me before the mountain? I, I had no idea, Kendra. Before you showed up. I thought I was strong, but I was just so alone, and it was you, all along, that I needed."

My throat burns. My eyes tear up. The ideas I want to express catch in my mouth. As I take a step toward him, I take in Ian Buckley, the boy I used to hate, all muscle and glistening brow and gushing eyes that somehow seem lit up in the darkness.

I stare. He stares back. Our appreciation of each other hangs in the air. It is an energy all its own, like magic, only greater—there is no rite accompanying this, no sigil or deal with dark forces. It is pure and incredible and feels so undeniably right that I am stunned by it, my thoughts an indecipherable blur.

Yet, though I could arguably stand here all night, I know that it would be selfish. We are still incomplete. There's something to be taken care of, if we want to remain strong in each other's eyes.

"Do this with me," I say, nodding to my bike.

"Okay," he says, and we ride off to see PJ.

PJ's front steps bear a single-toothed jack-o'-lantern, its flame flickering weakly.

When she opens the door, Samantha Wilson looks bad. Her skin, normally clear and freckled, is waxy and pale. Dark, tender skin rings her eyes. Her hair sticks out at all angles. Her hands flutter over to us and squeeze our shoulders in a shaking, unsure manner.

"He's been having a really good day today," she chirps as she leads us into her home. "He ate some soup, and he's been talking to his sister all day. And he even did some homework!" She laughs, as though the idea of PJ voluntarily doing homework was a miraculous sign of improvement.

As we pass the living room, I see PJ's father in an armchair watching TV and offer him a wave of salutation. He nods back at me, his eyes stony and ungiving. He will not even look at Ian. PJ's mother has gotten over it, but his father seems intent on reminding us, always: PJ, his only son, left with us, went somewhere, and got sick. We were there when the terrible thing happened.

We're always there.

Upstairs, we reach PJ's bedroom door, covered with a poster for the silent film *The Cabinet of Dr. Caligari*, which features a spidery black-clad man carrying a prone woman across a German Expressionist cityscape. His mother raps a knuckle twice against the door, and we hear PJ's breathy voice call out, "Just a minute!" There is some shuffling, a few bumps and footsteps, and then, softly, "Come on in."

While his mother looks exhausted and frantic, PJ looks simply awful. His skin is yellow-gray, his eye sockets and cheeks sunken and dark, though his bright eyes still shine out from those deep, shaded pits. He sits, propped up against a pile of pillows, his chest rising and falling with every slow, labored breath. Surrounded by the expensive camera equipment and colorful, vibrant film posters that fill his room, he is especially small and weak, daunted. When we come in, he smiles, or attempts to, and the hopes that had arisen from the repeated claims that he's been doing better sink low into my stomach and calcify.

"Kyra, sweetie, leave your brother alone," scolds PJ's mother.

"It's okay, I asked her to," rasps PJ. Next to his bed, PJ's sister is tightening two joints on a tripod holding up a camcorder. She smiles at us, her eyes large and bright but very sad.

"Hey, dude," says Ian hoarsely. "Hear you're feeling better."

"Oh yeah," says PJ, rolling his eyes with some effort. "Never better—" He lets out two deep, hacking coughs; his one hand goes to his mouth. The other, I notice, stays jammed firmly beneath the covers. After he calms down, he looks at his mom and says, "Could I talk to these guys alone for a second?"

"Sure," says his mom, overeager. "Come on, Kyra, PJ wants to hang out with his friends."

"I want to stay," she says, suddenly looking skittish and terrified.

"Go with Mom, just for a second," he says to her. Kyra nods and follows her mother out of the room. Once the door is closed behind us, I go to speak to PJ, but he holds up his hands as though to halt me . . . and my stomach cramps. My pulse quickens. It is as though hope has become a ridiculous concept.

The bite is a deep, infected black color, dry but still shining with a fresh coat of some foul liquid. From its edges creeps a web of black veins. His fingernails have turned a deep, bluish gray.

"They're gone," he says a little loudly. PJ's closet opens, and O'Dea reveals herself from between the racks of nice shirts and Christmas outfits. She also looks exhausted—eyes bloodshot, face even more wrinkled than usual. According to PJ's emails, she's been visiting him almost every night, and I do not wish to think about where she's been sleeping.

"This is sick," she says to PJ.

"Just turn the camera on," he says.

"What's happening here?" I ask as O'Dea crosses the room and presses a button on the camcorder. "PJ, what are you doing?"

"I'm going to film it," he croaks out, pointing to the camera. "When I change. I want to get it on camera, so we can know how it looks. It's the perfect ending." He goes into another coughing fit again, the sounds coming out from deep in his chest.

"But . . . but wait, man, you're feeling better!" says Ian, looking furious. "Your mom just said—"

"Lying," says PJ, shaking his head. "I've just been holding on for today. I'm going tonight."

The words sink into the room, taking the place of anything else that can be said. We stare at our friend, who looks back at us with a gaze of calm resignation. O'Dea will not make eye contact with him, staring at the ground and repressing a grimace. None of us wanted to know what PJ just told us, and yet somehow, he's been aware all day. All of our hoping and praying, all of O'Dea's magic spells, they didn't mean anything.

PJ's about to go. To leave us, his room, this mortal coil. Tonight.

And then, he's going to come back.

"PJ, we can't," says Ian gravely. "O'Dea's right; it's too much."

"You don't understand," he gasps, holding out a rolled-up sheet of paper wrapped around something solid. When I take it from him, I find a hastily scribbled note covering a small black metal cylinder, with a USB port jutting out of one end.

"What is this?" I ask him.

"Read it," says PJ. I smooth out the note and read:

PJ—If you're reading this, then you found the camera. Yeah, that's right, you had one hidden in your gear. I'm not going to lie; I'm stealing whatever you film. I won't use it in anything, but I wanted to see what happened down there. Good news is I also put a flash drive in your backpack

that recorded it all, so you have the footage, too.
Hope you can make some cool movies with it.
Sorry for sabotaging your gear, but admit it, it's
cool that you have a video recording of this.

> *Admit it,*
> *MELEE*

"I have it all on this hard drive," he says. "Kudus, Savini, even the mushroom. . . . It's the ultimate zombie movie. And this . . . this is its conclusion."

Ian and I stare at each other, faces draining of blood.

"What can we do?" I ask, almost to myself more than anyone else.

"You can get in the shot," says PJ.

TWENTY-ONE

PJ

Not yet. Almost, but not yet. I know. Food. I know.

Around me, my room blurs. My head throbs. My hearing goes fuzzy; one ear just stops working, turning instead into a high-pitched ringing sound that feels as though it's boring its way into my skull, my brain. A cold, searing pain travels from the base of my skull down my backbone.

Please. Please, I'm so close. Not yet. Just this last thing.

"You're good," says O'Dea in a soft, cracking voice as she peers into the eyepiece of one of the many cameras around me. Have to get all the angles. It's the perfect ending. I'm living my art.

It is so hard to breathe. I pull deeply, fill my lungs to the point of breaking, and speak directly at the black lens hanging before me, the eye of truth peering into the blurred, unsure world around me.

"Hello, my name is Peter Jacob Wilson, and I am a Gravedigger." Already, there's no air in me. Concentrate. Another deep breath, another sentence. Keep it going. "A Gravedigger is someone who is chosen by the powers that be to fight zombies, undead creatures that rise from the grave due to curses. Dark karma ruins parts of the world, and it wakes the dead. My friends Ian Buckley and Kendra Wright and I first discovered them on a school trip to the mountains of Montana."

I motion over to Ian and Kendra next to me. They do not look happy about being featured in my grand finale. Ian glances back and forth between the camera and me with openmouthed shock and sadness. And Kendra bears the same squinting frown that O'Dea's been giving me lately. Whether they like it or not, they can feel the infection spreading in me, feel what I am about to become.

"We encountered them again during a vacation we took in Puerto Rico, out on an island called Isla Hambrienta," I continue through the lightness in my head and chest, "and once more, in an underground city in Indonesia called Kudus. It was during this last trip that

I was bitten by one of these reanimated corpses." I raise my hand to the camera. The bite is black, barely painful. In my vision, it is the only thing in the room that is not blurred; the flesh of the bite and the veins around it seem to stand out, dark and solid, almost casting a shadow out of them that seems to darken the room and reach its hungry fingertips toward my friends. "In the week since it happened, I have been losing health gradually, and tonight, I can feel the infection spreading deeper. I think—I know—that tonight, the change will happen. I will die, and I will become one of these cursed monsters."

Ian puts a hand over his eyes and grimaces. From beneath it, tears roll down his cheeks. Part of me wants to reach out to him, let him know that I'm okay. This has been a long week for me, and I've thought long and hard on what's about to happen, and I'm ready for it. This is the inevitable.

For the first time in as long as I can remember, I'm not afraid.

A throbbing iciness shoots through me, emanating from my hand and my spine. No time to waste. Have to get it on camera.

"I just wanted to say," I manage to utter, "that I'm happy with this. I have had incredible adventures and have made the best friends any person could ask for. I've done my job as a Gravedigger, keeping people safe from the darkness and terror that waits for us out there in the world. And if I have any advice to anyone who sees this, it's that it's okay to be scared. There are monsters out there, terrible beings that exist only to spread pain and death and the end of everything that's great about being alive. That's scary. But you can't let the scary things win."

A sharp flutter, like a strong cold breeze, shoots through me, and I take a long, deep, gasping breath in response. Around me, the room drifts in and out of focus, the blood red and slime green of my movie posters blending and swirling together. A sound like rushing water fills my ears.

"You've gotta keep fighting," I say, my mouth and the words feeling out of joint. "But that doesn't always mean you have to fight. Sometimes, fighting just means being strong and doing the right thing. Being the person who . . . keeps the darkness from being stronger. When people, when the world, is evil and tries to break you . . . you have to stand in its way."

My hands tighten on the bedsheets. Someone, many people, call my name.

Finally, there's the fear—not overwhelming and gut-wrenching, but simple, standing in the background. But it's something different, mostly—it's fear with regret, fear that this is it, that the hundreds of thousands of things I want to say to my family and friends, to Kyra and Ian and Kendra and O'Dea and Josefina, they'll never get a chance to come out.

"Be strong," I say through chattering teeth. "They'll come for you, out of the dark. Don't let them take you. Let them know . . . what you can be."

As I say those words, my breath leaves my chest in a long, slow exhale, and doesn't come back.

The eye of the camera expands, growing larger and larger until it fills my field of vision and swallows the room in bottomless black.

Blackout.

PJ WILSON, 12, dead of a severe case of the zombie bites, falls—no, not falls, sinks, pulled by a steady force that only flows downward. Soon, he loses all sense of up or down, of warmth and the real world, of anything he can feel with any part of his body. This is less shadow or darkness than it is a void of all life—he is not adrift in a world of black, only a complete nothingness, entirely separate from all that he's ever thought was real. There is only silence and stillness and vast open truth.

Around him, things begin to move, rushing through the void and past whatever last remaining understanding of touch he still possesses. These shapes are swift and giant, like mile-long silent fish swimming through waters that encapsulate and flow through him. Some part of him registers that normally he would be deeply disturbed or upset by the sensation, physical or otherwise, of great creatures near him. At this moment, he is entirely without fear, knowing that such emotions are futile in this place on a level he does not entirely understand but in no way doubts.

Then, light, in two lines, meeting at a rough angle.

A door opens in the blackness. As it cracks, the light pouring out of it is blinding at first, bathing the formlessness on all sides of PJ in its harsh glare, until he can see into the door. A FIGURE, average height, skinny and silhouetted, stands at the open portal, one hand on the door's edge as though to keep it held wide. The sides of the creatures moving near PJ are briefly illuminated, revealing huge serpentine

coils that retract with a feral cry
as they're caught in the light. For a
moment, PJ catches something in his
peripheral vision—many eyes glittering,
teeth gnashing, skeletal designs on soft
repellent flesh—before these strange
beings dart farther away from him, deeper
into this constant void.

PJ drifts over to the door, floating
through the darkness as though he's known
how to do it all his life.

Close-up on the Figure, its facial
features invisible as it's entirely
backlit by the pure white light, leaving
him bathed in shadow.

                    FIGURE
              (deep, confident)
           Hello. I'm here for you.

                      PJ
                 Thank you.

The Figure extends a hand. When PJ
reaches his hand out, a BITE is visible,
throbbing with a dull and sickly
reverberation, like heat off concrete.

The Figure sees it, turns toward PJ's
face.

                    FIGURE
          Forgive me. I did not know.

                      PJ
     It's all right. I'll go anyway. I am
                    ready.

                    FIGURE
          No. You must not yet.

                      PJ
     They will take it. They will raise it to
        walk again. I am finished there.

                    FIGURE
     For most, that would be true. But there
          is something more to you.

PJ moves for the door, but the Figure
blocks his path. Slowly, tentatively the
Figure extends a hand and presses it to
PJ's bite, sending a deep sharp sting
into him and pushing him backward.
     Suddenly, PJ is floating back out into

the black current, the door remaining
open and stationary in the darkness but
its light seeming to travel with him. He
ascends, slowly at first and then rapidly,
blasting farther and farther up with the
light of that open doorway thrusting him
like a bubble, yanking him toward the
surface in a shriek of burning celestial
fire. The creatures from earlier, the
massive void beings, howl as he rushes
past them, shying away from the blaze
that seems to erupt from his very center
and pull him insistently toward the
surface of oblivion.

Fade in on a bedroom.

Everything is mushed together, way out of focus, a swirl of black murky shapes. Then, gradually, blurred forms begin to distinguish themselves from one another. The noises of the world fade in—a girl sobbing, slowly and loudly. The faint hum of a machine.

"We need to do something," says a voice. Male. Hard.

Ian. It's Ian talking.

The bedroom comes together—my dresser, my posters, my camera on its tripod, O'Dea's scarecrow form standing behind it with her arms crossed.

The sobbing stops.

"Wha—what does that imply?" asks Kendra.

After a pause, Ian says, "We need a knife. An axe, maybe a shovel."

"Ian, you can't be saying—"

"It's our job," he snaps. "We can't let him hurt anyone when . . . when it happens. PJ would have wanted it that way. He'd want us to get the change on camera, and then . . . stop it."

My mind strains at its petrified home. I focus on my heart, willing the warmth therein to pull me awake, but it remains still. Unbeating, immobile. My lungs won't inflate. I am here, but I'm not able to be here, unable to do anything but lie and watch.

"He—he might snap out of it. It might be some kind of coma or catatonic state."

"Kendra, he's *not breathing*," says Ian.

"No. You can't. PJ's a friend of ours, we can't—we can't—"

"O'Dea?"

"Do it, Ian," she whispers. "It's the only way."

Kendra sobs hard, loud, for all the room to hear. "How can you even think of this, Ian?"

"You think I'm happy about this?" snaps Ian, his voice finally cracking. "You think this is fun? Oh yeah, this is a real ball for me!"

Kendra's sobbing gets deeper, harder. O'Dea

whispers for Ian to do it, before he thinks about it.

"Yeah, Kendra, I'm having a blast! What'd I do today? Re-killed my best friend! What a rush! King of the world, Ma!"

No, no, no, hold on.

"Top."

The room goes dead silent. In front of me, O'Dea's eyes go wide and bright.

"PJ?" asks Ian's voice in a shaky whisper. Suddenly, his face darts in front of mine, his eyes scanning me for recognition. "PJ, man? Did you just say something?"

There. That feeling, that strength. You had it before—grab that. Use it as a rung on a ladder and pull yourself back into your body with it.

"Top of the world," I say, not even feeling my lips move.

Ian sits back with a start, face going pale. "What?"

" 'Top of the world, Ma' is from *White Heat* with Jimmy Cagney," I ramble suddenly, spilling out words that I can barely even grasp. " '*King of the world*' is from *Titanic* with Leonardo DiCaprio. You can only use one, even though both scenes involve someone throwing his arms wide open—"

Kendra squeals with joy, clapping her hands to her head. Ian sits back, breathing loudly through an exhausted smile. Then, both leap at me, arms thrust forward to pull me into a hug—

"NO!" I cry, thrusting my hands feebly up in front of me. The two of them stop short.

"PJ? What's wrong?" asks Ian.

And I say it before I can even think about it: "You're food."

There it is. Out on the table. Both of my friends back off slowly, mouths tightening in grim understanding. O'Dea nods, sadly sure of what's happened.

As they stand away from me, I climb out of bed. It takes some time to stand steadily—it's as though my whole body has gone asleep, every movement a mixture of complete numbness and cold, prickly sensation. Finally, when I stand on my own feet, O'Dea takes a step toward me.

"How do you feel?" she asks.

"Like death warmed over," I rasp. I hope for a smile from her. I don't get it.

"Do normal zombies ever talk?" asks Ian.

"Never," says O'Dea. Slowly, carefully, she lifts my bitten hand. "It must have been those awful mutated zombies. That, mixed with the cockroach poultice, my spells . . . maybe they changed the curse somehow. Created a new kind of zombie."

"Zombie two-point-oh," I say. "The latest edition."

"So . . . we don't have to kill him?" asks Ian.

"I don't think you should," says O'Dea. "The way things have worked themselves out . . . you're all three—Gravedigger, Warden . . . and Zombie—together as one."

"You don't sound too excited," I tell her, feeling stiffness in my jaw as I talk.

"Magic works in threes," says O'Dea, putting a hand to her chin. "And something like this . . . it's unpredictable. Before, these things had rules to them. Gravediggers weren't Wardens. Zombies weren't people. This is new. I'm just . . ." She snorts. "I'm scared."

"So, what's the next logical step?" says Kendra, her hand never leaving my cold shoulder (har-har).

"Honestly?" says O'Dea, lowering herself nervously into my desk chair. "Your guess is as good as mine."

The reality sets in. Not alive. Undead. Whatever I am, it's strange and different. Already, I can feel things in my body and heart changing. My spine aches, but in a good sort of way, solid and strong like a tree trunk. My jaw perpetually moves, as though I'm chewing thin air. I am the bump in the night, in my very core.

"Mirror," I say breathlessly.

"Over here," says Kendra, leading me to my dresser.

The mirror on top of my dresser shows a hilariously cinematic sight. My skin is perfectly pale, my eyes slowly going white in their deep, shadowy perches. The lines in my face seem even stronger, like canyons in my skin. Even my lips have gone slowly dark, threatening to turn a full unholy black. As much as I don't bear the urge for viciousness or brutality, I look like the creatures in the movies—sallow, stark, ready to set fear in the hearts of men.

Someone knocks at my door, and everyone but me starts. "PJ?" calls Kyra. "Are you okay?"

This won't do.

"I'm fine," I say, trying to sound as *fine* as possible. "Just . . . need some more time."

"I have no idea what to do," whispers Kendra.

Out of the corner of my eye, I catch my monster makeup kit, the cosmetic-filled tackle box I've been using for my werewolf movie. Digging through it, I find an underused product beneath the prosthetic gashes and rigid collodion—a pat of foundation I stole from my mother, meant to be the color of plain flesh. Normally, I use it to help blend in latex wounds to people's skin.

"O'Dea," I say, "can you make me look human?"

My friend smiles sympathetically, but then says, "PJ, I'm sorry, I just can't . . . you're a—"

"I got it," says Ian. He takes the sponge and dabs at my face. Doesn't even say anything about being a dude putting makeup on his best male friend, or about O'Dea not being able to touch me because of what I am. I can't blame anyone for feeling weird. This *is* weird. Every time Ian's hand comes to my face, I have to remind myself that he's not food.

As he applies makeup, I can't help but smile. This is

kind of hilarious in a bizarre way, isn't it? That has to be acknowledged—here is PJ Wilson, the world's first self-aware zombie, having his Living Guy makeup applied by his best buddy who's also destined to kill him. That's absolutely ridiculous. Truly absurd.

It would be a shame to go undocumented.

"O'Dea," I say, "get the camera. Kendra, can you upload the footage from the cave onto my computer?"

"On it," she says, snatching up the flash drive and bringing it over to my desk.

O'Dea takes the camera and tentatively peers into the viewfinder, mumbling, "All right, red circle's there. You're rolling."

"How's the light?" I ask.

"Pretty good," she says. "A little stark."

"That's fine, kind of appropriate. Okay, October thirtieth, Halloween eve," I say, training my pale eyes on the camera lens. "This is the life of Undercover Zombie, day one. Ian Buckley, our perpetual protagonist, is applying my makeup. Say hi, Ian."

"Yo," mumbles Ian, trying not to smile.

Kendra flies her way around my computer, opening the footage to the sounds of crunching and screams. Ian pushes my head to one side to smear makeup onto my dead ears. In the dark, under the eye of my camera, I talk about zombies while trying to feel like a human being.

It all feels surprisingly normal.